A GAME OF PLEASURE

Barbara Satow

PREMIUM PRESS AMERICA

NASHVILLE, TENNESSEE

A Game of Pleasure by Barbara Satow

© 2006 Barbara Satow
Published by Premium Press America

For information on Premium Press America books, call 615/256-8484.

ISBN 1-933725-03-6

Design by Armour&Armour
armour-armour.com

First Edition 2006
1 2 3 4 5 6 7 8 9 10

PORTIA'S PROMISE

The fullness of the bosom pressing his rib cage was evident through his shirt, his waistcoat, his coat, her coat, and whatever else she wore beneath it. Glorious.

Her sweet breath escaped in ticklish puffs from their joined lips, inciting Castleton to a more passionate embrace than he'd first intended. He tightened his grip, his mouth moving over Portia's to explore its silken contour.

For one heady instant she responded to him. Her lips pressed back at his and parted farther.

Castleton leaned into the pressure, his tongue stealing forward to lightly caress the curve of her lower lip.

This book is dedicated
to my mother,
Marjorie O'Malley,
for all her love and support
through the wannabe years

Acknowledgments

ON THIS, MY first book, I had a strong urge to thank everybody I've ever known. But my family (the Satows, O'Malleys, Mitolos, Sacharas, and Thomes) constitute a laundry list in and among themselves and I quickly realized if I thanked one friend, I'd have to thank them all, so ... if you know me, thanks. Your support means a lot to me.

I do have some specifics, though. Michelle Levigne and Jesse Long were my critique partners long before I knew what a critique partner was. Jesse has always been my authority on all things "horse." Thanks to all the good listeners in my life: Gretchen Crea, Katie Hudak, Cheryl Fedorcio, Cheryl Kloscak, Gina Todd, Annette Williams, Cathy Lussier, Gary Dumm, Sue Shestina, Eddie Columbia, Erin McCarthy, and Kristie Parker.

I began this book long ago, but never would have finished it if not for Romance Writers of America. Joining this organization changed my life—not because of the resources it offers, but because I've met so many wonderful people through it. My local chapter, Northeast Ohio Romance Writers of America (NEORWA) means more to me than I can say, and the special interest chapter The

Beau Monde has taught me just how much I still don't know about the Regency period.

They would be the first to point out there were no yellow roses in the Regency. I'm sure there are other inaccuracies in this book, although I've always done my best to get the details right. But I left the roses in to remind myself, and now you, that this is a work of fiction and some elements are the sole product of my imagination.

1

THE GAME WAS over, and Castleton had won. As he surveyed the grand assemblage in his ballroom, he knew he should feel ... something. Relief? Victory? Satisfaction for a job well done?

He shifted his splinted leg on the stool set before his chair and sighed. Unrelenting tedium was more the like. Though Sarah's debut was a bonafide squeeze—Margaret must be in transports—only a handful in the crowd held any interest for him. Those few friends and members of his family were scattered among the myriad acquaintances and social contacts he'd cultivated over the years to ensure this night's success.

I should have heeded Geoff's suggestion to be carried to the cardroom, he thought. Geoffrey Wilkes, his best friend from childhood, had read the situation in a trice.

"You'll be bored with only the dancing to amuse you. Let me call one of the stout fellows by the door and. . . ."

"I beg you, no," Castleton said. "It's bad enough this broken leg keeps me from circulating. The

9

surgeon insists I return to my bed at the supper interval. My sister-in-law would have the vapors if I hid myself away before."

"Very well," Geoff said, settling his solid form by Castleton's chair, a martyred expression on his face.

"But go play, if you like," Castleton urged. Geoff rarely came to Town without his wife. Were he Geoff, Castleton would revel in his freedom. Were he Geoff, though, he would never have married a woman like Alvenia in the first place.

"No," Geoff responded. "If you can bear being stuck here, I suppose I can, too."

But Geoff lacked Castleton's experience. As they silently watched the ballroom antics of his guests, Castleton remained inert, allowing numbing paralysis to wash over him.

Geoff fidgeted. He rubbed the toe of his dancing pump on an itchsome spot on the back of his silk-clad calf. His brown eyes drifted with increasing longing toward the cardroom door.

"So Evan has a cold," Castleton said, as if Geoff hadn't told him so upon his arrival. The Wilkes doted on their son, the youngest of their three children.

"Nothing serious, but Alvenia thought it best to remain with him." Geoff's attention fixed on Castleton's niece. "Sarah looks pretty tonight."

Sarah skirted the edge of the parquet dance floor, her arm linked with another debutante's. She looked fresh in her white gown, decorated along the van-dyked border with tiny yellow roses. A gloved hand absently adjusted a similar bud nested in a coronet of dark-brown braids.

Yellow roses accented the floral arrangements on the tables and the garlands festooning the chandelier and the mantelpiece—Margaret's idea to subtly showcase her daughter's gown.

No tricks or artifice were necessary in Castleton's estimation. Sarah's ready smile and sweet nature would seal her success, despite his temporary infirmity or her mother's perpetual nerves. But beyond this night. . . .

"I'm not sure Sarah is ready for this," Castleton said.

"She seems easy enough."

"This is just a party to her. I managed to persuade Margaret that she's still too young to fret about hordes of suitors beating down our door."

"Margaret's own pet fantasy, you mean?" Geoff responded with a laugh.

Castleton smiled at him.

"She can't be thinking of conquests the way she sticks by that stunning girl. Who is that?" Geoff asked.

"That," Castleton told him, "is Miss Vivian Barstow. Sarah met her at school, where they became immediate and inseparable friends. You must meet her. I have a strong suspicion she'll be Mrs. Frederick Christopher one day."

"No!" Geoff studied Miss Barstow, a vivacious honey blonde with a heart-shaped face and a curvaceous figure. Though also sixteen, she cast Sarah in the shade with her greater beauty and innate sense of style.

Geoff's attention drifted toward Frederick. Trying to match them in his mind, no doubt. Castleton's nephew conversed with a group of earnest young men, shrugging his thin frame around in his evening clothes in an effort to find some comfort in them.

"I never imagined Frederick in the petticoat line," Geoff said. "Is he really bold enough to pursue a beauty?"

Castleton laughed.

"He's the pursued, my friend. And Miss Barstow's strategy is cunning to the extreme. She merely appears a part of our family circle and defers to Frederick at every opportunity."

"David Carlyle! You abhor such machinations."

"Despite her scheme, her attachment is genuine," Castleton replied. "She requires no alteration of Frederick. And she admires Sarah. How can I dissuade someone who loves them for who they are instead of what they are?"

"The niece and nephew of Lord Castleton," Geoff murmured.

"Exactly." Despondence gripped Castleton. All his efforts to secure a lofty position in Society culminated in this night. Sarah and Frederick would be accepted anywhere, Frederick's awkwardness, Sarah's youthful enthusiasm, and the taint of trade on their fortune not withstanding. He should be happy.

"Your cousin Lesley would be proud of you,"

Geoff said in a soft voice. "Your bon vivant performance year in and year out. I imagine him gazing
down from Heaven, and wondering why he didn't
cast you as the lead in his little scenarios more often."

"I am but a poor understudy. Lesley would have
made a grand Lord Castleton. It was the role *he* was
born to play."

"Castleton!" His sister-in-law Margaret Christopher flittered up to him, turban quaking on her still-
dark hair. She looked too youthful to be the mother
of two grown children. Her stylish sapphire gown
molded a trim figure. Though well into her forties,
her rosy cheeks remained unlined.

She was sufficiently attractive to entertain
suitors of her own, if she desired it. But no thought
of replacing his late half-brother William had ever
occurred to the matron. Her hopes for the future
centered exclusively on her offspring.

"Castleton, I must speak to you."

"A good time for that game of whist," Castleton
told Geoff.

Wilkes rolled his eyes.

"Go on. I insist. I'll stake you if you lose, and
your wife will be none the wiser."

Geoff bowed to Margaret and withdrew.

"You must speak to Frederick," Margaret said,
her blue eyes skittering around each flocked and
mirrored wall in search of potential calamity. "He
isn't dancing with anyone. And he's ruining his
cravat!" she exclaimed as Frederick poked a finger
up through the folds of his neckcloth to loosen it.

"Can't we just settle for the prestige of snaring the elusive Mr. Christopher as a guest?" Castleton asked. "If it's any solace, he promised to dance the supper dance with Miss Barstow. Neither she nor Sarah will let him break his word."

"You are too lenient," Margaret replied with a shake of her head. "He must learn to overcome his reticence."

She made a beeline for her son.

This should prove interesting, Castleton thought, as Margaret dragged Frederick toward the nearest young lady sitting down. But Castleton cringed at every halting step discordant to the cadence of the small orchestra's stately music.

The boy did not dance well. Why should he display his awkwardness to satisfy some notion of correct behavior? The social niceties were Castleton's job. Unfortunately, without such occupation. . . .

Ennui gripped him. He leaned his blond head back on the stuffed chair, inwardly debating a glance at his watch to see how imminent the return to his bedchamber. *And it's a sad state of affairs when I crave my "prison" of the past three weeks.*

He needed diversion. Desperately. Before he calculated how many little pieces of wood made up the flooring beneath dancing feet. He'd already counted the one hundred sixteen candles glowing in the chandelier, lustres, candelabra, and sconces.

"What do you think of Miss Burke and Mr. Salinger?" The unfamiliar voice spoke so close to his ear, Castleton gratefully turned toward it. But the speaker did not address him.

The two elderly chaperons in the chairs beside him gazed past Castleton toward the dance floor. They were among the unfamiliar faces in the crowd tonight—Margaret must have used some approved Society Register for her guest list. He suspected the too-red complexion of the woman seated at his shoulder was the result of an inexpert rouging. A large cap, like a silken mushroom, spilled over the ears of the other woman.

"He'll be lucky if she accepts his suit now that he's lost the title," the woman in the cap responded, focused on the couple in question, who promenaded in the center of the room.

"What a tragedy," Mrs. Cherry Cheeks said. "Who would have dreamed Lady Haviland would bear a son at six and thirty?"

Castleton frowned. Six and thirty was not an excessive age. *He* was six and thirty, and considered sons a future expectation. He knew Evan Wilkes had made his debut to a more than thirty-year-old mother, and a swift consideration of the married women of his acquaintance proved to Castleton's satisfaction it was not too late an age to bear a child.

"Astonishing," Madame Mushroom proclaimed. "And now Mr. Salinger has no expectations. But how can Miss Burke jilt him? She's allowed him to court her exclusively for almost a year."

"As I've told my dear Melinda, never discourage

other suitors until there's an engagement. You never know when you will snare a more eligible partner."

"Mr. Salinger has other attributes," the capped woman mused. "A fine figure, for instance."

"My dear, that is all a sham," Cherry Cheeks replied with a snort. "He wears a corset, you know. And those calves. . . . ."

"Not real?"

"Great heavens, no! See how stiffly he moves—how mincing his steps—he's guarding against slippage."

Castleton studied Salinger carefully. His apricot coat molded lean shoulders. His knee breeches and white silk stockings were exceptionally tight. He executed the steps of the minuet with marked deliberation. But Castleton could detect no evidence to support the chaperon's assertion.

The red-faced woman cleared her throat. "I understand it's not the only part of his anatomy he pads," she said.

Castleton gasped. Some topics were too personal for speculation. The two chaperons tittered maliciously, and he turned toward them, intending to bestow the ringing set down at the earliest opportunity. Their attention was too much on each other to pay him heed.

And a laughing, hazel gaze beyond them roused Castleton's sleeping sense of humor.

This woman was nearer in age to himself, dressed in a simple gown of pale green. She wore no cap on her light-brown hair, so he assumed she was unmarried. Probably because she was more appealing than pretty.

But the merriment suppressed in her features held amiable allure, and the sparkle of her eyes kindled laughter within him. Castleton gazed toward the dance floor, lest he set his mirth free.

"Speaking of...." Mrs. Cherry Cheeks paused significantly. "Have you heard Major's Fitzhugh's injury has had a ... rather startling side effect?"

"No!"

The chaperons slanted their heads closer together, but Castleton could still decipher the whispered venom.

"It appears the major can no longer control certain physical reactions to women he finds attractive."

"You mean...?"

Castleton glanced over. Mrs. Cherry Cheeks raised her hand slowly from her lap until her fingertips angled toward the chandelier. Castleton's face began to rival hers in hue.

Across the heads of the chaperons, the hazel eyes widened. As her gaze locked with Castleton's, the woman in green trapped her lower lip between her teeth.

"How do you know?" Madame Mushroom whispered.

"It's happened thrice in public. He had to excuse himself at the theater last week the moment the actress playing Olivia took the stage. Guarding his ... jewelry, I'm told." Mrs. Cherry Cheeks crossed her hands over her lap in illustration.

Castleton cleared his throat.

The corner of the lady in green's mouth slid up as her teeth sank deeper below her lip. Her eyes generated agitating mirth. Castleton's mouth crept higher in response. He quickly looked away.

"Then, in Hyde Park, Lady Jersey broke a lace. She stooped to fix it and exposed an ankle. The effect was instantaneous!"

"Goodness me! And the third?"

"That is the most shocking. His close friend, Captain Parker, held a dinner party. Young Miss Parker decided to entertain the guests after the meal. She drew her harp to her breast and up popped Adam's needle. Fitzhugh stood to retreat but had to face the entire company. I'm told it practically pierced through his pantaloons."

I will not laugh, I will not laugh, Castleton willed, trying to focus on his empathy for Fitzhugh instead of the Cruikshank-like image building in his head.

He glanced toward the woman in green. Her efforts to quell her own merriment had added a becoming rush of blood to her round features. Castleton's renewed eye contact proved too much for her. She turned her head and barked, letting the noise taper into a weak cough.

Castleton tried to emulate her. He glanced up at the chandelier, hoping to suppress some of the noise by forcing his lips together. A horrendous snort emerged. The lady in green broke into a paroxysm of strangulated glee in consequence, and Castleton pushed his knuckles into his mouth to bottle his responsive laughter.

The chaperons turned away from each other to fix them both with curious stares.

A hand fell on Castleton's shoulder. He looked up into the craggy face of General Thompson, his superior from his Army days.

"Are you all right, dear fellow?"

"Yes," Castleton gasped. "There was, for a sudden, a most offensive . . . wind in this corner."

"I felt no draft," Mrs. Cherry Cheeks asserted, as the woman in green choked further.

Madame Mushroom patted her on the back. "Do you need a restorative, Portia?" she whispered. "Should I call for a servant?"

The lady in green smothered a last chortle with a sniff, then stated she was "fine now" in a soft voice.

Castleton resolutely turned from her tearful, humor-filled eyes to focus on the general.

"Forgive my tardiness," Thompson said to Castleton. "And I was sorry to hear about your accident. Bad break, that."

"Actually, it was common as breaks go," Castleton quipped. Though Thompson frowned, perplexed, a sideways cast of the eyes told Castleton his fellow eavesdropper had caught the joke. "The surgeon says it's healing nicely, though it will be some weeks before I can dance a reel."

"Ah," Thompson said, "that reminds me. . . ." The general bowed to the woman in green. "Miss Kirby, you owe me a dance from the Elden party."

"I'm afraid my aunt wished to leave early, sir," Miss Kirby said, delicately wiping the last evidence of her outburst from the corner of her eye. "But I would be more than happy to discharge my debt this evening."

"Then let us join the set forming," the general replied.

Miss Kirby rose to reveal herself of middling height, broader in hip than the current fashion liked, though a well-rounded bosom added balance to her figure. She flashed Castleton a smile in passing that warmed him toe to crown.

Having captured his interest, she compelled his observation. After a few moments, Castleton judged Miss Kirby an excellent dancer despite her lack of height and slight excess of breadth.

"So kind of General Thompson to take pity on Portia," the red-faced chaperon said.

"She's such a sweet girl," the capped woman replied.

"Hardly a girl! She passed thirty on her last birthday."

"Such a shame she has nothing to recommend her to a man." Madame Mushroom sighed. "But it's brave of her to continue hoping."

"Oh, she knows her situation is hopeless. She's no fool," Mrs. Cherry Cheeks said. "But her attendance provides Charlotte Andrews with an excuse to haunt the cardroom, doesn't it?"

Castleton considered Miss Kirby with new eyes. A spinster—perhaps past prayers—but nothing to recommend her? Humor was not the equal of birth, beauty, or fortune in Society's eyes, but it was a vital quality in any woman he fancied.

He resolved to have Thompson introduce him to the lady when they quit the floor. But the dancers were across the room when the music ended. Thompson drew Miss Kirby into a circle, where she conversed a while before disappearing in the sea of revelers to some other unseen corner.

Castleton was obliged to endure the gossiping women beside him until his guests withdrew for supper, at which time his wish to return to his bedchamber became a stupefying reality.

"THERE HAD BETTER be cards, Portia," Charlotte Andrews whispered three weeks later, as she scanned the line of guests waiting on the threshold of the Harveys' drawing room. "Such a meager affair. The majority of the company are but youngsters."

"Shhh," Portia cautioned as they stepped forward. "Caroline Applegate assured me her mother would attend. Mrs. Black will broach the subject if no one else does."

"Do you see her yet?" Charlotte asked and cast her capped head around in search of the distinguished matron.

Portia didn't bother to look. She knew a prior engagement would delay the Honorable Mrs. Black's arrival, but kept this report to herself. She could use an inquiry to the Applegates to engineer an escape from Mrs. Cray and Mrs. Trent. Her aunt seemed duty-bound to establish her in their vicinity at every engagement. Their chatter had become nigh unbearable, especially since that nearly embarrassing night at Sarah Christopher's ball.

That was Lord Castleton's fault, she thought, and smiled at the memory. His expressions had been priceless from the moment he'd focused his abstract attention on the gossips beside him.

Castleton stood in the reception line before her now, one arm linked with Margaret Christopher's and the other leaning heavily on an ebony cane, as he listened to his niece's easy prattling. Lithe and elegant, his pronounced limp was the only sign of having been abed for six weeks. His deep blue eyes scanned the company with a dread equal to Charlotte's.

At least that's what Portia guessed. Castleton had mastered the trick of disguising his true feelings behind an amiable social veneer. He proved an interesting puzzle to decipher on most occasions. He was one of her favorite subjects for observation in the pageant of human behavior that entertained Portia most nights.

Castleton's party nearly reached their hosts when Sarah exclaimed, "Oh, there's Vivian!" and deserted her mother and uncle to greet her friend.

The ostrich feathers in Margaret Christopher's headdress trembled. "Sarah," she hissed. "Oh, dear. . . . ."

Castleton squeezed his sister-in-law's arm once

before releasing it. "You follow her in," he said in a low voice. "I'll make your excuses."

With red face held high, Margaret stalked after Sarah. She gestured toward the abandoned reception line as she reached her daughter's side, her lips pursed in censure. Sarah looked back too, guilt-stricken. But Miss Barstow came to her friend's defense with a wheedling smile that soon had Mrs. Christopher softening. Margaret totally abandoned her pique when her own particular friend, Phoebe Ballinger, joined their party.

"Lord Castleton," Mrs. Harvey exclaimed, drawing Portia's attention back to her immediate surroundings. "How wonderful to see you about again!"

"How wonderful to *be* about," Castleton reflected as he bowed. The candles above flicked threads of light into his thick blond hair.

"I saw Sarah pass by." Mrs. Harvey's voice held no resentment. "Such a lovely girl. You and Margaret must be well-pleased."

"We are," Castleton said. He glanced around the room and stilled as he spied Mrs. Cray and Mrs. Trent with heads together on the far wall. Obviously, they'd left an impression on him. He directed a deceptively sweet smile at his hostess.

"I'm afraid I'm not as mobile as I wish yet. I need to find a perch out of the way. Perhaps. . ." He pointed to the wall opposite the chaperons near the salon entrance. Portia paid Castleton an inward compliment on his stratagem. It would likely become the cardroom later.

"Of course!" Mrs. Harvey exclaimed. She tapped her husband on the arm just as he reached for Portia's hand to greet her. "Dearest, please see Lord Castleton to his chair."

"That isn't necessary," Castleton said.

"No, no, dear fellow. Let me help you." Harvey beamed at Portia apologetically. "You'll excuse me, Miss Kirby, won't you?"

To Portia's great surprise, Castleton's head snapped around at her name. His deep eyes brightened with clear recognition. His smile was so direct and dazzling, Portia instinctively ducked her head to hide her blush and reciprocal smile.

"Of course not," she murmured. The air grew heavy in a pause—as if Castleton waited for some further response. But when Portia looked up, Harvey was supporting him away by the elbow.

Portia shook Mrs. Harvey's hand and thanked her for the invitation. As expected, her aunt led her toward the chaperons' corner. Portia turned her head to sigh and noticed Castleton grinning sympathetically at her.

Yes, it's my turn now, she responded in her head as she smiled back. But unlike Castleton, she could move about.

Portia spied Caroline Applegate in the rear of the chamber, seated beside her ethereal daughter Serina. Already a half-dozen men buzzed around the beauty, including poor Arthur Ponsby, a young man Portia had lately befriended.

"I'll ask Caroline when her mother is expected,"

Portia whispered in her aunt's ear. Charlotte nodded as she sank down beside the ruddy-featured Mrs. Trent.

After exchanging greetings, Caroline asked: "Will you attend the musicale at Lady Sidwell's, Miss Kirby?"

"My aunt dislikes musical programs, ma'am," Portia answered as she settled into the chair beside her.

"Then come with us," Caroline exclaimed. "You can help me fend off these young men who drown my Serina in attentions."

Which is the precise reason you asked me, Portia thought, nodding assent. She wished she had the nerve to proclaim herself a spinster outright. She'd accepted the truth nine years ago when her only serious suitor, the Reverend Avery Greenwood, had died unexpectedly. She'd been almost happy to withdraw from London after that to care for her ailing parents.

Her mother had died later the same year and her father four years after. Portia would still be living a life of country seclusion if her brother James hadn't married an overbearing woman who resented Portia's lot as their Dependent.

Her life was far better than she'd hoped when she'd hit on the idea to live as her aunt's companion. Nothing exciting happened on the average evening, but she was happy to be living in London instead of with Maria in Surrey. Portia had carved herself a comfortable niche in the corner of ton functions—a pleasant-enough guest to help make up the numbers, though her only contact with her hosts was usually the greeting at the door. Knowing pity prompted many of the invitations she received, however, Portia feared an open declaration of her permanent single state would reduce their number significantly.

Having procured Portia's promise to second her as a chaperon, Caroline launched into a litany of Serina's latest conquests. Portia listened, nodding and smiling at the proper intervals to keep Caroline beaming.

The Applegates' sole mission this Season was to see Serina wed to the wealthiest man of high rank she could attract. Serina's brother had gambled away the bulk of his inheritance after their father's death. Caroline wanted Serina wed before the extent of Nicholas Applegate's debt was discovered.

Arthur Ponsby really has no hope of engaging her interest, Portia thought as he clipped the side of her slipper in an effort to maneuver into Serina's line of sight. A kind-hearted and intelligent young man, Ponsby was clearly out of his element in London's social milieu. He looked bumpkinish in his tight coat and fashionably high collar. His stocky build and blunt features screamed country—nothing there to interest many young ladies, let alone Serina or her mother.

"Miss Kirby, I'm so sorry! Did I injure you?" Ponsby stammered.

"No, you didn't," Portia lied with a bright smile. "How do you do, Mr. Ponsby?"

"Well, ma'am. Thank you." His brown eyes drifted in Serina's direction, and his slight jowls drooped as yet another suitor got between him and his obsession. Portia pitied him.

She could see Mrs. Black just outside the drawing room door. If Caroline remained true to form, she would rise to greet her mother. Portia would have to time it correctly to appear happenstance, but. . . .

"Any more news about your sister's wedding?" Portia asked, gesturing to the empty chair beside her in clear invitation.

Ponsby sat, his gaze still fixed on Serina, as he answered, "I received a letter from her yesterday. She's having trouble convincing Father a touch of elegance is worth the outlay. She wants me to write and beg him to relent."

"And will you?"

Caroline stood up. Before she took more than a step away, Portia slipped sideways into her chair, earning the glare of more than one young swain who coveted that place at Serina's side. Portia grasped the sleeve of Ponsby's black jacket and pulled him into her now-vacant seat.

Ponsby nodded. "It's Jane's day, after all. And by falling in love with a local gentleman, she spared Father the greater expense of a London Season," he said.

"What a good way to put it." Portia rose, blocking the chair beside Serina from a frontal assault. "Well, I should return to my aunt now. . . . ."

Ponsby rose and bowed to her.

Young Sidwell pushed between them in a bid for the seat of honor, but Portia latched his arm. "Mr. Sidwell, would you be so kind?"

Sidwell looked at Portia as if her head were on fire. Portia motioned Ponsby toward the empty seat with a flutter of fingers behind her back. She sensed his movement as Sidwell bowed in defeat and offered his arm to her. She turned back to catch Ponsby's flush of grateful pleasure.

And then, as her head swung around, she noticed Castleton smiling at her. Portia turned away quickly, her heart hammering. Had he seen what she'd done? She peeped back, and Castleton's smile broadened to a grin. Yes, he had.

Portia directed her attention to the floor.

So what if he had? she thought as she sat back in the chaperons' corner. He'd maneuvered a situation to his liking more often than she could count. Usually to defeat the wiles of some matchmaking mama. Castleton excelled at that.

But Portia had to admit the results of Castleton's machinations were, in general, more satisfactory. Ponsby appeared to have no idea what to say to Serina. She tossed her golden head at his one attempt to engage her, then steadfastly ignored his presence at her side. Ponsby eventually surrendered the seat of honor to Mr. Giles Dodd and trod into the refreshment room, his broad shoulders slumped.

Portia used the call for card players and its resulting shift of the crowd to follow him. She spent the better part of fifteen minutes coaxing him to something less overtly distressed.

When she stepped back into the drawing room, she noticed Castleton was still seated by the salon doorway, his attention focused in her direction. Most of the walls were draped with finely woven tapestries, but there was nothing beyond her of particular interest. Portia glanced back over her shoulder, perplexed. There was nothing before her of interest, either.

He can't be looking at me, she thought.

But . . . what if he was? The idea offered such exciting possibilities.

Her aunt would be in the salon. If Portia strolled over to glance inside, she would draw close enough for a brief politeness. It wasn't as if she was approaching Castleton—that would be so impertinent. But if he was looking at her—which seemed likely by the way he straightened as she stepped toward him—and he wanted to, perhaps, greet her. . . ?

Mr. Harvey appeared at her elbow and bowed. "The young people would like to dance, and I'd hate to disappoint them. Would be so kind, Miss Kirby?"

"Of course," Portia assented, changing course toward the pianoforte. In addition to pleasantness, she held a reputation as a useful guest. She was loath to disappoint.

So much for engaging a dashing baron in small talk, she thought as she sifted through the music on the rack. Miss Harvey appeared to lack proficiency in her instrument. Portia sighed and elected to play from memory instead.

She started with some country dances—romping songs to get the blood flowing and the toes tapping. Then she played a drawn-out quadrille so the young men might flirt a bit with the lady of their choice. No one had ever flirted with Portia in her salad days, but she remembered how much she'd wished they would. And the Season was well underway; could she hazard a waltz?

She looked up from the keyboard to assure herself every young lady present had leave to dance it—she wouldn't play a waltz if all didn't have an opportunity to take the floor. Portia hadn't waltzed much herself—the dance had come into fashion only two years ago—but it was her favorite. And she imagined with the right partner it could be so romantic....

She started from her reverie with a jolt. Lord Castleton was smiling at her again. Smiling as if he'd been smiling for some time, and almost as if he could read her thoughts. She dropped her eyes to her fingers. He definitely watched her. But why?

MISS KIRBY BECAME more interesting as the evening progressed, Castleton decided. Who would have guessed her spinsterish exterior concealed the heart of master tactician in the matchmaking arts? The way she'd exerted herself for the cloddish Mr. Ponsby, and now with her choices of music.

The mothers in the room must be in transports, he thought, glad his leg excused him from participating. He'd most likely be betrothed to some little chit by the time the dancing ended if Miss Kirby had her way.

She played with a skill and passion Castleton had rarely seen in a lady. At one point in her performance she shut her eyes and a smile of such sweetness appeared on her lips, Castleton found himself smiling in concert.

The hazel eyes opened to survey the company and caught his look squarely. Portia fixed her attention on her fingers, not lifting her head again for two whole sets. And then, as she declared she must rest awhile, she assiduously avoided looking in Castleton's direction, drawing a smile from him again.

I must know if she's as engaging tête-à-tête as she is from a distance, Castleton thought. He beckoned his host to his side. "I should like to compliment Miss Kirby on her performance. Could you arrange an introduction?"

Harvey smiled and rushed off to obey. Portia shot a suspicious look in Castleton's direction as Harvey spoke to her. But she nodded, took their host's arm, and allowed him to lead her to Castleton's chair. Castleton rose with the aid of the cane and sketched her a bow.

"Miss Portia Kirby, you are, perhaps, acquainted with Lord Castleton?" Harvey said.

Portia regarded Castleton with a steady gaze and replied, "We were introduced some time ago."

Castleton frowned. It must have been quite some time ago. He owned his memory better than most but could recall her face and voice only from recent weeks.

"At Lord Everton's fireworks display," Portia supplied helpfully. "To celebrate the first anniversary of Nelson's victory at Trafalgar."

Castleton laughed. "Eleven years is 'quite some time,' indeed," he replied. "I hope you will forgive my faulty memory and allow me to renew our acquaintance."

"Since our original acquaintance consisted of no more than the introduction and a few commonplace exchanges, I should say it has already been renewed."

Harvey gasped at a statement that, but for its tone, sounded like a set down. But Castleton recognized it as simple truth and took no offense.

He smiled and gestured to the chair beside him. After a moment's hesitation, Portia sat down and Castleton resumed his seat. Harvey scurried away.

"You play superbly, ma'am," Castleton began. Portia nodded acknowledgment. "But your skills as a matchmaker leave something to be desired. Your young friend did not use his gift of proximity wisely."

She looked as if she might dissemble for a moment, but thought the better of it. She shook her head.

"I did not expect he would," Portia replied with

a sigh. "Mr. Ponsby tries too hard. And the desire to please is not a quality Miss Applegate is inclined to prize at this time."

"Then why did you do it?" Castleton asked.

Portia smiled.

"It's a quality I admire," she told him. "And, though it may have done more harm than good, I'm glad he had an opportunity for Miss Applegate's attention."

Castleton smiled in turn.

The pretty blush returned to her pale cheeks, and Portia rose self-consciously. "I should find my aunt," she said.

"She does quite well without you," Castleton said. He could see Charlotte Andrews just beyond the salon door, discarding her cards with absorbed delight. "I, on the other hand. . . ."

"Do you require some assistance?" Portia asked.

"No," he said. "I only desire you should sit back down."

"What for?" Realizing at once how gauche she sounded, her cheeks deepened to a less-fortunate crimson.

"To tell me all about Miss Burke and Mr. Salinger, of course," Castleton replied without censure. "Or better yet, tell me about those old gossips and how they know every misfortune that befalls their fellow man. Poor Fitzhugh. I'm acquainted with him, you know. I don't know how I'll face him with any equanimity. Who can I possibly discuss the particulars of his infirmity with?"

"Not I," she asserted. "Mrs. Cray and Mrs. Trent were shockingly vulgar. I could never discuss anything so . . . private with a mere acquaintance."

"Then I must get to know you better, mustn't I?" Castleton said in a soft voice. "If I wish to bare my soul."

After a nonplussed beat, Portia laughed and resumed her seat beside him. She spent the rest of the evening at his side.

And as Castleton lost track of time, he realized he'd found his new diversion, at last.

2

CAROLINE APPLEGATE SEATED Portia in the front row of delicately curved parlor chairs before taking her beautiful daughter off to circulate among Lady Sidwell's guests. Portia took no offense at her desertion. She could see as well as Serina would be seen. Her proximity to the front of the room might also allow her to actually hear the music when the program began.

Her heart fluttered with residual pleasure as she observed Castleton's arrival. He was handsome in his blue superfine—not the same coat of Sarah's come out, but as elegantly styled. He had his sister-in-law on his arm, also attired in dark blue, while the smiling Sarah Christopher and the sparkling Miss Barstow entered the room before them.

Their young eyes surveyed the decoration and the company with enthusiasm—a striking contrast to poor Serina, under strict orders to engage the notice of men of high rank instead of enjoying her evening or her surroundings. Portia mentally applauded Miss Christopher and her friend for their easy, natural manner.

She laid Sarah's poise at Castleton's door. Margaret Christopher flustered too easily and her son was too timorous to have fostered her unconcern for Society's strictures.

Castleton was unimpressed by pomp and status, probably because he'd never expected to become a titled gentleman himself. Her night of conversation with him confirmed what Portia had long ago surmised; he was amusingly irreverent. With the exception of her cousin George, she could not recall laughing so much in a gentleman's company.

Yet, Castleton had weighed her words as if they were full substance. He'd made Portia feel quite important, and if he could do that for a dab of a spinster with nothing to recommend her, what feelings of worth could he foster in a girl he'd doted on since childhood?

Lord Castleton's notice had been exhilarating, though his objective had been his own pleasure. Something in their shared laugh gave him the idea Portia was amusing.

He led Mrs. Christopher to her friend Mrs. Ballinger, then ascertained Sarah's whereabouts. Satisfied his charges were well-disposed, he surveyed the company.

Portia ducked her head as his eyes swept in her direction, smoothing her primrose gown to cover her inattention. She did not wish to oblige his notice.

He had been agreeable company. Portia hoped

she'd entertained him in return. But to expect a recurrence of his attention would be highly presumptuous. He held a large acquaintance, and was more likely to find a friend to converse with here than at the Harveys'.

So it was with some surprise and shortness of breath that she observed a pair of gentleman's shoes and the tip of the cane she knew Castleton leaned on this evening beneath her downcast gaze. She lifted her eyes to Castleton's smiling face.

"How do you do, Miss Kirby?" he asked as he bowed to her.

"Very well, Lord Castleton," she replied. She rose and sketched him a curtsey. "And you? How is your leg?"

"It could use a brief respite at the moment, if you will oblige," he said, indicating the chair beside her.

Portia nodded. They sat together, he stretching his lame leg before him.

"I don't see your aunt tonight," he said, glancing around the room again.

"I came with the Applegates."

"Ah, then there will be no cards."

"I'm afraid not," Portia replied with a laugh. "But there generally aren't at musical evenings."

"My sister-in-law tells me I am in for a treat. Madame Lussier has a superb voice."

"She's very good," Portia replied. "But she's been a popular feature at musicales this Season. I fear her program is already too familiar to enchant. You'll be fortunate to catch one note in three above the whispers."

"It's deplorably rude," he agreed. "I usually shun these evenings because I find such behavior in an audience annoying."

"I wonder you bothered to come, then," Portia said. He turned toward her with a raised brow, and her face reddened. "I'm sorry. That was not what I intended."

"What did you intend, Miss Kirby?"

Portia lowered her eyes. "I should think an evening like this would bore a gentleman of your tastes and interests. Since it is your custom to shun them, I only wondered why you chose to amuse yourself so. I should not have expressed my curiosity so bluntly, however."

"No," he replied. "But I shall satisfy your curiosity, badly expressed or not. The surgeon wants me to remain at home in bed until he's certain my leg is healed. I am heartily sick of my bed, and my house, and my servants for company, and wish to resume a more active lifestyle.

"After much debate, I agreed to restrain myself to a few quiet activities where I can remain seated for much of the time, like the theater or a musicale. When I am better, I'll return to shunning, but for the moment I am too happy to be here."

"Is it very bad?" she asked, gesturing at his boot.

"Not very," he said. "The bone is knit but still fragile. At least, that is what Mr. Mulgrew says. But it's been six weeks since I've indulged in exercise, and the muscles are weak. I shall have to rely on the cane a while longer, I'm afraid."

"I heard you broke it taking a fence," Portia said.

"Then you heard incorrectly. Have you ever seen my horse?"

A simple yet daunting question. Portia had seen Castleton riding any number of times. He had a good seat. At least, that's what George had remarked. Portia thought anyone who could perch with confidence atop a creature with a mind of its own had accomplished something she could not.

But beyond one fact she could not distinguish Castleton's horse from any other in London. Nonetheless, she offered it. "It's ... black, isn't it?"

"Yes." Castleton grinned at her. Portia was momentarily dazzled. Golden hair, deep blue eyes, lean cheeks, strong jaw, perfect mouth—and when he smiled. . . . She wondered if she could recall his smile well enough to sketch him. She had never dreamed she would ever sit beside him, look into those eyes, and have that smile flash for her benefit.

"I'm afraid I have no interest in horses," she said to disguise her pointed attention. "Black is all I recall."

His blue eyes sparkled. "I acquired him during my brief return to the Army after Napoleon escaped Elba. He's a war horse, born and bred. He was a wonder on the battlefield. Cannon shells exploding around him, the smell of blood and powder. It unnerved me, but Caesar stood it all, stalwart and unfazed.

"So imagine my surprise when he shied on Rotten Row one morning because a squirrel dashed across his path."

"A squirrel spooked your horse?" She compressed her lips tightly together, but her cheeks swelled with repressed merriment.

"Go ahead. Laugh," he said. "Had I not broken my leg in the bargain, I would join you."

Portia was still laughing when Caroline Applegate and Serina returned. Both wore a familiar, predatory look. Castleton had eluded too many snares over the years to worry for him, however.

"Lord Castleton, will you be joining us? It would be so delightful, wouldn't it, Serina?"

Serina fluttered her lashes. Castleton's features changed . . . but didn't. Still smiling, still exuding easy charm, his eyes lost some of their depth, and there was a new aloofness. He rose.

"I am afraid not, ma'am," he said. "Knowing Miss Kirby's proficiency as a musician, I only wished to secure her opinion of tonight's program."

"Madame Lussier has a lovely voice," Caroline exclaimed. "But did you know Serina is also gifted with musical talent? You must come some night and let her play her harp for you."

"A harpist?"

Serina smiled and nodded. Portia nearly choked as an image of Castleton pretending appreciation for one of Serina's schoolgirl performances intruded in her imagination. Castleton glanced down at Portia, and his eyes crinkled with shared laughter.

"I'm afraid I never developed an appreciation for that particular instrument," he continued, avoiding the subject of the implied invitation. He glanced beyond the Applegates toward Margaret and Sarah in the general crowd behind their backs. Portia could see they paid him no heed, but Castleton used their position to engineer his retreat.

"Ah," he said, "I am summoned by my family. If you will excuse me, ladies." He bowed to the Applegates and then back at Portia, who smiled conspiratorially at him before he withdrew.

He secured seats for the Christophers and Miss Barstow well away from them. Portia later wished he could have contrived a way to take her, for the worst whisperers in the room were Serina and her mother. Instead of Madame's fine soprano, she heard evaluation after evaluation of the men in the company.

"I'm sure Giles Dodd will ask me for a drive tomorrow," Serina told her mother. "I think him very agreeable, don't you?"

"Giles Dodd is amiable," Caroline told her. "And he's very well-to-do, but let's not be too hasty in singling out one gentleman. Especially when one could have fortune *and* a title."

Caroline turned her head in Castleton's general direction. Portia wondered if he noticed, and what his reaction might be. She dared not look herself. Eye contact would bring on a fit of giggling that would utterly embarrass her.

"Lord Castleton?" Serina said. Her surprised tone mirrored Portia's own feelings on the subject.

"Castleton would be quite a feather in your cap, my love," Caroline whispered. "Though the nephew's pockets are better lined, and he is closer to your age."

"I've seen nothing of Frederick Christopher since his sister's come out," Serina replied. "And Lord Castleton is much better looking, even if he is old."

"We must contrive a way to engage him during the interval," Caroline decided. "In another week or two, and he'll become as elusive as the nephew."

Portia could stand it no longer. She had to laugh at them, thinking they could ham-handedly accomplish what more subtle and worldly women had attempted over the past eleven years.

Though the music continued, she excused herself to retire to the refreshment room. Six liveried servants behind the artfully laden tables snapped to attention at her entrance, obliging her to disguise her laughter as a cough again to set it free.

Serina should marry the level-headed Mr. Dodd and be done with matter. But Portia could neither advise, nor expose, the folly of their new plan. Meddling would only infuriate Caroline. The Applegates were Portia's best means of attending amusements her aunt did not care for this Season.

If Madame remained true to form, this aria would be her last selection before the interval. Portia surveyed the aromatic platters and fruitful tiers. A servant raised a cover in response. Portia shook her head. She could not bring herself to lift a plate and fill it without an invitation from her hostess.

"Do you plan to partake or just observe?" Castleton's voice purred in her ear.

Portia turned in surprise. "I ... had to cough," she stammered.

"I noticed. Though your coughs and your laughs could be mistaken for the same by the keen observer."

"Can they?" Portia smiled. "I will remember that."

Castleton smiled in reply.

"What about you, Lord Castleton?" Portia said. "Did you come here to be served? The pastry looks very well."

"It does." He limped toward the table and directed the servant to transfer a few of the delicate puffs to a plate. He surveyed each salver, taking two of each selection, including an empty plate that he placed beneath the full. His intention came clear when he asked Portia if she wished wine or lemonade.

"You will have to carry it for us," he said. "The plates are all I can manage with the cane in hand."

Portia accepted two full wine glasses from the porter and followed Castleton to the door.

The steady buzz of normal conversation replaced the mixture of whispers and song in the music room. Their presence in the refreshment room startled Lady Sidwell, who met them on the threshold. *No doubt seeing all is in order before inviting her guests inside*, Portia thought, embarrassed.

Castleton smiled at their hostess, unperturbed.

"Ah, Emily," he said. "Everything is quite delightful. I hope you don't mind, but I decided to grab my victuals now instead of holding up the rest of the company."

"Oh, Castleton, how kind of you," Lady Sidwell said. "And how thoughtless of me. I should have made arrangements to see you served, so you didn't have to walk about."

"If I don't use it, I will never get it back," Castleton replied, tapping his leg lightly with the cane. "And as you can see, I've conscripted a delightful companion to my service."

Lady Sidwell gave Portia a grateful nod. Portia followed Castleton in dazed silence, allowing him to lead her to a secluded alcove near the terrace entrance with an arched stone seat and a very small table set before it.

He settled Portia in the curved section of the bench before sitting on the extreme end. As the Applegates approached, he casually stretched his bad leg to rest on the opposite edge, making it impossible for them to do more than nod as they passed.

"Now," Castleton said, setting the empty plate before Portia and offering her the full one to pick from. "What can I tempt you with? You must take the pastry, since you expressed your delight in it, and I've been told red meat heightens the blood. Since you blush so prettily. . . ."

"You're a terrible man," Portia exclaimed without thinking.

Castleton grinned broadly, as if she'd paid him a compliment.

"You have our hostess apologizing for *our* rude behavior," she continued, "and made certain the rest of my party may not join us. . . ."

"Which I'm sure vexes you to no end," Castleton replied, grinning more broadly still. "I would have gladly given up that beautiful music to hear what amused you so vastly, and to know what finally overset your resolve not to laugh."

Portia gasped.

"It was about me, wasn't it?" he continued. "Come. Confess. I'm to marry the fair Serina by Eastertide."

"You or your nephew," Portia replied.

Castleton's amusement died. "Because Frederick's pockets are plumper?" he guessed.

Portia nodded.

"It will be a cold day in Hades before I abandon Frederick to calculating women like them."

Frederick will be meeting very few young ladies, Portia thought wryly. The Christophers might attend ton functions for their entertainment value, but most of the young women here tonight would have matrimony in the back of their mind. Mr. Christopher's fortune was one of his most attractive attributes.

"Serina Applegate is a tender and affectionate girl in private," Portia said. "But her mother expects her to make a spectacular match. Once she settles on a suitor, and can be herself again, I believe there will

be far more broken hearts than those that courted
Serina outright."

"You give her far more credit than she deserves,
ma'am," Castleton said. "There is nothing I despise
worse than a fortune hunter. And any man who
chooses his wife on looks alone is doomed to disappointment."

Portia laughed at this pronouncement, drawing
a frown from him. Surely he could not be serious?
What had he known of *her* the one time he'd been
captivated? Anything beyond her beauty?

"Louisa Penbrook was the Rage in my first
Season," Portia hazarded. "Do you remember her?"

He did. She could see it in his face. The softness
in Castleton's eyes betrayed a residual affection.

He'd been handsome then too, though his face
did not hold the character it did now, in Portia's estimation. And he hadn't been about in Society much,
being newly home after spending all his adult life in
the Army. He could have rivaled Arthur Ponsby for
awkwardness, and yet his eagerness to embrace this
new world mirrored his niece's enthusiasm.

Castleton had worked to establish himself in the
best circles for the sake of his family. And central to
his new world had been Louisa Penbrook, soon to
be the Duchess of Carne and then no more when
she died in childbirth at age twenty.

"I knew you would," Portia said, ruthlessly shat-
tering his fond memory. She didn't know why she
told him. She'd taken no offense, even at the time.
A plain woman came to expect such behavior from

men. But Portia owned it had something to do with the fact he could remember a woman dead ten years now with obvious clarity, and yet not recall ever being introduced to herself, though they'd probably attended a hundred mutual social functions in the course of the same time period.

"You never took your eyes off her the first time we danced."

"The first. . . ?" Castleton's jaw slackened.

"I had to cast around in my memory," she said. "But in all I'm sure we danced four times that Season. And twice in the Season that followed."

Castleton balked.

"That can't be," he began, even as he realized it could be true. He'd done his duty to his hostess whenever asked in those early years, partnering girls who would otherwise sit down. He flushed. "Was I so uncivil? Allow me to beg your pardon."

"You weren't uncivil," Portia assured him. "Your ability to carry on a credible conversation with your attention directed elsewhere was quite impressive. You even paid me a compliment on my appearance."

"Thank goodness I wasn't totally rag-mannered. What did I say?"

"Well, I was wearing white, of course—a ghastly color on me—but my cousin George had presented me with a bouquet of pink rosebuds earlier in the day. I broken it apart to ornament my headdress and the front of my gown, which was . . ." she reddened, but continued, "cut a bit too daring for my comfort."

Castleton arched a sly brow at her.

"Anyway, you said something like 'it's a pity young ladies must wear white because the blush of roses became me.'"

"And you have taken my advice all these years," Castleton remarked with a wave in her direction.

Portia looked down at her primrose gown and laughed. "Oh, yes," she replied in high tone. "Every time I don this gown or another like it, I think of you."

"And yet, you must have mistaken me, ma'am," Castleton said. "I think I must have been remarking on the roses in your cheeks when your color is high, as now."

"Oh." Portia blinked at him, then laughed. "You *are* dreadful. I don't know whether to thank you or cut you cold."

Castleton grinned. "I'm sure I deserve both. Now what of the other dances?"

"I really don't recall them all that well," Portia lied. In truth, each of those dances had been the highlight of her evening. But she would not tell him so, any more than she would tell him she'd pressed one of those roses in a book to safeguard the memory of his words. And as she had forgotten that piece of girlish sentimentality until now, she guessed the book was still tucked on a shelf in her brother's library with the rose inside it. She would have to look the next time she visited Surrey.

"Well, that I don't recall them at all is particularly vexing in light of the enjoyment your company has afforded me of late. I wonder how many other remarkable people I have ignored in the past eleven years?"

Portia pinked again, but smiled at him. "Quite a few, I'm sure."

"Uncle David," Sarah exclaimed somewhere from behind him. "Here you are. We've been looking for you everywhere."

Castleton turned and rose to bow to Vivian Barstow. He gently chided the girls for interrupting his conversation with Portia, and made sure the young ladies were known to her before asking what Sarah wanted.

"There are four new specimens in bloom at Kew," Sarah exclaimed, as she latched his arm.

Castleton rolled his eyes. "Sarah's passion is botany," he told Portia. "Every spring she drags me about the countryside looking for clippings for her garden. She corresponds with Sir Joseph Banks."

"He's greatly expanded my herbarium," Sarah explained. She turned back to her uncle. "So may we go tomorrow?"

"Unfortunately not," Castleton replied. "My inability to ride has made me conscious of the deficiency in our carriage horses. I've made arrangements to go to Tattersall's tomorrow."

Sarah's face fell in disappointment.

"Perhaps you could persuade Frederick to take us," Vivian ventured.

Sarah brightened at the suggestion.

"Frederick accompanies me," Castleton said. "He's done extensive research on my behalf."

"So there's no chance he'll cry off," Sarah finished glumly. "We will have to content ourselves with a visit to Soho instead."

"You make an exception for Miss Barstow, Lord Castleton?" Portia asked as the two young ladies departed in lower spirits than they had come, and he resumed his seat.

"I don't...?"

"Your dislike of marriage-minded females," Portia returned.

"Quite observant of you, Miss Kirby," Castleton replied with a laugh. "No, I like Miss Barstow very well. More to the point, Frederick does, too. But if she waits for him to seek her out...."

"Then your errand to find new horses is genuine."

"Yes, it is."

"Then you might...." Portia ducked her head. Castleton waited for her to compose her thought, curiosity plain on his face. "You might wish to consult with Arthur Ponsby," she rushed on.

"Why would I wish to do that?" Castleton asked.

"Because..." she gazed around to be sure no one paid them heed, and then lowered her voice to be certain of it. "Because horses are the true source of his family's income," she confessed. "His father breeds them as a 'hobby', but it's a very lucrative one. Mr. Ponsby arrived in Town with only fifty pounds to cover immediate expenses and seven horses to take to auction. His pockets are now so well-lined he regularly searches for breeding stock at Tattersall's to take back to Northumberland."

"And he has prosed on and on to you about horses although you have no interest in them and cannot tell one from another."

"It's a topic that relaxes him to a natural manner," Portia conceded. "But his knowledge on the subject is profound, and he speaks with enthusiasm, not conceit. I wouldn't suggest him to you otherwise."

Castleton's face reflected his doubt.

"You've just wondered how many other remarkable people have escaped your notice," Portia reminded him. "Please believe me when I tell you Arthur Ponsby is one of them."

"No, Miss Kirby," Castleton said, surprising her. "Since this is the second time you've championed him in our brief acquaintance, I must conclude Mr. Ponsby is something more than remarkable. Exceptional, perhaps."

Portia smiled at him again, wishing her complexion did not betray heightened emotion so easily. She'd blushed more in these two nights with Castleton than in the past five years together.

CASTLETON NOTICED PONSBY straight off when he and Frederick arrived at Tattersall's the next day. In his casual leather breeches, shirt with an open collar, waistcoat of forest green, and square-cut coat of brown, he could have been mistaken for a groom. The outfit suited Ponsby much better than high fashion. And Castleton had to own his hands as his eyes roamed over the back of a large bay with confidence.

"We seek beasts with matched looks and movement," Frederick said, consulting his notes. "And must pay particular attention to the teeth and hindquarters. . . ."

"Or ask someone who knows better," Castleton said, spying his friend Lord Sefton sheltering under the arch surrounding the cobblestoned courtyard.

Even with the slight hunch of his broad back, the earl was a tall man. His reputation as a horseman was known throughout London. Castleton hoped Portia would forgive him as he hailed the peer and explained his errand of the morning.

"Carriage horses?" Sefton said. "There's only one worth a look in this lot. The bay with the left sock." Sefton waved his hand in Ponsby's direction. "I watched that country youngster put him through his paces. He's a high-stepper, for certain, but a little tender on the right. That and the markings require a careful match, and there's none to be had, unfortunately."

"There's another bay with a sock over there," Frederick said, pointing to an animal staked some distance from the rest.

"Fenton's Bright Promise? A damned waste of horseflesh."

Castleton looked the horse over. It was an excellent match to the other bay in size and coloring, although Bright Promise's sock was on the horse's right. His untrained eye could see no defect. "I'm afraid you'll have to enlighten us."

"That horse could have been a great hunter in the right hands," Sefton said. "But those hands were not Dwight Fenton's. What a good horseman recognizes as spirit, Fenton took for willfulness. He whipped the drive out of him. And now he's left with an empty shell that he'll be lucky to get any money for."

Castleton decided to stay for the auction anyway, so Sefton could point out what they should look for in the future.

The earl expounded on the virtues and vices of the horses brought to the courtyard for the next half-hour. There were some good race horses, he said, and hunters. Castleton nodded politely but paid him little heed, knowing Frederick stored every word with scholarly zeal.

He focused instead on Ponsby, talking with great animation to one of Tattersall's grooms. The groom nodded and crossed the courtyard to retrieve a carriage whip from its place on a demonstration gig. He sauntered the yard in a broad circle, stopping at last at Bright Promise's shoulder.

A snap of the whip behind the horse's ear proved Sefton correct. The horse tensed, but did not move. The groom shook the whip, intentionally trying to spark some reaction. Nothing. At a light flick of the whip against the horse's rear flank, Bright Promise took but two steps forward, then stopped dead.

A few potential buyers who noted the

demonstration grumbled in disgust. Ponsby nodded
to the groom—he'd seen enough, too—but Castleton
was struck by the satisfaction in his swarthy face.

Mr. Tattersall did his best to extol Bright Promise's virtues when he came to the block. Silence met
his request for bids. The horse would have gone
unsold if Ponsby hadn't shouted, "Fifty pounds."

"That boy's either too plump in the pockets or
too soft," Sefton said in a low voice.

"Perhaps he means to breed him," Frederick
said.

"He don't strike me as that green," Sefton said
with a laugh. "That horse is gelded."

Frederick colored at his mistake.

Ponsby claimed his property and stood aside,
lightly stroking his new acquisition and speaking in
his ear. He ignored the rest of the auction until, with
determination, he outbid all others to purchase the
second bay. Even so, Sefton felt Ponsby's bid of two
hundred and fifty guineas was a bargain.

"A really good team will go for seven hundred
to a thousand pounds," he told them. "If there'd been
a match. . . ."

"I'm not so sure there wasn't," Castleton said,
summoning the groom who'd taken up the whip on
Ponsby's behalf. He asked the purpose of the earlier
demonstration and was told the young gentleman
wished to see which direction the horse would take
when rattled.

"A good carriage horse will move forward," the
groom explained. "Or, better yet, stop."

"Then he means to make a pair of them," Frederick exclaimed.

The groom nodded.

Sefton shook his head. "Fenton ruined that horse."

"He did his best," the groom agreed. "But if any man can bring him back, it's that lad. Look you now. Young mister's just talkin' but the horse is listenin' for all he's worth."

Ponsby placed the second horse on Bright Promise's left. The bay side-stepped, but immediately stilled at Ponsby's soft nay.

"Get used to him there, my boy," Ponsby said, stroking the bay's nose. "He'll be joining you soon if I have my way."

Frederick crossed the yard and asked, "Do you really mean to make a pair of them?"

"I mean to try," Ponsby said. "Much will depend on this fellow."

He raised Bright Promise's drooping head and affectionately scratched his nose. When he took his hand away, Castleton noted, the horse's head stayed raised.

"I should like to see how you do it, if you wouldn't mind my observing," Frederick said.

"I don't mind." Ponsby introduced himself to Frederick, who, in turn introduced Ponsby to Castleton and Sefton. Ponsby's bow reflected more of his usual self-consciousness. But understandably so. It wasn't every day a young whipster was introduced to the leader of the Four-in-Hand Club.

Sefton questioned Ponsby about his training strategy.

"He's been badly trained and badly treated," Ponsby said. "He needs to know me first, what I expect of him and what I will *not* do. I intend to drive him on long reins until we are used to each other. Then we'll see what we will see."

Sefton nodded but still looked doubtful. "I find myself very interested in the outcome of this experiment. Keep me informed, Frederick."

"Yes, sir," Frederick said, as Ponsby blinked in amazement.

After Sefton took his leave, Ponsby turned to Castleton. "Miss Kirby mentioned you were looking for a new carriage team."

Castleton blinked in turn. "She did? When was that?"

"This morning. In the park. I . . . My father has a team I believe he wishes to part with. If you like, I could send for them. No obligation, of course. But if they suited . . ."

Castleton smiled. "If you think your father really wishes to part with them, then I would be interested in taking a look. Or, if you don't mind, having Sefton look at them for me."

"Oh, no, sir," Ponsby stammered. "I mean . . . it would be an honor to show them to Lord Sefton, if nothing else. My father takes great pride in his stables."

"Yes, Miss Kirby mentioned something like that to me."

They fixed a time for Frederick to observe Bright Promise's first training session, and Ponsby promised to send for the carriage horses by that afternoon's post. Then Ponsby took his leave to see to his new team, and Castleton and Frederick journeyed back to Curzon Street, Frederick eager to begin his education in the ways of breaking horses.

"Ponsby seems a good fellow, doesn't he, Uncle David?" Frederick said.

"Exceptional," Castleton replied with a sly smile. He could hardly wait to relate the morning's activity to Portia's appreciative ear.

3

A S SOON HE was off his feet, Castleton realized he'd spent too much time on them. His leg
throbbed in reproach and would not bear his weight
for the whole of the next week without protest.

When he arrived at the Seftons' ball eight nights
after the auction, he immediately sought out Portia,
finding her, as expected, in the farthest corner of the
massive, gilded room.

She wore the green gown again, but there was
something more attractive in her appearance this
evening. Castleton studied her carefully—easy to do
with her head bowed—and decided it was her hair,
loosely arranged to frame her round features with
charming tendrils.

She looked up when he cleared his throat and
offered him the seat beside her. "Your limp has wors-
ened," she observed.

"Amazing. How could you tell without looking
at me?"

Portia smiled. "The best time to survey the
company unobserved is at their arrival," she said.
"You were too preoccupied with our hosts to notice."

"Ah," Castleton said, unaccountably pleased she'd looked. "I had a setback. But a few days' rest has put me right again."

"I'm glad to hear it. Though I thought, perhaps, you had graduated from sedate entertainments."

"You missed me?" he asked with an arched brow.

Portia turned her face away. She spoke in such a low voice, Castleton barely heard the words. "I noted your absence."

Castleton smiled. He gave her a moment to compose himself.

The tabbies—Mrs. Trent and Mrs. Cray he now knew, though he didn't know which was which—had their heads close together, the furor of their conversation like the hum of bees at a picnic.

"What has them all a-twitter?"

"Mr. Pritchert was seen kissing Miss Sanderson at Vauxhall last evening. Both are unattached, and he publicly stated he wouldn't offer for her, or any woman, for such a paltry reason."

"And what do you say to that, Miss Kirby?"

"I think he must feel some attraction to have done such a thing, but to marry for one kiss seems excessive."

"You shock me, ma'am."

"I do not," Portia asserted with a light laugh. "I suspect you feel as I do about the situation."

"How so?"

She glanced at Ponsby, shifting in his unflattering clothes and predictably gazing at Serina

Applegate from afar. "I often encounter Mr. Ponsby in the park, exercising his horses. He lavishes much affection on them, including kisses, and yet I feel no obligation to wish him joy."

"Heaven forbid," Castleton chuckled, much amused.

"People kiss their dogs, their children, their siblings—in the scheme of intimate behavior, a kiss is of no moment."

"Placed in that context, I must agree. But there are kisses, and there are *kisses*. . . ."

"And since neither of us witnessed this kiss, I prefer to give Mr. Pritchert and Miss Sanderson the benefit of the doubt."

"And I, in turn, bow to your wise counsel."

She smiled in broader fashion than normal. Castleton marveled at how animation transformed her features. He couldn't say she was pretty, but. . . .

"A ray of sunshine in an otherwise dreary landscape," a voice drawled above them. Castleton frowned, then blinked as George Mahew, one of the most notorious rakes of his acquaintance, took Portia's hand in his own and kissed it.

She seemed pleased. In fact, her face held an expression Castleton could only describe as deep affection, and it eclipsed animation as a transforming attribute. Mahew's green eyes swept over Portia, and his handsome features split with a dimpled grin of appreciation.

"The company is too staid for my blood," he said. "I will languish on the sidelines partnerless if these iron-hearted women have their way. But you'll oblige me, won't you, Portia?"

"If the evening is not to your liking, why don't you leave, George?"

"Alas," Mahew slanted his eyes in the direction of Lady Burrow—his lover and the rumored source of his present income, Castleton recalled. That Portia could interpret this look, yet still smile at Mahew and allow him to hold her hand in his, gave Castleton pause.

"So, what say you, cousin?" Mahew persisted, making the reason for their intimacy clear. "Will you take pity on me?"

"The first dance?"

"A simpering minuet? Lord, no. Let's say the first waltz?"

Some unspoken communication passed between them. Portia nodded. Mahew kissed her hand again before withdrawing. Her troubled gaze followed him across the room.

Then, as if recalling he sat beside her, she turned a token smile on Castleton. "I'm sorry. What were we discussing?"

"It's irrelevant." Castleton said. "The topic is now George Mahew."

"Why?"

"Because he's not generally received in such a warm manner," Castleton retorted, realizing the whole exchange had disturbed him deeply.

"He is my cousin," Portia replied, nettled. "He always treats me with respect and courtesy. If you intend to warn me about his reputation, I probably know far more about his amours than you. And, no, I don't approve and have frequently told him so. But beyond our relation, I consider him a friend. . . ."

"Enough," Castleton said. "I don't wish a quarrel. You care for him. Obviously."

"Not in the way you imply, sir. He's like a brother to me."

Castleton held up his hand, and Portia fell silent.

"I hope," he said in as mild and reasonable tone as he could muster, "if an occasion arises to champion me, you'll be as passionate. To be frank, after the first shock you knew him wore off, it's only his choice of dance I object to."

"It's unusual," Portia agreed, cheeks burning with emotion. Her eyes sought out Mahew again. "The waltz, I mean. Not dancing with me. He usually does when we are in the same company. And, I assure you, no one will remark on it."

"No one has before," Castleton replied. "Or I should have known of your loose nature before this."

Portia blinked, then laughed. "Yes, I'm George's good point. He may be a rakehell, but he's kind to his spinster cousin."

"Not difficult, I'm sure."

"I suspect," she continued, letting his compliment pass without acknowledgment, "George wishes to speak to me privately."

"About what?"

"I don't know. Nothing dire, or he would have drawn me off."

"But not so unimportant he could not wait until the morrow to call on you," Castleton mused.

"George doesn't call on me," Portia said, levelly. "We always meet in public and then for but a few brief moments."

She changed the subject to his prospective carriage horses, scheduled to arrive on the morrow. Since the reception line was breaking up, Castleton excused himself on the pretext of making arrangements for Sefton to see the new team.

In truth, he needed to regroup. He was having difficulty concealing his feelings for Mahew from her. And the fact he *had* feelings troubled Castleton more. He barely knew Portia Kirby, though he found her pleasant company.

He liked her.

But this seemed more than liking. Their reunion had been the major fixation of his inactive week. He'd abandoned his family at the door to look for her this evening. From the moment Castleton caught her laughing glance, she'd been in his mind, chasing away despondent reflection about why he still played Society's game.

After obtaining a confirmation from Sefton, Castleton took refuge in the cardroom. After two bad hands, he relinquished his place at the table and elected to watch instead.

A table beyond, Charlotte Andrews bounced in her seat, an astonishing display of eagerness in a woman of sixty. She laid her cards out and collected her winnings, her lined face alive with satisfaction. Castleton wondered if she was also related to Mahew. Not likely. If so, Mahew would be duty-bound to visit her on occasion. No need to safeguard Portia's reputation.

The orchestra played the first movement of a waltz out in the ballroom. Castleton limped over to the door to watch.

"I PITY CASTLETON," Mahew said as he steered his cousin onto the crowded dance floor. They whirled in perfect time to the music; Portia was a good dancer and, since he'd taught her, Mahew always felt a swell of pride whenever she took the floor.

"Why?" Portia inquired. "His infirmity is temporary."

Mahew observed Castleton limp to the card-room doorway and fall into a brown study as he watched them dance.

"But it denies him the honor of holding you in his arms."

"George!" Portia laughed. "If he could dance, it would not be with me."

"Don't be so sure, coz. He's spent a great deal of time in your company of late. Beyond the realm of mere acquaintance."

"How on earth would you know...?" He twirled her past Mrs. Cray and Mrs. Trent. Portia sighed. "Can people find nothing better to talk about? He's merely bored. When he is better...."

"No," Mahew said. "That man has partaken of

your friendship. He won't relinquish it willingly. I know I would be lost without it."

Portia's eyes softened. "What's wrong, George?" she asked.

Mahew glanced at Lady Burrow, standing near the wall, her hand artfully pressed on the back of an empty chair. He hoped she would sit if the need arose. But this would likely be her last public appearance, and he knew she wanted to relish it.

"She's dying," he told Portia.

Portia glanced at Lady Burrow also. Illuminated by the full light of a wall sconce, her pallor was golden, any color supplied by a rouge pot and the careful application of cosmetics. Her hand gripped the back of the chair like a lifeline, though only the set of her jaw betrayed any pain or discomfort.

"I'm sorry. I know you care for her."

"She thinks we should break off now," he told Portia, his misery plain, "so I cannot witness her decline. Once she is bedridden, she'll be lost to me anyway. And though two years is more time than I've devoted to any woman in the past, I find I cannot abandon her. She needs me. I *want* her to need me."

"Have you told her so?"

He laughed. "The game isn't played that way, my dear."

"The time for games is over," Portia replied. "And if I were dying, knowing I was genuinely loved would comfort me greatly."

"Lord knows, her husband won't offer such consolation," Mahew said. "I suppose I will have to contrive some way we can be together. Thank you, Portia."

He drew her closer, almost an embrace, then lifted his head and amused her with an anecdote about the Prince of Wales.

ALTHOUGH MAHEW HAD caught him watching and arched his brow at Castleton in a way that greatly irked him, Castleton could not take his eyes off Portia and her partner.

Mahew cut an elegant figure, accentuating Portia's fluid grace. Their ease of manner disquieted Castleton, despite Portia's assertions. Their laughter changed to something serious. Then, to Castleton's alarm, Mahew drew her closer, a near embrace, before they were all smiles again.

Perplexing. Their intimacy was neither sexual nor improper, but Castleton found himself reacting as if it were.

He studied Portia's shining eyes, her heightened color, her easy movement, her smile that broke open with laughter at some sally of Mahew's. None were the normal attributes of beauty, but something in their combination spoke to his senses. And then, to writhe because they were displayed for another man's benefit. . . .

I'm jealous, he realized with a shock. But how could that be? Jealousy implied some claim of her on his part. Five weeks ago he hadn't even known she existed.

Perhaps that's it, Castleton thought as he limped to the refreshment room. Portia was his hidden treasure—an amusing companion and golden friend discovered in the recesses of the ton. But George Mahew had always seen and appreciated her worth. It was as galling as those dances that he could not recall no matter how hard he tried. It bespoke a shallowness and short-sightedness in himself he'd never suspected.

And because the idea he'd allowed a diamond beyond his reach to blind him to the pearl in his grasp was foremost in Castleton's thoughts, he found the mirroring behavior of Arthur Ponsby disturbing that evening.

Ponsby stood on the threshold of the refreshment room, wringing his gloved hands behind his back with indecision, as Serina Applegate balanced the attentions of two other swains eager to serve her from the table.

"Ponsby." Castleton had to call more than once to gain the young man's attention.

Ponsby stammered an apology. "I was distracted," he said.

"I noticed," Castleton replied. "A very pretty distraction."

"Beautiful," Ponsby corrected. His features fell with the hopelessness of it. "She is very beautiful."

"But not kind," Castleton said.

"Sir?"

"She sets them against each other to feed her vanity," Castleton explained. "The more heated their exchange, the greater her delight. One must wonder if this behavior would carry throughout her life. Might she, for instance, pit child against child to prove which loved her best?"

Ponsby's mouth fell open as Castleton stepped closer.

"Good looks always fade with time," Castleton murmured in Ponsby's ear, "but good manners do not."

Ponsby studied Miss Applegate with new eyes as he digested this comment. He absently agreed to bring the carriage team around to Curzon Street at eleven the next morning.

Castleton left him to reassess Serina's worthiness, finding his good deed only brief solace to his own reflective thoughts.

AFTER GAZING AT her image in the looking glass for ten minutes, Portia reluctantly loosened her smooth knot, softening the hair around her full features. She clasped her best pearl necklace around her throat, then sighed.

She thought she'd grown beyond this folly. She was not hideous, but she had no beauty. From the age of twenty on, her goal had been to present a neat and modestly pleasant appearance to the ton. But here she was, ten years later, wishing she were taller or slimmer or had some outstandingly lovely feature to enhance. And why? Because Castleton sought her company.

She'd always thought him so handsome. And these feelings—if only she had some beauty or style—had similarly gripped her eleven years ago. Only then she'd been too shy to carry on a credible conversation.

The frank tone of their dialogues left Portia feeling quite unguarded. She liked him very well. Too well, in fact. She was a diversion; when Castleton was healed he would be gone with, perhaps, the odd nod across a room to remember her by in future.

But her life, with which she had been perfectly content, would become a little darker and vastly duller.

And so she wished for some measure of loveliness. An armor against his inevitable desertion. A lure to keep their acquaintance a while longer. A solace that her worth extended beyond his notice.

Portia shook her head at the looking glass image. "Enjoy it while you can, for it *will* end, and you'll be no worse off than you were before."

Still, a pang mingled with the elation in Portia's heart as Castleton crossed the Beauchamps' drawing room, knowing he limped in her direction for the fixed purpose of speaking to her, and his warm smile and the keen shine of his deep blue eyes were for her benefit.

"You must congratulate me on my acquisition," he said after an easy bow over her hand.

"You purchased Mr. Ponsby's team," Portia replied.

"I had to." Castleton laughed. "As Ponsby led

them up my drive, Sefton said *he* would buy them if I did not, and my head groom would have wept with vexation had I let them slip away."

He sat beside her. His suppressed amusement indicated he had a tale to tell, and he would remain beside her until its finish. Portia hoped it was a long story.

"Sefton practically salivated when he learned this wasn't Ponsby Senior's 'best' pair. Although I was sorely tempted to ask your young friend why he buys breeding stock if his father is under strict orders from Mrs. Ponsby to limit the size of his stable. But I refrained."

"Thank you." Portia would not have revealed Ponsby's circumstances if she hadn't thought she could trust Castleton. Despite his easy manner, she knew he kept his counsel. But to tell him so would betray her study of him these past eleven years. Castleton might misconstrue that. Until recently, he was just another player on Society's stage.

"Frederick thought Sefton was being hasty, however," Castleton continued. His eyes danced. "His research indicated we should test them on a rig first."

"He didn't say so?"

"I'm afraid he did." Castleton sighed. "I thought Margaret would sink into the ground."

"Your sister-in-law was present?" Portia asked, confused.

It appeared his entire family was present, including Miss Barstow, who suggested calling out

a landau. Sefton drove Castleton and the Christophers in the carriage while Ponsby rode beside.
"When we got to the park, Sefton decided traffic was
light enough to 'spring 'em.' I thought we lost Ponsby
there."

"I highly doubt that," Portia said, then grew hot
thinking Castleton might take offense. She would
blush far less if she would curb her tongue. And
why it should always fly loose when he was about
remained a mystery.

And yet, as the corner of his mouth curved
up into his lean cheek and his eyes crinkled with
amusement, she wondered if this was the reason. He
certainly enjoyed seeing her blush.

"No," he agreed. "Ponsby fell back to accommodate traffic on the path. His mount and his skills as
a rider impressed Sefton, as well. I suspect he'll offer
Ponsby membership in the Four-in-Hand Club if he
succeeds with those bays."

"Oh, do you think so?" It would be the making
of Arthur Ponsby. Nestled in a branch of society
united by his genuine passion, Portia could envi-
sion him achieving sorely needed confidence. For a
moment, she was so lost in vicarious joy she did not
register Castleton's probing look.

"You really like him, don't you?" he asked softly.

"I do," she said. "He's good, kind, decent, and
caring. If we prized those qualities as we do looks,
address, fortune, and birth, we would be a much
better society."

"You're most certainly right," Castleton replied,

and for a moment Portia felt a communion between them so deep it snatched her breath away. Then his eyes creased with humor again. "But whatever shall I do about my title?"

Portia blinked. Should she say he was much more than a baron? That he had each of Arthur's good qualities in addition to those prized by Society, and beyond them all a humor and confidence that raised him high in her estimation regardless of his rank? But that would be far too familiar. And though truth, Castleton might question her motives for such flattery.

Portia blushed. Again.

"I like him too," Castleton said, relieving the pressure of the situation. "And that's good, considering he's about to become a fixture in my home."

"He is?"

"Most certainly. The more Sefton expressed his admiration for Ponsby's horsemanship, the more determined Frederick became to remedy his own deficiency on the topic. Ponsby offered to teach him to drive. And then there's the shopping excursion."

"Excuse me?"

Ponsby had accepted Margaret's luncheon invitation before Sefton refused. Noticing his silence, Sarah drew him out and learned he was considering the money for the horses.

"I see you are curious but too polite to ask." Castleton said. "Sefton told me anything less than a thousand was a bargain. Ponsby offered them for seven-fifty, and I accepted. But I got the impression I surprised him."

"Well, actually...last night he mentioned his father wanted six hundred for them," Portia confessed, "but I suggested he ask for eight hundred, in case you wished to talk him down."

Castleton laughed. "And here I thought you were my friend."

Portia warmed at the label, but would not apologize. "If your pockets cannot bear the extra amount, I can speak to him. . . ."

"I can bear the expense," he replied with a smile. "But will the additional money line Ponsby's own pocket?"

"Most likely," Portia said. "Why?"

"Because he excused his inattention by wondering which merchant on Bond Street sold the best lace mantillas."

"Oh, for his sister Jane," Portia exclaimed. "She wants one most particularly but their father thinks it too extravagant for a country wedding."

"Just so," Castleton said. "He asked Miss Barstow to recommend a shop, and she offered to help him choose one. Ponsby would not accept her assistance unless Sarah and Frederick accompanied them. Frederick choked at the notion of shopping with his sister, but Ponsby thought nothing of it."

"Jane is one of four sisters, and Arthur's very close to them all. I have a feeling, as the only son, they've run herd on him all their lives," Portia replied.

"He must be very close to his mother, too," Castleton said. "He promised Sarah a prize rose bush. Does his mother love him sufficiently to relinquish such a treasure?"

"I don't know," Portia replied, astonished. "They are her passion. She has great pride in the acclaim she's won for them."

"Well I hope she will oblige. Otherwise, I fear he'll deliver a barrel of manure to my doorstep."

Portia blinked.

"It's the secret of her success," Castleton explained. "Out of that vast stable, one horse on a special diet produces the most potent fertilizer."

Portia laughed.

Castleton continued: "As it is, Ponsby intends to contact their groom for the feed mix. And Stubbins is so enchanted with our new team he'll probably indulge Sarah and change the diet of every horse in our stable. I suspect our acquaintance with Ponsby will cost far more than the expense of the horses alone."

Portia thought her laughter might burst her stays. And while she could mentally hear her mother chiding how unseemly and unfeminine it was to laugh so in public, Portia couldn't contain her mirth. Arthur Ponsby would never fit well in Society; Portia had known it from the first. And yet among Castleton's unique family, he'd found a fashionable place where he could be himself.

PORTIA'S LAUGHTER HELD a peculiar music. Light and flowing like a breeze on an uncut field.

Entrancing. Her eyes shimmered beneath the light of the candle sconce above them, which also burnished golden hues in the shine of her light brown hair.

She wore it in the looser style, the one Castleton found attractive, though he suspected long, unbound locks would suit her better still. Soft curls teasing at her sloping shoulders and the curve of her back, caressing the swell of her breast. . . .

Castleton paused, astounded at the tenor of his thoughts.

Portia touched a hand to her lips in an effort to suppress her merriment. Her other hand came down on his sleeve, midway down the forearm, and though it exerted no pressure, seemed intent on bracing her to composure.

Castleton stilled, recognizing the emotion stirred by the light contact. Desire.

But why? He searched her face and form for a reason. This broad, bright smile brought the line of her full cheek higher and exposed fine, even teeth. Her mouth was her best feature, he decided. Mobile and expressive. The eyes were next. Large, and shining with intelligence and understanding— much more beguiling than shape or hue. The rest was commonplace, but those features—the eyes, the smile, a trace of bone in the full cheek, and the texture of her hair—drew him. And the softness of her—the idea of exploring the curving contours of her figure. . . .

"I'm glad you like him," Portia managed,

returning Castleton to his senses. "Otherwise, you'd be wishing me to perdition."

"Never," Castleton replied, and knew at once his tone was too intimate.

The laughter died, the hand snatched back to her lap, her gaze dropped to the floor and, other than a brush of a finger to the corner of her eye, all trace of her outburst vanished.

Spirit quelled, Portia was at her plainest. And yet, the pace of Castleton's heart did not abate. That brighter creature was inside her. If he exerted himself, he could coax it out again. And he'd just begun to know her. With time, what other delights might he draw from her?

He scanned the room for a neutral topic.

"Your aunt is particularly social this evening," he commented. Charlotte Andrews beamed and nodded to the Fortiscues, then joined the conversation of the group behind her.

"Her monthly allowance is gone. No cards for a sennight."

"How will she survive?" Castleton murmured.

"She's putting out feelers for the summer," Portia said. "We can always stay with James and Maria, but like to avoid that option whenever possible."

"Is your brother such an ogre?"

"James is a dear," Portia replied. "It's Maria who's the monstrous one. And then, not monstrous as much as overbearing."

"I have a friend with such a wife," Castleton said.

Portia nodded. "Alvenia Wilkes."

Castleton turned. "You know Geoffrey and Alvenia?"

"Only by sight," Portia said, her face flushed. "And sound."

"She does have a voice, doesn't she?"

"Since Nature bestowed the voice, it must be forgiven. But her opinions and the superior manner in which she delivers them . . . I wonder if she knows her voice is unpleasant, so she structures her content to suit its timbre."

Castleton widened his eyes in surprise. It was his own evaluation of Mrs. Wilkes, formed by eleven years' contact. The Wilkeses spent very little time in Town, though. Alvenia must have held court in one of Miss Kirby's corners for Portia to hold such a decided opinion of her.

"I'm sorry Captain Croft took his family abroad," Portia said. "We spent last summer at their house in Plymouth. I enjoyed the seaside very much."

"Have you been to Brighton?"

"Nowhere so fashionable," Portia replied. "But I'm sure you must have gone there."

"To satisfy my curiosity about the Pavilion," he admitted.

"What did you think of it?"

He shook his head. "It has touches of prettiness, but the effect of the whole. . . ." Castleton held her eyes with his own. "There is something to be said for simplicity."

Portia sensed the intended compliment, and her response disturbed him. Her features cooled back to mere acquaintance, and she turned her attention away from him.

So much for flirtation, Castleton thought, if a tiny gallantry produced such chill results. And did he truly wish to step up to another level of intimacy?

Turned so, the tendon of Portia's neck tightened into an inviting curve, brushed by the curled ends of upswept tendrils. Castleton had a strange yearning to trace his fingers up that line and across her jaw, to gently turn her back to him. . . .

For what purpose?

I don't believe this. He rarely indulged in passionate fantasy. Experiences with Women of Low Virtue in his Army years had taught him he did not require sexual intercourse for its own sake. He'd never kept a mistress, and the few encounters he'd had since attaining his title were characterized by brevity and a mutual desire for impermanence at the outset.

He *liked* Portia. Their friendship had substance. She was good-humored, insightful, intelligent, and fiercely loyal. The way she championed the downtrodden Ponsby or defended her reprobate cousin bespoke an underlying fire beneath her soft exterior. Slipping beneath her guard revealed a vibrant rainbow of emotions beyond her pale propriety.

She—and the rest of the room—would most likely laugh if they knew he found her attractive. And yet, the longer she kept her face away the more Castleton longed to touch her. To claim her attention and her person for himself.

The frown of angry displeasure she wore when at last she turned back unnerved him, however.

"Have I offended you, ma'am?" he asked.

Portia blinked and focused on his face. "I'm sorry. I fear I'm too used to my own company. I was lost in a thought directed elsewhere, I assure you."

"And to whom was it directed?"

"Lord Burrow," Portia replied.

Castleton frowned and let his gaze drift over her head.

Burrow stood near the doorway, conversing with three members of Parliament. His wife stood beside him, charmingly attired in pale blue with intricate silver cords binding her upswept hair. From time to time, Burrow patted the hand clinging to his black evening jacket. He inclined his head so its salt-and-pepper strands brushed her ladyship's guinea curls, and said a word in her ear that had her draw up straighter.

"He's particularly attentive tonight," Castleton said, wondering why this rare display of affection should disturb Portia so much.

"He's a cold, unfeeling monster," Portia said venomously.

Castleton stared at her, shocked.

"Look at her very carefully," Portia urged in a low voice.

Castleton studied Lady Burrow. She shifted, and her perfect features momentarily tensed. Her gaze drifted to the chair behind her. As if sensing her movement, Burrow tucked her hand tighter into the crook of his arm. He did not look at his wife, but must have said something meant to call her attention back to the gentlemen before them. Lady Burrow flashed them a wan smile and made some comment. But within the span of seconds her eyes strayed back to the chair with a growing measure of longing.

"She appears to be in some discomfort," Castleton murmured.

"She's gravely ill," Portia told him. "George told me so the other night. He also said her physician counseled her to stay at home in future. But Lord Burrow must feel he needs to make the most of his investment. She is no more than an ornament to him."

"Did your cousin tell you that, too?"

"My eyes told me," Portia returned. "He struck her once for having wine spilled on her gown. Someone backed against her in a crowded room; it wasn't even her fault. But Lord Burrow drew her off to a quiet room and struck her with a fist to the small of her back. To punish her without marring her visible beauty."

"You witnessed this?!"

Portia nodded. "They didn't notice me; most people don't. He dragged her away before I could say a word.

"The next night we attended the same soirée. George was there, too. I didn't tell him what I'd seen, only that she appeared to be in pain, and would he please inquire after her for me. When they became lovers, Lord Burrow's physical abuse stopped."

"How do you know?" Castleton asked.

"Because George says nothing. And I hear every verbal transgression he can pry from her. Lord Burrow must have thought twice about marking her anywhere while another man bedded her."

"You assume Burrow knows of your cousin's relations with her," Castleton said.

"Oh, please," she said in withering tones. "That man reports the Prince Regent's expenditures to the penny each Parliamentary session. Nothing escapes his notice. He tolerates George's attentions because it shows George for a rake, but, at the same time, doesn't his wife attract the handsomest lovers?"

A chill gripped Castleton. "Did you know?"

"I'm sorry?"

"Did you know Mahew and Lady Burrow would become lovers when you sent him to inquire after her?"

Portia reddened appreciably. "I suspected they would deal well together. Their backgrounds are similar, and George feels himself so low on the social ladder, any opportunity to play knight errant tempts him. If he were here, he would be furious."

"But he has you to be furious for him," Castleton replied coolly. "Pray, excuse me."

He rose and bowed to her before withdrawing.

What is the matter with me? Portia scolded inwardly. *I must appear a veritable abbess for suggesting I'd drawn Lady Burrow and George together.*

Castleton limped the breadth of the drawing

room, and Portia's breath quickened. It was worse than she expected. Castleton had abandoned her to join Lord and Lady Burrow. *Oh, Lord*, she prayed. She'd forgotten his own penchant for gallantry.

To Portia's astonishment, however, Castleton smiled at the peer. His social smile—though he directed a warmer one at Lady Burrow. Castleton had Burrow and the three MPs laughing at some anecdote within minutes. Then he directed a comment to Burrow, who responded with an oratory. Castleton nodded. The MPs asked Burrow questions. Castleton stepped back toward Lady Burrow and allowed her husband the floor.

Castleton spoke to her, and Lady Burrow responded politely. As she talked, Castleton stepped backwards. Lady Burrow twisted to maintain eye contact.

Burrow glanced at his wife, registered Castleton's position, and relinquished her arm. Castleton took another step backwards. Lady Burrow adjusted accordingly, pain in her expression.

Castleton called to Burrow. He indicated his leg and the set of chairs along the wall. Burrow nodded. Castleton guided Lady Burrow to refuge, finally glancing toward Portia.

He winked.

Portia's eyes misted as she nodded to him. In her head she composed and recomposed a sentence to convey her gratitude without betraying how much what Castleton had done affected her. He would return. Glances indicated he intended a retreat as soon as Burrow was too absorbed to notice. In the meantime, he drew Lady Burrow out in a way that might have made George jealous.

"Portia!" Her aunt stood beside her, cap askew.

Portia stood and adjusted the lace back over the iron curls.

"A lure was taken. Tunbridge Wells with the Barkers. He's a formidable opponent, although his wife is weak. But I hear he has a sister who's a decent hand."

"That sounds delightful," Portia murmured.

"I've sent for the carriage," Charlotte said.

"Already? I mean. . . ." Portia gazed in Castleton's direction. He was totally focused on Lady Burrow.

"I'm very tired, and there's nothing else here to amuse," Charlotte complained.

"Of course." Portia offered her aunt her arm. Taking leave of their hosts seemed quickly done. And yet, Castleton waited by the doorway when they turned to exit.

"Good evening, Mrs. Andrews," Castleton said, bowing to her aunt. "Leaving so soon, Miss Kirby?"

"I'm afraid so," Portia replied.

"That's too bad." His gaze fell inward, as if weighing something in his thoughts. The inattention was so swift, Portia wondered if she'd imagined it. "Perhaps you and your aunt would join my family at the theater tomorrow. Covent Garden?"

"I have no use for such affairs," Charlotte answered with a frown. "I tend to sleep more than I watch."

"And you, Miss Kirby?"

She searched his face. She loved the theater, and to attend with him would be so marvelous. But. . . . "I'm sorry," she said. "It's kind of you to offer, but I've made other plans."

"Another time then?"

Portia doubted there would be another time, but nodded.

Castleton smiled at her. "Then I bid you good evening."

Later she would wonder at her boldness. But her carefully thought-out sentence could not be uttered with her aunt at her shoulder. And she could not leave without some gesture to relieve the fullness of her heart.

She extended her hand out to him. "Good evening."

Castleton's smile broadened. His palm made contact with hers from below, and Portia instantly closed her fingers, hoping her eyes held sufficient gratitude to explain the familiarity. But then, to her amazement, Castleton raised her hand to his lips and placed a light kiss on her knuckle.

"Good night, Miss Kirby," he said as he relinquished his hold. "Until we meet again."

4

"AGAIN" WAS FOUR nights later, at the Duchess of Wallace's cotillion. The social event of the Season, a thousand men and women crammed rooms large enough for hundreds only. Portia's invitation surprised her; she was as new to these rooms as any debutante. And although her aunt thought it a lot of fuss about nothing, Mrs. Applegate made room for Portia in their carriage.

Portia repaid the kindness by sitting at Serina's elbow while her mother circulated the crowded floor.

By the time Castleton's party arrived, crowds obstructed Portia's view of the door. Even Frederick attended, though he wandered off when he spied Arthur Ponsby by Lord Sefton.

Considering her proximity to Serina, Portia had expected Ponsby to approach her. But Lord Sefton had pounced on him as he crossed the threshold, introducing him to a half-dozen Corinthians. By his relaxed manner, Portia guessed their topic to be horse flesh. Joined by Frederick, Ponsby shook hands with the horsemen and walked off with his friend in Castleton's direction.

After bowing to Castleton and Mrs. Christopher, Ponsby turned toward Sarah, who, it appeared, had replaced Serina in his affections. They spoke for several minutes—commonplaces by Sarah's manner—but Portia'd never seen Ponsby so happy. His eyes dropped to his feet, but lifted again as Sarah nodded.

Then Frederick drew Ponsby off to another group of young men. But from time to time, Ponsby glanced in Sarah's direction, and smiled to himself with satisfaction.

Portia hoped Lord Castleton liked Ponsby very well. Sarah would be an excellent match if he could engage her notice. Compared to his pursuance of Serina Applegate, he was already a leap ahead. He could apparently hold a conversation with Sarah despite his feelings, and had, if Portia read the situation correctly, asked her to dance and been accepted.

Castleton did not look around, so Portia studied him at her leisure. He was mending. He only placed weight on the cane after three or four steps, and his limp was barely noticeable. Hailed on all sides by friends and acquaintances, he greeted them in turn with smiles of pleasure. Then he led Margaret into the next room, where Portia could see him no more.

It has begun, Portia thought, smoothing the skirt of her best gown to hide her disappointment, though, in truth, there was no one to observe it.

"HAVE YOU EVER seen such a crowd, Margaret?" Mrs. Ballinger remarked, fanning herself and everyone else about her. Phoebe was as stout as Margaret was slight. Her hair was prematurely white, though her brows were black as soot.

"Not this Season," Margaret said. "So clever of you to place us near the window, Castleton. If it's this close here, I can imagine what the heart of the drawing room is like."

"Sweltering, I'm sure," Castleton said, pleased for once his leg gave him an excuse to take refuge in a remote chair.

"Castleton, I am most vexed with you," Lucy, Duchess Wallace said as she stepped into their corner. The dainty matron had a waifish figure and a luxurious head of chestnut hair. "Have you quarreled with your friend?"

"I've quarreled with no friend I can think of," Castleton replied with a frown.

"I asked her particularly for your sake, and yet you skulk in another room. What else am I to think?" Lucy asked.

"What friend?" Margaret asked, perplexed.

"Why, Miss Kirby, of course."

"She's here?" Castleton asked, scanning the swells of the other room. He could not detect Portia amidst the sea of faces, despite careful scrutiny. "I confess, I never saw her; though I don't know how I missed her. Such a meager turnout," he said.

Lucy laughed. "Well, I hoped that was the case, and your point is taken about the company. Perhaps we can arrange a more intimate gathering for the pair of you, in the future. Supper, maybe, or a night in our box at Vauxhall?"

"Most obliging of you, Lucy," Castleton said. "I'll extend your invitation to her when we speak. If I can find her."

"Find who?" Frederick asked, arriving just then with Ponsby.

"Miss Kirby," Margaret said in a flat tone.

"Oh," Ponsby said. "She's with the Applegates. In that bower-like place beyond the floral arch."

"If she's with the Applegates, you must be sure," Castleton quipped.

Ponsby flushed, and his dark features took on a guilt-stricken cast. "I haven't spoken to her this evening. Between Lord Sefton and Frederick I've met so many people and. . . ."

Sarah stepped into their corner on the arm of Cecil Lane. Her blue eyes sparkled, and her smile dazzled. One of the dandy set, Lane lived not far from Frederick's house in Kent, where the family usually made their home. Lane had fascinated Sarah since infancy, though they'd had little discourse since her come out.

Sarah's life-long infatuation took on a different dimension with her new status as a young lady, Castleton realized. He hoped she'd grown out of her crush. Cecil was a shallow coxcomb.

"Thank you for the dance, Mr. Lane," Sarah said demurely. She smiled at Ponsby. "I believe this dance is yours, sir."

Ponsby nodded and offered Sarah his arm.

Castleton noted the softness in the young man's eyes, and the squaring of his shoulders as he led Sarah into the drawing room.

If the choice is a vain coxcomb or a bumbling horse trader for a nephew, Castleton thought, *please, Lord, make her a child again. I don't think my heart can take this.*

"Castleton," Margaret was saying, "I find what the duchess said disturbing...."

"As do I," Castleton said. "Poor Miss Kirby with only the Applegates to keep her company."

"Shall I fetch her over, sir?" Frederick asked.

"No." Castleton smiled to himself. "I have a better idea."

BREATHLESS FROM THE last set of dances, Serina resumed her seat next to Portia, plying her fan with rapid strokes and smiling at her swains with proprietary pleasure.

"No, no, no ... I must sit down a while."

"The musicians intend to wait for you," Portia said with a light laugh, for she could see their shadows in the gallery above the dance floor, stretching and refreshing themselves.

Serina concealed her mouth with her fan and leaned in close to Portia. "I wish they wouldn't. It's terribly warm in here."

"It is," Portia agreed in low tones, "and I have not been exerting myself as you have. Perhaps a glass of punch?"

"I've already had six. I shall have to retire to the withdrawing room if I consume more."

Caroline pushed through the revelers and straightened her feathered turban. "My love, why are you sitting down?"

"I'm tired, Mama."

"Be tired at home. Every eligible man in the kingdom is here tonight. If you don't dance, you should circulate among them."

"But, Mama...."

"Don't argue with me, miss. On your feet. A woman who is always sitting down...."

Caroline glanced at Portia. Portia suppressed a grin as Serina popped upright. There were worse fates than being an acknowledged spinster, but probably not to Miss Applegate.

Portia wished she were more secure in her spinsterhood. She wanted to rise herself, walk the room, and, perhaps, discover Castleton's location. She had a notion he was far more comfortable than she in this airless quarter.

"Excuse me, ladies."

All three turned in astonishment as Frederick Christopher sketched them an awkward bow. Caroline beamed. Serina straightened. Portia pitied the poor fellow bumped from Serina's dance card. A wealthy man in his own right, heir to Castleton's unentailed properties, and not one to fix his interest with the ladies, Frederick would be a plum in Serina's pocket.

"May I have this dance, please, Miss Kirby?"

Three pairs of eyes rounded at this pronounce-ment, none more than Portia's. She rose, and in doing so, observed Castleton grinning at her from the door of the salon, although Mrs. Christopher, standing beside him, frowned deep disapproval.

That dreadful man, Portia thought as she placed her hand on Frederick's and allowed him to lead her to the floor. Even worse, the orchestra struck up a waltz. Panic crossed Frederick's face as he drew Portia into his arms.

The second time he trod on her foot, he begged her pardon.

"It's quite all right," Portia said. "Like any phys-ical activity, dancing requires practice for profi-ciency. And since you were coerced to this in the first place. . . ."

"Ma'am?"

"I haven't known your uncle long, but I suspect we're here at his request and not an inclination on your part."

"He did ask me," Frederick said, amazed. His shoulders relaxed. "When he learned you were here, he expressed a wish to speak to you. I offered to escort you to him but he felt that would be presump-tuous. . . ."

"So he suggested you dance me about and end somewhere in his vicinity," Portia finished.

Frederick laughed, relaxing further. "Exactly so!"

Portia cast a disparaging look in Castleton's direction, only deepening his broad smile.

"Well, Mr. Christopher, you are faced with an

awkward dilemma. Which is more important to you? The affection of your uncle or your duty to your dance partner?"

"Miss Kirby?"

"It's very warm in here, and I have sat in that closed corner all evening. My thirst greatly excels my desire for your uncle's company. You would make me very happy if you danced me toward the refreshments instead."

"Ma'am!" Sobriety replaced the momentary flash of laughter in his blue eyes. "It would be a dilemma, wouldn't it? A lady's wishes should always be respected. But I owe my uncle my allegiance, and in light of his infirmity...."

"Infirmity? He has a bad leg on the mend and a prankish sense of humor I suspect he indulges far too much. But there is nothing 'infirm' about him."

"No," Frederick smiled in Castleton's direction. "He's simply splendid, isn't he?"

"He's a remarkable man," Portia agreed. "But so are you, Mr. Christopher."

"Me?"

"It's not every day a young man chooses to dance with an aging spinster over a diamond of the first water."

Frederick blinked, and Portia directed his attention to Serina Applegate. Although revolving in the arms of Giles Dodd, she watched them with a frown on her lovely face. She spoke furiously, no doubt critiquing Frederick's performance as a dancer. Frederick stumbled as he sensed her disapproval.

"I did not snub her," Frederick stammered. "I . . . I don't dance in general. . . ."

"Such a shame. When you don't think about it, you do quite well," Portia said.

Frederick flushed. "It must be you, ma'am. I mean . . . dancing takes two partners. . . ."

"Gallantry, too. You shall turn my head."

Frederick laughed. "I'm so rotten at all this," he confessed. "I would rather be home reading than stuffing myself into a tight jacket, negotiating through crowds, and making small talk. I hate small talk the most."

"I sympathize. I was positively tongue-tied at your age."

"Not so long ago, ma'am," Frederick said.

"Very kind," Portia replied with approval. "Do you know the remedy to shyness? You take a person—say, Arthur Ponsby—and you observe what interests him—like horses. Then you approach him, and express a desire to know what he knows. . . ."

"But that's how we met," Frederick exclaimed.

"Is it? Then you know what to do, don't you?" Portia said.

"But what. . . ?" Frederick glanced at Vivian Barstow, dancing in the arms of the Honorable Percy Carr. Society became her, Portia observed. Her spirits were high—her features animated.

Frederick quickly looked away again. "What if the person's tastes and interests appear to have nothing in common with you?"

"Then you make a commonality. For instance,

you require dancing practice, Miss Barstow requires partners. Beg her pardon as you begged mine, step on her toes a few times, and let her teach you what she knows."

"You make it sound so easy," Frederick said.

"I admit, it is far easier when you are not attached to the person in question."

"Miss Barstow and I are not attached," Frederick stammered. "There is no courtship between us."

"Attachment is a matter of heart, not a matter of courtship," Portia told him. "And a lack of attachment is probably why Miss Barstow dances so easily."

"Ma'am?"

"Unlike Miss Applegate, her aim is not to captivate. She just wants someone to dance with her. For that reason, I suspect she would dance with you regardless of your proficiency. And as you become more adept under her tutelage, who knows? It may have pleasant consequences for you both."

Frederick gazed at her intently. "It is no wonder my uncle seeks you out, ma'am," he said. "You are very wise."

"An attribute of advancing age, I fear. As for your uncle...."

The music drew to a close. Frederick glanced at Castleton once, then offered Portia his arm. "Thank you for the dance," he said. "May I offer you refreshment?"

"Bravo," she replied with a light laugh. "Let's compromise, shall we? I will agree to your leading me off the floor in the direction of your family, if you will be so kind as to run to the refreshment room and fetch me a glass of lemonade."

Frederick escorted Portia to his mother and his uncle. Portia avoided Castleton's dancing eyes. Mrs. Christopher's distress must be dealt with first.

"Very prettily done," Castleton said. "I have never seen you dance so well, Frederick. Have you, Margaret?"

"It was well done," Margaret admitted reluctantly. She looked Portia over with troubled eyes.

"Frederick is a delightful young man," Portia said. "Too bad he's cursed with such an uncle."

Margaret's eyes widened in surprise.

Frederick laughed. "She knew, sir. She knew you'd sent me. And she wanted me to take her to the refreshment room to spite you, but I intend to fetch a glass for her instead. Would you like something? And you, Mother?"

"It's a capital idea, isn't it, Margaret?" Castleton asked.

Margaret nodded.

Frederick bowed to them all and dashed off to accommodate them, skirting the dance floor to expedite his errand.

"I fear I've been meddlesome, ma'am," Portia said as soon as he was out of earshot. "A spinster's habit. I beg your pardon."

"I don't understand you," Margaret replied in a faint voice.

"I told your son if he wished to improve his

social skills, Miss Barstow would make an excellent tutor. I hope you are not opposed to that."

"Oh, no," Margaret said. "Vivian is an excellent girl. We are all very fond of her."

"I feared you would take offense," Portia continued, "not because of whom I proposed, but because I implied he needed alteration. He really is a dear boy, and does you great credit. Both your children do."

"Oh. Oh, thank you," Margaret smiled at last. "But we should all be lost without Castleton's guidance."

"Even when he is so devilish as to compel that poor boy dance with me?" Portia asked in a light voice.

"Even so," Margaret admitted with a rueful smile.

They conversed on neutral topics—the decoration, the heat, and Miss Bingley's dress, or lack thereof. While shockingly spare, they agreed it was probably much cooler than their own finery. Frederick returned with glasses in hand, a frown of concentration on his face.

"I hope I did not spill much," he said as his uncle took the lemonade from him and dispensed one each to the ladies. Margaret took her leave of them with Frederick some moments later, and Castleton invited Portia to sit in his cool corner.

As soon as she was settled, Portia drank her glass empty.

"You were thirsty, weren't you?" Castleton asked.

"Perishingly so. The disadvantage of 'the thick of things.'"

"Then it was kind of you to oblige me."

"I didn't oblige you," Portia replied. "I obliged your nephew, who seemed torn about the matter, and I obliged myself. I suspected you were better situated than myself, and I still wished to thank you for your kindness to Lady Burrow. It was so very good of you to exert yourself on her behalf."

"Before you canonize me, you should know my motives were purely selfish. I'd just had the most intriguing revelation about you and wished to explore it at my leisure. But I thought you would not be easy if Lady Burrow remained standing, so. . . ."

"A revelation? About me?!" Portia exclaimed. "What kind of revelation?"

"That you are a student of human nature. You amuse yourself by picking us apart like Latin texts to see what we are about."

Portia gasped.

"Don't deny it," Castleton continued in airy tones. "How else would you know the best way to allay Margaret's fears was to compliment her as a mother and invoke Miss Barstow's name?"

"Lord Castleton, I . . . really . . . that is to say. . . ." She rolled her eyes. "You are a dreadful man."

"I knew it," Castleton could not keep the triumph from his voice. "And what a perfect night to put your knowledge to the test. The whole of London is here, and I'll wager you could tell me more about each one of them than they could tell me about themselves. Whom shall we start with?"

"This is not a game, my lord," Portia replied stiffly.

"No. It's diversion. Something a bit too dear to us both."

She compressed her lips tightly. *By God*, he thought, *there's a hint of steel in her, as well.* The more Castleton learned, the more he liked her. But what of her feelings?

"Then tell me about someone who won't take exception. Tell me about myself."

Portia widened her hazel eyes. "I couldn't...."

"Of course you can." He rested his index finger on the tip of her chin and turned her face toward the dance floor. He leaned close to her ear and purred, "Pretend I'm one of those mother hens you sit with. My charming but sadly freckled daughter dances with Baron Castleton. Quite a catch by all accounts."

"Oh, *quite* a catch," Portia replied in a brimming voice.

Castleton smiled, too. He changed the register of his voice to a high falsetto. "Are you acquainted with him, Miss Kirby?"

Portia choked back a laugh.

"Pray, pray what can you tell me about him?"

"What is there to say, Mrs. Tabby?" Portia countered, drawing a chuckle from her audience. "You see it all before you. Good looks, exceptional manners—though he hides a tendency toward prankish levity under his smooth exterior. Most vexing."

"Is that so? What can you tell me of his character?"

"He is a sportsman of some note," she said. "Accounted to be a bruising rider, a dead-on shot, and a punishing boxer." Portia's voice dropped to a lower register. "He has a fondness for paper boats."

Castleton froze. "Excuse me?"

Portia kept her face carefully turned away. "When his nephew was a child, he took the boy to Hyde Park where they would sail paper boats of their own making on the Serpentine. When Frederick outgrew the practice, Lord Castleton brought his niece. And now that she is grown, he enjoys delighting strange children with gifts of boats from time to time. It made me wonder why he pursued an Army career instead of one in the Navy."

"By God, madame. . . ." Castleton cut off his comment, noting the redness of her countenance. He'd asked for this, after all.

"He sounds a bit rattlepated," he continued in Mrs. Tabby's voice. "Though he appears to hold children in some affection."

"He is a loving guardian to his brother's family," Portia said. "I can name two dozen men here tonight who do not lavish one-tenth the consideration on their own children as he does to those under his protection."

"That is too good of you," he murmured, and Portia turned back to him. Her eyes were soft.

"I mean. . . ." Castleton composed himself.

"I mean, it's good to know he'll treat my girl well, should she win his heart," Mrs. Tabby said.

"She will not win it," Portia stated flatly.

"You seem very sure of that, missy," Castleton drawled in peevish Tabby tones.

"I am."

"How so?"

Portia turned again. "His affection is not given lightly," she replied. "He is well-liked and respected. His acquaintance is large, make no mistake. But he saves his love for those who earn it. His family, certainly, and but three or four close friends."

"You could set up on the streets as a seeress, Miss Kirby," Castleton said. "In the next breath you'll be telling me what Miss Tabby could do to nab me properly."

Portia reddened.

"You have an idea, don't you?" he pressed. "Come now, tell me. How can my Mildred snare Lord Castleton's affections?"

"Mildred?"

"Don't evade the question."

Portia sighed. She looked him in the eye, her face suffused with ... pity? "If your Mildred wants to win Lord Castleton, she must never forget the key aspect of his nature. The key aspect of one's nature colors everything they do and dream, you see."

"Do you know the key aspect of my nature?"

"I believe so."

"And it is?"

Portia drew a deep breath. "Lord Castleton is but

a role—a game you play with strangers. If Mildred wants *you*, she must win David Carlyle."

Dear God in Heaven, Castleton realized. *I'm in love*.

CASTLETON WOKE THE next morning in high spirits. For the first time in years he directed his valet in the choice of the day's attire. He summoned the upper footman as he dressed and told him to have a posy sent to Miss Kirby of Leicester Square.

"That would be Miss Portia Kirby, my lord?" the young man asked with a pucker of confusion on his face.

"Yes," Castleton replied. "Is there a problem?"

"No, my lord." The footman rushed off to discharge his commission—the quicker to spread the word below stairs of this odd attention to a spinster when his staff hoped daily he'd cast his lure to some little girl, Castleton had no doubt. Let them talk. It didn't bother him. Loving Portia had surprised him, too.

He'd let life lead him where it willed with satisfactory results. He'd made only two monumental decisions in his life: his profession at age seventeen and whether or not to assume his title upon returning to England after William's death.

He wondered if even Portia knew how troublesome this last had been for him. He'd been acknowledged Lord Captain Castleton for two years. But he still considered that estate in Hampshire as his uncle's, and his fortune was only a means to see to it that his dependents—tenants, servants, family—lived in comfort.

Castleton felt no ancient duty to marry for succession. Tertian fever had killed his uncle and two male cousins in the space of a week to make *him* a baron, after all. And marriage as a means to increase one's property—he'd marched across India in knee-deep mud, living and fighting beside some of the lowest but most honorable men alive. Substantial property was not a requirement for his happiness, either.

His discontent came clear only when his leg rendered him immobile. Alone and friendless at his own ball, he thought no one knew him beyond his Castleton persona.

But Portia did. Perhaps she'd always seen him. He'd never felt lonely, but the idea of sharing his life with a woman who understood who he was and saw the world as he did filled Castleton with elation.

He would make Portia Kirby his wife.

Though aching to see his beloved at the earliest respectable hour, Castleton delayed his visit until the afternoon—a time for one's more intimate acquaintance. Doubtless his marked attention would cause Portia some disquiet. But once she realized his attentions were sincere, she would surely yield to him. He'd been told since his salad days he need only make his choice and the lady would be his. And it wasn't as if he had to beat a line of fellows off the path to Portia's door.

Mrs. Andrew's butler, a stout fellow with a notable lack of hair, blinked like an owl as Castleton asked to see Portia. The servant ushered Castleton into the sitting room, quaintly furnished in the style of fifty years ago, though the pieces were well-made all around.

On the mantel, a vase of sturdy lilies and fern fronds complemented the old-fashioned decor. Castleton stepped closer to examine them (and take one more glance in the mirror at his cravat) and discovered his own card beside the blooms.

He should have specified roses. The footman, perhaps misunderstanding Castleton's intentions, had sent a bouquet better suited to one's mother than one's love.

Portia arrived a moment later. Castleton smiled brightly at her. She had her hair in a prim knot. The sprigged muslin gown she wore did nothing to enhance her figure. Her hazel eyes held a frown— she was adorable.

She did not offer her hand, but instead dropped a formal curtsey. "Lord Castleton, this is ... unexpected."

"But not unwelcome, I trust," Castleton replied.

"No, of course not," Portia said in the most unconvincing of tones. She offered him a chair and seated herself, her back poker-straight and her hands clasped tightly in her lap. Her eyes glanced up at the mantelpiece to register the time on the carriage clock, then briefly flitted toward his flowers.

"Thank you for the lilies," she said. "They were also ... unexpected."

Castleton's smile died a little. She sounded ... displeased.

Portia's eyes drifted back to the clock. Timing his visit.

Maybe it would be best to remove to less-intimate surroundings, he thought. "I wonder if you care to take a turn in the park with me," he asked.

"I've been to the park today," Portia said.

"We can go to Green Park instead of Hyde Park, then. Or anywhere else you prefer. Just a breath of air. It's too fine a day to be indoors."

Portia shook her head. "I'm sure you can find some other friend to bear you company," she said. "At such a fashionable hour, one might be tempted out just to be seen abroad with you."

"And wouldn't you like to be seen abroad with me?" Castleton asked with an arch smile.

"Not particularly," Portia said. His shock must have reflected in his face. She apologized immediately. "How graceless of me. I'm sure you tendered your invitation out of kindness. But such attentions are not necessary. Indeed, we both know how some people find such ridiculous things to talk about. I doubt it's occurred to you, but someone could mistake our acquaintance for something warmer if you drive me about."

"You think so? And what if that happened?" Castleton asked, apprehension replacing the euphoria that had buoyed him all day.

Portia laughed. "It's too ridiculous. It would be like Mr. Pritchert offering for that girl on the basis of a single kiss. What the ton expects and what common sense dictates are often quite the opposite of each other, as well you know.

"You have offered me your friendship, and I thank you. But as your friend, I ask you not to make us the subject of gossip. Your reputation can bear it, but mine won't."

"Then it appears I'll have to seek other company for the afternoon," Castleton said, striving to keep his tone light. He rose, and she popped to her feet, a relieved smile on her face.

"Thank you again for the flowers," she said as she offered him her hand to bow over. "It was very thoughtful."

Her polite gratitude felt very much like a boot to Castleton's backside, propelling him out the door.

5

CASTLETON DIRECTED HIS coachman to drive on to the park, where he traveled in total abstraction, unintentionally cutting more than one acquaintance thanks to his introspection.

Portia had no idea of the depth of his regard. A gross understatement. And if he pursued her, she would cut him cold. It was almost laughable. Castleton was a prize of the Marriage Mart, and yet the woman he desired would have none of him.

That's not entirely true, he told himself. *She'll accept your friendship. But anything deeper....*

What could he do? He couldn't give up just because she wouldn't accept his attentions.

Portia liked him. She might not be in love with him, but she found his company agreeable. And Castleton knew she was more open with him than a mere acquaintance. The groundwork existed.

I need information, he decided. *No general worth his salt charges into enemy territory without learning all he can about his foe.*

"So, this is the team I've heard so much about."

Castleton looked up. George Mahew rode beside his carriage.

"Quite a handsome pair," Mahew went on, running his green-eyed gaze over the chestnuts. "Did Ponsby train them?"

"I don't know," Castleton replied, his tone frosty in spite of himself. "Why don't you ask your cousin?"

Mahew's dimples framed a rueful smile. "She'll want to know why I am curious, and she won't approve of my answer."

"Why do you want to know?"

"Odds are six to one against him succeeding with Fenton's cast off," Mahew said.

"Ah."

"And yet, I'm tempted to wager on him. He brings that bay out every morning. Walks him round the park without a vehicle. It's most comical to watch, although Portia doesn't think so."

"You were in the park with your cousin?" Castleton asked in as light a tone as he could manage.

"My dear fellow, Portia is just as diligent about her morning walk as Ponsby and the horse," Mahew said. "You'd be stunned at the number of times I've dragged myself out of bed to arrange a 'happenstance' meeting."

"Would I?"

Mahew grinned deeply, as if he sensed Castleton's unfounded feelings of rivalry.

"She's here and gone by eight. She comes sans chaperon and doesn't want it talked about."

"No," Castleton shifted in his seat. "She doesn't like to be talked about."

Mahew continued to ride beside Castleton's carriage. Though a part of him wished Mahew elsewhere, Castleton inwardly debated about pressing him for more information about Portia. Mahew was certainly acquainted with his cousin's character, although Castleton didn't want to know how intimately.

But Mahew might report an interrogation back to his cousin. At this early stage, Castleton wanted nothing to tip his hand.

Mahew cleared his throat, and Castleton looked up at him. "Portia told me what you did for Lady Burrow," Mahew said hesitantly. "I hope you will allow me to express my gratitude."

"Her distress would have gone unnoticed except for your cousin's observation of it," Castleton replied with a shrug.

"And would have gone unrelieved, but for you," Mahew insisted. "I love Portia"—the easy way this phrase rolled off Mahew's tongue chilled Castleton— "but she would have fumed all night in that corner instead of coming to Amy's aid herself."

"I'm not so sure about that," Castleton said, remembering how Portia had engineered Ponsby's seat beside Serina Applegate. "I've seen her bestir herself on another's behalf."

"Oh, so have I," Mahew said. "In fact, I've been her instrument of interference more times than I can count. But I'll wager whatever you observed was done with subterfuge. Portia confronted no one, nor did she intervene directly."

"That's true," Castleton replied. But he could not see how this aspect of Portia's character would help him win her heart.

"Do you know I had to drag her into the shrubbery at Vauxhall to teach her to waltz?"

Castleton stared at him.

Mahew's dimples returned to his cheeks. "She wore the same appalled expression at the time," he quipped. "Thought we'd be caught, we'd be compromised, and I'd have to offer for her—you should see your face. Never mind the circumstances—Portia loves to dance. And she asked me endless questions about waltzing. But she had no intention of learning the steps until I forced her. And do you know why?"

"She didn't want to trouble you?" Castleton guessed.

Mahew shook his head. "She said she didn't need to know because she's 'on the shelf.' No one would ever ask her."

"Except you," Castleton said.

"And you," Mahew retorted. "Through your surrogate."

Mahew noticed Lady Burrow ahead on the path before Castleton could formulate a credible reply. He excused himself to canter up to her carriage, leaving Castleton to ponder their conversation for the rest of the afternoon.

* * * * *

CASTLETON ROSE BY seven o'clock the next day and had Caesar brought from the stables. He set out at a sedate walk, until he was certain the rhythm of riding and its stresses on his leg were tolerable.

He made two circuits of the park grounds before he found Portia. She sat on a folding camp stool beside the Serpentine, a sketchbook in her lap and a faraway look on her face.

"There she is, Caesar," he whispered, leaning forward to stroke the stallion's jaw. "My opponent. What, do you suppose, is the key aspect of her nature?"

How many mornings had she'd been here? Certainly enough to acquire knowledge of his paper boats. She wasn't sketching much, he realized. Instead she watched two lively boys caper near the water. Their weary nanny called caution at frequent intervals.

Portia sat up straighter, focusing on the approach of a young couple on the footpath. The girl was in her mid-teens; the youth nearer twenty. Both were soberly dressed. Servants, Castleton guessed, with the morning off.

As they drew closer, Portia considered her sketchbook with singular attention.

The girl had her hand tucked in her young man's arm; the boy covered it with his own. Portia peeped up from her work and smiled warmly when their fingers twined and the girl leaned her head on the young man's shoulder. He led his sweetheart off the path to avoid the scampering children.

Portia returned to her sketches as they ambled by, but raised her head to watch their retreat with a glowing expression.

Castleton urged his horse forward, keeping the pace slow and steady. He waited for her to recognize him before raising his hand in greeting. Portia rose off the stool and looked at her feet, as if caught in mischief.

"Miss Kirby, this is a pleasant surprise," he said as he gingerly dismounted.

"Lord Castleton." Portia curtseyed. "What are you doing here so early?"

"Following the surgeon's orders," he replied.

"He's given you leave to ride again?"

"No." Castleton grinned at her. "I'm engaging in an activity where I'm sitting down for much of the time. I came early to avoid discovery."

Portia suppressed a grin of her own. "I won't tell."

"Thank you." He led Caesar into the grass and dropped the reins. He gave the horse's flank one last pat before joining her.

"Is this the horse that threw you?" Portia asked.

"Yes, that's Caesar," Castleton replied.

"He's so . . . large."

"He is," Castleton said, amused. He held his hand out toward her sketch book. "I did not mean to interrupt your work. May I?"

Portia surrendered the book with a self-conscious blush. As Castleton idly turned the pages, he wondered how he might keep it there. Warmth suited her.

The drawings were more of people than places, with the common folk who populated the park in the early hours best represented.

"You have a superb eye and a deft touch," he murmured, then noted an earnest compliment was one way to keep her color high. He glanced toward the two little boys and smiled. "Might I borrow a page?"

Portia smiled back and nodded.

Castleton carefully ripped out a back page and returned the sketchbook. He creased it against Caesar's saddle, speaking to Portia as he transformed the paper before her fascinated eyes.

"My maternal grandfather was a yachtsman. Unfortunately, I did not inherit his sea legs. When it became clear nothing would curb my *mal de mer*, Grandfather taught me to make these. I plied my high-seas adventures in more manageable puddles and streams."

Where his flowers had failed, the paper boat succeeded. Her features opened in soft pleasure as she accepted it from him. Castleton reveled in the broad smile that illuminated her round face as she offered the boat to the boys.

The little gentlemen squealed with delight as Portia crouched by the water's edge to demonstrate the craft's seaworthiness. When she stood up and looked at Castleton again, the shine of kinship in her eyes nigh took his breath away.

How many times had she watched him perform this ritual?

An inkling of what he must do to win her formed in his thoughts. Castleton took his leave of her, riding into the park, then circling back so he could observe her from a distance.

The serving couple ambled back in her direction, making coy love to each other. Portia seemed keenly interested in their welfare. How many mornings had she waited for them to pass by?

The world is a theater to her. But for a brief moment she'd participated in the theatrics, and it had delighted her.

Castleton smiled. Mahew had it right. He must make Portia an actor instead of an audience. And hope she loved it so much she would be loath to part with it. Or him.

"Time to marshal our energies," Castleton told Caesar as he guided him toward the gate and home. "Tonight the siege begins."

LORD CASTLETON WAS different. Not in any way Portia could easily determine. Everything seemed magnified—the shine of his eyes, the warmth of his smile. There was something more ... intimate in his expression.

It must be the return to full vitality, she thought. He certainly suffered no ill effects from his clandestine morning ride. He entered Mrs. Digby's grand salon that evening without a cane, and only the barest stutter flawed his step as he crossed the room to greet her.

He'll be gone soon, she thought. Indeed, she took the flowers and his odd invitation for a drive as the first signs of his departure from her sphere. They must be small gestures of gratitude for keeping him occupied these past few weeks.

Portia would miss him. So, despite the disquiet his deep smile roused in her heart, she answered it with one of her own.

He wore black. It accentuated the blondness of his thick hair, and his eyes were startling points of color in his handsome face. Portia wished she was better matched to his exquisiteness. Her gown of silver grey, which had seemed so flattering in her dressmaker's mirror, seemed positively Quakerish now.

After exchanging commonplaces, Castleton confirmed Portia's fears. He had an appointment with the surgeon on the morrow.

"I hope I never see his puckered visage again in my lifetime," Castleton asserted.

"What will you do with all that freedom?"

He gazed at her in a disconcerting fashion. "I have a plan or two," he said.

Portia nodded encouragement to continue just as Mrs. Trent and Mrs. Cray arrived in their corner.

Castleton rolled his eyes and rose. "I must be feeling better," he said. "I'm tired of sitting by the wall. Miss Kirby, will you oblige me in a turn about the room?"

He offered his arm to her. Portia rose. She placed her hand on his sleeve, and he drew her away at a stately pace. Portia thought he meant only to lead her to another corner, but 'a turn about the room' became a genuine promenade.

She could not help feeling self-conscious. She could not remember the last time he'd been so attentive to a woman not of his own family, though she knew he'd only drawn her off to escape the Ladies Cats, as he had christened the gossipy chaperons.

"What mischief can we pursue this evening, ma'am?" he asked, casting his gaze around the room.

"Must we pursue mischief?" Portia answered with dread.

"Indeed. I've been good too long and you a great deal longer."

Castleton altered course with a wicked grin on his face. He steered them toward Mr. Cheever, a portly MP from Lincolnshire. Portia had expressed her contempt of him on a recent evening. She tried to pull away but Castleton's hand came down on hers, tucking it firmly into the crook of his arm. He kept her fingers trapped with his own as they descended on Cheever.

Castleton hailed him as if they were on friendly terms, though Portia knew he disliked Cheever as much as she.

"I understand you've had more trouble in your district," Castleton said in a bland voice.

"Strikers. Nothing the militia can't handle," Cheever asserted, breathing the words out between wheezing puffs. "Damned rabble. Making a fuss about nothing."

"I thought it was only next to nothing," Castleton replied. Cheever blinked at him, and Castleton smiled sweetly. "The drop in wages to seven shillings a week seems a pittance. I wonder how men with families survive on such a sum, don't you?"

Cheever snorted, either an expression of humor or disgust at Castleton's "ignorance." He said, "If they don't like their situation, they should give their job to men who are willing to work."

"Lord knows there are enough of them about," Castleton said. Cheever frowned, sensing the intended slur but unable to comprehend the censure beneath words delivered so innocuously.

Portia cringed. This conversation could only result in discord, and she wanted none of it. She tried to slip away again.

Castleton tightened his hold and turned in her direction. His eyes sparkled with deviltry. "Miss Kirby, you said something the other day about the plight of factory workers, did you not?"

Blood rushed to Portia's face. Damn the man.

"I would hardly call it a 'plight.'" Cheever snorted again. "Though, as the weaker sex, it behooves a lady's sensibilities to think well of any man."

Portia stiffened.

"I can't recall your exact words," Castleton continued as if Cheever hadn't just insulted her. "But it was so well expressed."

Portia attempted to draw away again. He was perfectly dreadful. He knew exactly what she'd said. And knew she would never repeat it to Cheever. If

Castleton did in her stead, she would sink into the ground.

"It was something like 'if we believe the workers in our cotton mills serve no purpose worth compensation. . . .'" Castleton shook his head. "No, it won't come to me. Help me out, ma'am."

"I should like to," Portia said, struggling for a puzzled tone to match his, "but I do not recall it." She forced a smile. "We are not only weaker but prone to lax tongues, I fear."

Cheever smiled back at her and nodded. Portia knew he would. Now if she could only escape. . . .

"Margaret looks somewhat lost, wouldn't you say, Miss Kirby?" Castleton's attention had diverted to his sister-in-law, who indeed looked about her as if desperately seeking something. Castleton released Portia's hand and bowed. "I must discover what has agitated her. Pray, excuse me."

And he withdrew, leaving her alone with Mr. Cheever.

Portia fumed at the abandonment, even as she mustered another weak smile for Cheever's benefit. Without Castleton to fuel its flame, the conversation withered.

"So. . . ." Cheever said at last. "I suppose we'll soon be wishing Castleton joy."

"I beg your pardon?!"

"Nothing firm yet?" His stays creaked as he bowed. "I must instead beg yours."

Portia shut her slack jaw tight with concentrated effort. Was Cheever so stupid to believe Castleton courted her? *Or maybe*, she thought, her heart hammering in her chest, *he thinks I've set my cap for him.* But to correct Cheever's mistake was as useless as telling him he "should walk around the streets of London naked for a week if he thought the workers in England's cotton mills served no purpose worth compensation."

"Lord Castleton hasn't singled out any young lady that I've noticed," she fumbled. "But when he chooses a wife, I'm sure I will join his many friends to wish him joy."

Cheever frowned, perplexed.

Portia excused herself with a curtsey and scurried away, not stopping until she reached the haven of the withdrawing room. She accepted some lavender water from the maid attendant to soak her kerchief, and stood before the full-sized window, breathing in its scent and the cool night air.

How could Cheever have come to such a conclusion? But Portia herself had realized the honor Castleton paid her with their promenade. And then.... Of course. Castleton had gripped her hand throughout the conversation. Though he'd done it to prevent her escape, such familiarity should not be tolerated from a mere acquaintance. Had anyone else noticed? And misunderstood?

She took a deep breath. She was being foolish. Cheever's opinion counted for nothing, which is why Castleton made sport of him this evening. No one could possibly think she expected anything of Castleton save friendship.

How fortunate she'd declined his invitation to drive out. Should she tell him? Warn him they must end their discourse before more credible tongues uttered such absurd sentiments?

Tears pricked at Portia's eyes at the idea of relaying Cheever's assumption. She'd already broached the subject once. Wasn't that sufficient? To broach the topic again indicated it preyed on her thoughts. Castleton might misconstrue her motive.

The withdrawing room door opened. Portia stilled herself as Margaret Christopher poked her turbaned head inside, looked about, then shook her head at someone beyond her and withdrew.

Portia crept to the door and peered out. Castleton and Margaret lingered in the hallway just beyond. She could not hear their conversation, but Castleton was obviously trying to calm Mrs. Christopher's agitation, even as he looked about in the hopes of some discovery of his own.

Could he have sent Mrs. Christopher to see if I was here? The moment the thought entered her head, Portia dismissed it as utter fantasy. Mr. Cheever's sentiments had unbalanced her.

She needed time to compose herself. The Digbys had a lovely garden with a temple-like gazebo in its center. Portia slipped out the window so she could walk out there a while, knowing she could return by the terrace doors in the conservatory, adjacent to the far end of the salon where Mrs. Trent and Mrs. Cray sat.

A steady breeze rustled her hem, and the skin

above her long gloves raised in goose bumps. Portia quickened her step to reach the confines of the shelter, but slowed as she recognized the muffled sounds of tearful distress coming from within.

After a moment's inward debate, Portia crossed the threshold of the gazebo and let her eyes adjust to the change of light.

Sarah Christopher sat in the cushioned recess near the window, her face buried in her gloved hands. Despite the remoteness of her refuge, she muffled her sobs. Sarah's presence explained Margaret's distress, and Castleton's searching glances.

Feeling wretched herself, as well as foolish for thinking Castleton might miss her, Portia couldn't walk away without discovering what had upset a usually carefree girl.

"Miss Christopher? Sarah?" Portia touched Sarah's arm.

Sarah raised her head and swiped the tears from her eyes. Portia sat beside her and offered her the scented handkerchief.

"It's nothing," Sarah began. Her lower lip trembled, and tears welled in her eyes. "I am so foolish."

Portia impulsively placed an arm around the girl's slight shoulders. "Why would you say that?"

The cause of Sarah's tears appeared to be Mr. Cecil Lane—the crush of Sarah's girlhood. Portia knew who the young man was. With chiseled Grecian features, he was one of the few dandies who wore his fancy dress with so much style as to appear natural.

"Oh, Miss Kirby, he truly seemed to like me better than any other young lady. He's acknowledged me whenever we've been in each other's company. He asked me to choose his buttonhole in Mrs. Bellow's conservatory because I could spot the superior bloom. And after we danced the allemande he said I was a 'dashed pretty little chit at times.' That's high praise from Cecil.

"Tonight he drew me out here. 'To ask me something particular,' he said. I thought. . . ." Sarah had to force the words from her lips. "He wanted to know if Vivian entertained any serious suit, then asked if I could speak to her about him."

"I suppose it won't help to say he's not the man for you?"

Sarah shook her head and blew her nose. "There is no man for me. I don't understand it. The other girls have suitors; they talk of nothing else. All I had was Cecil."

"Who is flawed to the extreme," Portia stated strongly. "Don't discount yourself because of his short-sightedness. Mr. Lane puts too much stock in appearances to recognize the appeal of an unaffected young lady."

"You think Vivian's 'affected'?" Sarah asked, bristling.

"Affected?" Miss Barstow herself appeared in the doorway, frowning in Portia's direction. "They are looking for you everywhere, Sarah," Vivian said stiffly. "And I thought you might be in the garden. But I had not expected to be insulted. . . ."

Portia laughed in spite of herself. "You're not affected in the least, Miss Barstow, but I believe Cecil Lane is quite so."

"La, yes," Vivian replied. "I've never met anyone so puffed with their own consequence."

"He made inquiries about you this evening," Portia told her.

"Me?" Vivian blinked and then her expressive face took on militant expression. "Oh, Sarah ... not to you?!"

Sarah nodded.

Vivian took the seat on Sarah's other side, and drew Sarah's gloved hand in both her own to squeeze it. "That nodtop! He has no sensitivity at all!"

"I'm sure he did not realize...." Sarah began.

"He had better not," Vivian countered strongly. "Ooh. I should give him such a set down."

"I believe your indifference will be set down enough," Portia asserted.

"Unless you wish...." Sarah stammered.

"Sarah!" Vivian giggled and gave her friend a spontaneous little hug. "Dearest, I'd sooner wed a spaniel. But you know what we should do? We should buy you the most fetching gown, crop your hair, and make Cecil Lane wild for you so you may snub him."

Sarah managed a wan smile for her friend.

"Come now," Vivian pressed, "it's a famous idea. Don't you agree, Miss Kirby?"

"Actually, no," Portia said.

Vivian stiffened in surprise.

"You could pull it off, Miss Barstow, but such behavior is foreign to Miss Christopher. I can't see her acting the grand dame with any comfort or confidence. Besides," Portia turned to Sarah, "if he's wild for a charade, he's not wild for *you*, just some creature of fancy.

"Your best revenge is to find some man who loves you as you are, and to be wildly happy with him. But to affect Mr. Lane, I'm afraid he must also tie a most fascinating cravat."

Vivian and Sarah both giggled, just as Castleton and his sister-in-law discovered them.

"Here they are," Castleton announced, arching his brow in Portia's direction. "Gossiping in the dark with Miss Kirby."

"Sarah, I've been quite worried," Margaret admonished.

"I'm sorry, Mama." Sarah bounced up and hugged her mother.

In closer proximity, Castleton must have noticed the trace of tears. His face creased in concern, and he brushed his finger tips across Sarah's cheek. "What's it toward, pet?" he asked in a kindly tone.

Sarah glanced back at Portia and smiled warmly at her. "Nothing to signify, sir."

"We ... we were discussing an outing," Vivian explained with obvious improvisation. "To Kew."

"Not that again." Margaret puffed a sigh. "If it were a pleasure outing, Sarah, I might agree. But I will not subject our friends to hours and hours of 'geniuses.'"

"Genuses," Castleton corrected.

Margaret rolled her eyes. "If you wish to study flowers surely something more local will suffice."

"Sarah wants to see those gardens," Vivian replied as she rose and placed a hand around Sarah's waist.

"And we would like to oblige her," Castleton said in turn, his tone temperate. "But it requires a free day, which neither of us has at present. Perhaps when the Season is over."

Vivian bit her lip and turned toward Portia. A smile of satisfaction lit her face. "What if Miss Kirby accompanied us?"

CASTLETON BORE GREAT fondness for Miss Barstow, but he had a sudden urge to wring her neck. Sarah's throat also was in danger of mortal squeeze as she pronounced this a marvelous idea. She begged her mother to accept Miss Kirby as a chaperon.

Margaret looked to Castleton for guidance.

"I don't believe—" he said, frowning.

"I shall happily escort them if you think me adequate to the task," Portia told Margaret, cutting off the end of his sentence. "I haven't seen Kew in ages. My aunt dislikes such excursions."

Although this step was tantamount to an announcement that Portia was unmarriageable, Castleton could do nothing. Protesting would not only be insulting, it might also tip his hand.

He shrugged, and Margaret took the gesture as approval.

The ladies conversed for several minutes, making plans to meet at Curzon Street the next morning. But the prospective outing dampened the rest of Castleton's evening. The girls spread word of the trip among their friends. Rather than see her as his future mate, Society regulated Portia to spinster once again.

Because of the proposed early start on the morrow, all decided to make a short night of it. On arriving home, Sarah scampered up the main staircase, followed by Margaret, who cast back many concerned glances in his direction. Castleton crossed the foyer to his study, untying the knot of his cravat. He poured himself a brandy, sat before the fire, and retrenched.

After a half-hour's brooding, he decided he must press on. Portia's insistence she was on the shelf had been an obstacle to surmount before she agreed to play chaperon. And Society had treated her as such before Castleton came into her life. Both would learn their mistake when he played his hand.

Meanwhile, he might use her declared spinsterhood to his benefit. A chaperon, after all, should not need her own chaperon.

A tap on the door roused him from his reverie.

Margaret stood in the doorway. She still wore her evening dress, and her twined hands suggested she'd worked herself into a state of great agitation. "David, I must speak to you."

"Of course, Margaret. Please sit down."

Margaret lowered herself into the chair opposite and clasped her hands in the her lap. Something very serious, Castleton thought. He wondered if the reason for Sarah's tears had been discovered, though it appeared Portia had soothed whatever sadness had produced them.

"It's about Miss Kirby."

Castleton sighed. "Miss Barstow should not have put her in such a position. But she has a steady temperament, and I've no fear for Sarah's safety in her care."

"It's not Sarah I'm concerned about." Margaret licked her lips. "I know you only befriended Miss Kirby as a way to amuse yourself while you recover your strength. But I fear your marked preference for her company has been . . . misinterpreted."

"How so?" Castleton asked.

"Mrs. Krieg wondered if Miss Kirby should be included in our invitation to her ball. She all but asked if you were engaged."

"I see." An unforeseen development. His preference might be news to himself, but the sharp eyes of Society had already drawn their conclusion. And while open speculation could sink him, it did have its silver lining. As his suspected fiancée, Portia might fulfill the position of chaperon without the mar on her character he had feared.

"Of course, it's the most ridiculous notion," Margaret said with a little laugh. "But, you know, once talk starts. . . ."

"Yes?"

"And think how awkward it would be if that poor woman also thought...." Margaret stopped mid-sentence, struck by something in his still manner. "Castleton, you're ... not courting her."

"Actually, I am."

"But, you can't marry her!" Margaret protested.

"Why not?"

"She's ... she's antiquated."

Castleton laughed. "She's younger than you or I, my dear."

"She has no style. No address."

"No, she doesn't. But she has a quick mind, a ready smile, and an extraordinary knowledge of people. I think you will like her very well when you know her better."

"What of children?"

"What of them? Lady Haviland bore a son at six and thirty. And if there is no heir, Frederick can inherit all but the land."

"But would such a person make you happy? Please consider. You could have any woman in London as your wife."

"Yes," he said. "It's quite likely I could. But I want Portia. I love her, Margaret."

"Oh, David," Margaret's tone held no joy at his pronouncement. "And does she return your regard?"

"Not yet," he said. "So I would appreciate it if you would treat her with great kindness and courtesy."

"Of course, I will not be uncivil," Margaret said, her head drooping. Castleton reached across and squeezed her hand. "But I cannot think her a good match for you."

"Give her chance. I'm sure she will surprise you, as she surprised me."

Margaret nodded and rose, but remained unconvinced.

6

PORTIA SET OUT for Curzon Street the next day at a brisk walk—so refreshing after years of moderating her step to the pace of a dawdling maid or her aunt. She passed more than one nodding acquaintance—and all nodded back with equanimity, an indication her own need for a chaperon had ended long ago.

This declaration opened a world of possibilities for her: trips to a museum or the circulating library at her own convenience; perhaps she could attend an afternoon salon. She'd always wanted to see what one was like.

She stood at the door of Castleton's mansion before she realized it, and was told Miss Sarah would be with her presently as she was ushered into the sitting room to wait. Since her social intercourse with the Carlyle and Christopher families had always been formal functions, Portia looked about with interest.

It was a light and airy room, furnished in mahogany and chintz. She could imagine the family there in an evening, Sarah seated at the pianoforte in the corner, or maybe pressing flowers at the work table while her mother sewed, Castleton and Frederick in the stuff chairs flanking the marble fireplace reading....

Portia picked up the book on the adjacent table and flipped to the frontispiece, decorated with a fine etching of the famous racehorse Eclipse. This must be Frederick's seat.

A gilt-framed landscape hung above the mantelpiece. Portia admired the artful placement of the Tudor manor house in the wooded parkland, wondering if such a lovely place really existed or was the product of an artist's fruitful imagination.

"That is Welton," Margaret said from the doorway. "Castleton's estate in Hampshire."

"It's beautiful," Portia replied with a smile, then noticed no answer in Mrs. Christopher's features. The matron had dark circles under her blue eyes, and her whole appearance looked thrown together, as if she'd just risen from a sleepless night.

Second thoughts, Portia guessed with a sinking heart. She hadn't realized how much she desired this outing.

"Castleton has left the house already," Margaret stated.

"He mentioned an appointment with his surgeon," Portia replied. "I'm sure all is well. He seems quite recovered, and eager to pursue more masculine enterprises. Poor man. He's been so bored by what passes for amusement to us, hasn't he?"

"He hasn't found it all ... disagreeable," Margaret

said. Her tone placed the onus of responsibility on Portia, implying it wasn't necessarily a good thing.

I wonder if Mrs. Christopher and Mr. Cheever are on speaking terms. Portia sighed. "Well his recovery will be somewhat of a relief to me. His spirits are too high for my temperament."

"Don't you like him?"

"Oh, I like him very well. I just think ... no, I *know* he can find more suitable company to pass the time of day."

Sarah's arrival ended their conversation. The word *sunny* crossed Portia's mind as she surveyed Sarah's white muslin skirt, yellow spencer, and buttercup-trimmed straw bonnet.

Portia had worn her dark green pelisse and a poke bonnet with a plain satin ribbon: sober clothes to fit her sober role.

"Do you have a parasol, Sarah?" Margaret asked as she inspected Sarah's dress and hat, then adjusted a soft brown curl to better frame her daughter's rosy cheek.

"I'm sure my bonnet will be sufficient, Mama."

"You will be out of doors for much of the day. Society does not admire a tanned complexion," Margaret returned.

"Miss Kirby did not bring a parasol."

"A regrettable oversight," Portia said. "I'm sure I'll miss it on those open lawns."

"I could lend you something," Margaret replied stiffly.

What an encroaching mushroom she must think

me. Portia forced a smile to her lips and shook her head. "At my age no one looks, but you should listen to your mother, Miss Christopher. I'll wager Miss Barstow won't forget her parasol and will be quite shocked if you forgo yours."

Vivian arrived a minute later, a flurry of lavender with the daintiest parasol clutched in her gloved hand. "Oh, Sarah," she exclaimed, "Are we taking the chestnuts? They are outside."

Sarah glanced at her mother in surprise.

"Your uncle ordered them with the landau," Margaret said.

Sarah clapped her hands, delighted. "He is such a dear. Everyone will turn to watch us drive past. Let's hurry."

Sarah kissed her mother's cheek. As she stepped toward the front door, Portia reminded her about the parasol.

"La, Sarah," Vivian exclaimed. "Don't forget that. It's positively cloudless."

Sarah rushed from the room and returned presently with two parasols. One matched her yellow spencer. The other was white trimmed with pastel green fronds. She held it out to Portia.

"If it's so important, ma'am, you must have one, too. I have nothing to match your outfit, however."

But Vivian assured her the lighter green would complement Miss Kirby's apparel, and Portia gravely accepted the parasol as too good of Sarah. With one last farewell to Mrs. Christopher, they stepped out to the carriage and were on their way at last.

Portia insisted she sit behind the driver so Vivian and Sarah could "be seen." Portia marveled how two seemingly different young ladies could blend so seamlessly. They laughed a great deal and often finished each other's sentences.

Portia envied them. She'd never had a bosom friend, except George, though it would be highly improper to term him so.

Since her official spinsterhood had only just begun, Portia related easily to the minor adversities of their first Season. By the time they glided up the tree-lined drive toward Kew's sweeping lawns, both were calling her "dear Miss Kirby."

The head gardener greeted their arrival and immediately drew them off to the sheds. Or Sarah, rather. Portia and Vivian trailed at every step. Portia did her best to follow the conversation but was soon lost in confusion of plant names and families, their native climes, and what measures were taken to approximate those conditions on English soil.

Vivian drew her back. "Don't try to understand, ma'am," she said. "It will make your head ache. Just let your senses appreciate what your intellect cannot."

Portia took a deep breath of loamy air, scented with exotic, unfamiliar florals. Most everything was green, but here and there a burst of color or a knobby bud delighted the eye.

Vivian linked her arm and sighed contentedly. "I did not expect to like it here the first time Sarah brought me," she said. "But it's so refreshing to the spirit."

After an hour's instruction, Sarah and the gardener parted ways, the sturdy man agreeing to pack some cuttings and seedlings away in Castleton's carriage. Sarah latched Portia's other arm and guided her toward the broad lawns. "Now, ma'am, you must let us show you Kew's delights."

The young ladies tramped her up walks and through bowers. Sarah knew the gardens intimately, offering the name of any plant Portia admired. Here and there a folly or a temple framed in nature's bounty added interest to the greenery.

"What next?" Sarah asked.

"The pagoda," Vivian exclaimed. The young ladies scampered through the thick tree line, leaving Portia behind.

She dawdled, basking in the sunshine sifting through the leaves and the plethora of bluebells populating the less-developed sections of the property. They reminded her of the woods surrounding her father's small estate. How she had loved to ramble with a book in hand, or play explorer with James.

Walks in Hyde Park were a poor substitute for those hikes. And on visits to Surrey, Maria demanded Portia's companionship and felt a stroll in her own rose garden to be altogether taxing.

Portia wondered what it would be like to own a property with acres and acres of park land and her own little temple to read in or sketch on an afternoon. *And don't forget the palatial mansion and the coach and four to drive me from one end of my estate to the other,* she thought derisively.

She would have to content herself with outings like this. It wouldn't take much coaxing for Portia to play chaperon again.

Reminded of her duties, Portia focused on her charges. The gap between them was growing rapidly. In fact, the girls practically ran. Portia closed her borrowed parasol to better clutch her skirts and increased her pace accordingly.

As she left the stand of trees, she realized the young ladies raced toward a distant figure. He raised his hat to them, letting sunlight glint off his golden locks. His own rapid gait revealed the slight hitch in his step.

Castleton. Portia slowed. *What is he doing here?*

He embraced Sarah, linked arms with her, then gestured in Portia's direction with a wry inclination of his head. Both girls turned, surprised at the distance between them. They dragged Castleton toward her.

Portia curtsied as Castleton approached.

"Good afternoon, Miss Kirby," he said, bowing.

"Isn't this a wonderful surprise, ma'am?" Sarah exclaimed.

"A surprise," Portia echoed, omitting the adjective.

Castleton's grin deepened. "Mr. Mulgrew has granted me leave to engage in moderate exercise. And since Kew had the most charming company this afternoon. . . ."

Vivian giggled.

"I hope you don't object if I join you," Castleton finished.

"No," Portia said, trying to keep her uneasiness from her voice. Something about the whole seemed ... calculated. "But wasn't the ride here more than moderate?"

"It would have been, had I ridden," Castleton said. "I came by boat. And I can return with you in the carriage. So it's only tagging after Sarah I must heed."

"We were on our way to the pagoda," Sarah told him.

"Great heavens," Castleton said. "That will finish me in ten minutes. Moderate, Sarah. Not a climb."

Sarah's face fell.

Vivian took Portia's arm and guided her to Castleton's elbow. "Why don't Sarah and I climb the pagoda while you stroll with Miss Kirby?" she suggested.

"An excellent plan, Miss Barstow," Castleton approved. "Judging by her dawdling, you and Sarah have traipsed her hither and yon all morning."

"I'm not tired," Portia said. "I was merely absorbing the delights of the landscape."

"Then allow me to absorb them with you." Castleton offered her his arm as the girls scampered past another gardener on the way to their destination.

Portia watched them cross the lawn to the towering building, her disquiet intensifying as Castleton grasped her hand.

He tucked it in the crook of his arm and leaned down toward her. "You will miss nothing," he assured her in a low voice. "It's a ten-story climb on a staircase wide enough for one."

"I should not leave them."

"What harm can they come to? There is no one about," he said, discounting the gardener who seemed wholly absorbed in his work. "If Margaret were here, she would not make that climb."

He guided Portia back toward the shade of the tree line. "Have you enjoyed your botany lesson?" he asked.

"Very much. Sarah is amazingly well-informed."

"Not amazing. In Kent she had only Frederick for company as a child, and he is always studying something. Sarah's interest in flora thrived long after Frederick's waned."

"And you did not discourage her," Portia replied, a little envious. How many times had her mother confiscated books from the circulating library she'd deemed too cerebral? *Men don't like bookish women, Portia.*

"I think an informed mind is far more appealing than an empty one," Castleton said, exposing the fallacy of her mother's assertion. "And I see nothing wrong in pursuing something one feels passionately about."

His blue eyes caught and held her own. The wood seemed suddenly airless. Portia struggled for breath, intensely aware of Castleton: his height, his figure, his perfect symmetry of features, the muscles of the arm beneath her hand, the way he altered his step to accommodate her stride.

Despite the diligent gardener beyond the trees and the knowledge Sarah and Vivian would return presently, they were alone. And though the height of foolishness, it felt iniquitous.

"If we strolled the lawn, Miss Christopher and Miss Barstow could see us from the top of the pagoda."

"And we might entertain them by fainting from the heat. That sun is punishing. Aren't you warm?"

Portia slid her hand off his arm and clutched at the buttons of her pelisse. "I'm fine," she said, though she was suddenly so very warm she thought she might swoon.

"Where is the carriage? By the sheds? We can walk back to it and stow your wrap away."

"That isn't necessary." Portia took two steps away from him, the need to put distance between them so strong she could not convince herself to do otherwise.

Castleton latched her arm. "What's wrong?"

"We should be where the young ladies can see us."

"I assure you, the young ladies are giving *us* no thought at all. They'll take all of twenty minutes to complete their task. I would rather spend that time in the shade, wouldn't you?"

"We should not be alone here," Portia blurted.

"Ah. I see." His eyes sparkled with amusement and something more unsettling. "You think I have designs on your honor."

"No, of course not! It's just. . . ."

"Yes?"

"Yesterday *I* required a chaperon. This feels . . . improper."

"I suppose it would look so to anyone who happened upon us," Castleton mused. "Or would it? Consider, ma'am. Two people of middling years strolling a garden path. Would you really spare them a censorious thought?"

"No," Portia replied, breathing a little easier.

"It's positively lowering," he said in theatrical tones. "The average passerby would likely mistake us for some old married couple on holiday. I'll wager we could even do something dreadfully shocking, and no one would remark on it."

"Shocking?"

An unholy grin lit his face. He knocked the parasol from Portia's hand, and startled her further when his arm circled her waist. The arm tightened, drawing her body into contact with his.

Portia's head snapped up, and her lips parted in shock. The reaction placed her in perfect alignment for his unexpected kiss.

HER CURVES FIT Castleton better than any coat Weston ever fashioned for him. Her figure was riper than he'd imagined. While the hip he splayed his hand upon was generous, it curved up and inwards. Allowing for the bulk of her clothing, her waist must be incredibly small. And yet the fullness of the bosom pressing his rib cage was evident through his shirt, his waistcoat, his coat, her coat, and whatever else she wore beneath it. Glorious.

Her sweet breath escaped in ticklish puffs from their joined lips, inciting Castleton to a more passionate embrace than he'd first intended. He tightened his grip, his mouth moving over Portia's to explore its silken contour.

For one heady instant she responded to him. Her lips pressed back at his and parted farther.

Castleton leaned into the pressure, his tongue stealing forward to lightly caress the curve of her lower lip.

Portia wedged her hand between their joined breasts and pushed away. One look told Castleton he'd made a capital error. Her eyes were bright with fury, not with a lover's passion.

She stormed down the garden path. Castleton paused long enough to recover her parasol and pursued. By the time he drew alongside and pulled her to a halt, his leg throbbed.

"I think I strained it," he murmured through gritted teeth. He dropped the parasol to rub his calf. He dare not loosen his hold on her.

"It serves you right," Portia seethed.

"Come now, Miss Kirby. Didn't you say a solitary kiss was of no moment?"

Her flushed and angry countenance remained unconvinced.

"Pretend I am a mongrel."

"An apt comparison." Reluctant laughter escaped

her lips, but the bruised look in her eyes said he was not forgiven. "If you meant it as a jest, I don't think it was funny."

"But you laughed."

"Only at your relationship to dogs." Tears shimmered on the surface of her eyes. "I don't appreciate being made sport of. . . ."

"I wasn't making sport of you," Castleton asserted.

"Then why did you. . . ? Why *did* you?"

A hundred answers sprang to mind—including the truth—but instinct warned him any suit offered now would be rejected.

"I was . . . curious."

"Curious? Curious!?" Portia shook her arm, but he held firm.

"Yes, curious. I am a man, you are a woman, we deal well together. You were worried about your reputation. I wondered if anyone had ever stolen a kiss from you. Then I wondered what you would do if I did. Unfortunately, now I know."

"It was very bad of you"—at least now her tone was only troubled—"not to mention dangerous. What if someone saw us?"

"I suppose they would expect me to offer for you. But you wouldn't marry me for such a paltry reason. What do you suppose *that* would do to your reputation, Miss Kirby?"

Portia thought about it a moment. "Actually," she said, "It would raise my consequence considerably. I'd progress from unknown to notorious in one rash act."

"Then perhaps I should kiss you again, more publicly."

Her cheeks pinked to a very becoming shade. "What you say may mean nothing to you, but it smacks of ridicule to me."

"My dear. . . ." He tried to take her hand, but Portia pulled away. Castleton sighed. This would not do at all. "I truly meant no harm," he said. "I beg you to accept my apology."

Portia searched his face, and he mustered every ounce of remorse in his being to show in his expression. She nodded, but only placed fingertips on his arm when he offered it again. She withdrew from conversation, answering his innocuous remarks about the weather, the landscape, and whatever neutral topic popped into his head with polite monosyllables. After a while, Castleton gave up, and they walked together in silence.

And if a casual passerby saw them now, they would appear two strangers forced into each other's company by some grudging sense of politeness. He had lost a lot of ground in this engagement, and he did not know how to gain it back.

THERE WAS NO sign of either Miss Kirby or her uncle when Sarah and Vivian emerged from the pagoda.

"Where can they be?" Sarah asked.

"I'm sure they are nearby, enjoying each other's company." Vivian's tone suggested she knew something Sarah did not. She probably did. Vivian understood people.

Sarah, on the other hand, still had not relinquished Cecil as her paragon of manhood. Except Miss Kirby's comment about the cravat tended to make her smile. It held a sad truth. If Sarah focused on Cecil's vanity, perhaps....

She looked around again for her uncle and her chaperon. The landscape was deserted, save for the gardener working this area and another man walking across the lawn toward him.

Here was a gentleman to dash Cecil's elegance to pieces. He was likely in his thirties, with a broadshouldered frame and his bottle-green coat nipped inward, accentuating narrow hips. His buff trousers molded strong limbs. His boots gleamed, and his hat topped his curling brown hair at a rakish angle.

And his cravat. Sarah stared at the deceptively simple folds. Cecil would certainly envy that neckcloth.

The man addressed the gardener, who gestured in Sarah's direction. The man looked at her.

Sarah caught her breath. His face was oval, with high cheekbones, yet a squared chin saved him from beauty. Sarah grabbed Vivian's arm as he advanced. His eyes, which held Sarah's as he approached, were the most amazing shade of green.

"Who is he?" Sarah asked.

"I don't know," Vivian said, losing some of her poise and looking around for their companions herself.

The man bowed. Now that he stood within arm's reach, Sarah sensed something else about him. He was supremely melancholy.

"Excuse me, ladies," he said. "I am seeking Portia Kirby."

"Miss Kirby is with us," Sarah replied. She looked around again. "She's walking with my uncle. Perhaps he needed to rest."

"Your uncle. . . ?"

"Lord Castleton," Vivian replied.

"Castleton. Of course." A ghost of a smile touched his lips. *He has dimples*, Sarah realized. He would be devastatingly handsome if he smiled. But a true smile seemed beyond him at present. He gestured in the direction both she and Vivian had indicated by their glances. "That way?"

"I believe so," Sarah said. "Is something wrong?"

For the first time, he looked at Sarah as if he saw her. His eyes were warm. Accessible.

"Nothing to concern yourself about," he said. "Good day to you, Miss Christopher." He nodded to Vivian. "Ma'am."

He stepped away as quickly as he'd approached, leaving both girls astonished.

"He addressed me by name," Sarah said in amazement.

"Of course he did, goose," Vivian chided. "You're Castleton's niece. But he did not give his name in turn."

"He is very elegant," Sarah said, assessing his retreating form. "I would have remembered him had we been introduced."

"Yes," Vivian agreed. "And so I suspect. . . ."

"What?"

"That he is not a gentleman."

JUST WHEN CASTLETON thought the day could not get any worse, he broke the tree line and found George Mahew but a dozen yards away. Sarah and Vivian stood beyond him, watching the rake and whispering to each other. Their manner suggested Mahew had addressed them. Margaret would be furious if that got out.

Portia immediately quit Castleton's arm and walked toward her cousin. Mahew held out his hand and she took it, her expression suffused with tender concern.

Castleton bristled.

"I'm sorry to intrude," Mahew said, "But Mrs. Andrews said I could find you here. . . ."

"I thought he did not call on you," Castleton said.

Portia discharged one dangerous look in his direction, then returned her attention to Mahew. She reached out and lightly brushed her cousin's cheek. "What's wrong, George?"

Mahew pressed his lips together. For the first time, Castleton noticed the pain reflected in his visage. *He's going to cry*, Castleton thought, surprised.

Portia latched Mahew's arm and guided him back toward the trees. Away from Castleton.

Sarah and Vivian joined him. "Who is he, sir?" Vivian asked.

"George Mahew."

Vivian gasped.

"I don't know the name," Sarah said in a perplexed tone.

"I was right. He isn't proper company," Vivian replied.

"Miss Kirby is familiar with him," Sarah remarked, as they all watched Mahew throw his arms around Portia.

Portia did not push *him* away. In fact, she drew Mahew's head to her shoulder, grasping his neck at the nape and rubbing her other hand in a soothing rhythm across his shoulders.

Castleton tensed. Though she clearly dispensed comfort, her acceptance of Mahew's embrace cut him to the quick. In comparison, the connection between them seemed so fragile. *A dagger to my heart would be less painful.*

It was Mahew who broke away. He brushed at his eyes, and folded his arms.

Portia placed a hand on his sleeve, and Mahew shook his head at her. She glanced at Castleton then, and breathed a troubled sigh. One last speech had Mahew nodding, before she deserted her cousin at the trees and returned to speak to them.

"Your inclination to come today may have been an act of Providence, Lord Castleton," Portia said. "George has suffered a tragedy. The loss of . . . a close friend."

"Not...?"

Portia nodded, cutting off his question in deference to the young ladies at his side.

Castleton found himself softening in sympathy.
Mahew had seemed sincerely attached to Lady
Burrow. And though expected, this death seemed
untimely. Castleton wondered what had occurred.
But Portia obviously wanted no questions.

"If you could see Miss Christopher and Miss
Barstow safely home," she said, "I would be most
grateful."

"You're not going with him, Miss Kirby?" Vivian
exclaimed.

"He's my cousin," Portia replied. "It will be fine.
Although I think this will be my last outing as a
chaperon. I've done a wretched job."

"He did not introduce himself to us," Sarah
said. "He was most polite, and is obviously in great
distress."

"He drove out in his curricle," Portia told
Castleton. "He will see me home if you will lend the
young ladies your escort."

"He could just follow us back," Castleton said.

"And be introduced to your family?" Portia
returned. "I'm sure Mrs. Christopher would enjoy
that. You needn't worry for my safety." Her tone
hardened further. "It isn't as if he intends to lure me
into the shrubbery and make love to me, after all."

Castleton flinched, then nodded. What else
could he do?

Portia returned the parasol to Sarah with thanks

for its use and for the invitation. She returned to Mahew's side, and, when last Castleton saw her, Mahew's arm was about her waist and her head rested on her cousin's arm.

HE KISSED ME.

Portia tried to listen as George told her how word of Lady Burrow's death had reached him from an unsigned note that he suspected came directly from husband.

"I thought it a prank, at first," he said. "I drove past the house. The wreath was on the door, the street muffled. I spoke with a maid near the servants' entrance. She said Amy took a second dose of laudanum by mistake. I . . . I don't think it was accidental, Portia."

"She was in great pain," Portia murmured. *Lord Castleton kissed me. He drew me into his arms and kissed me. And such a kiss. Nothing like Avery's. Nothing like the one you stole at James's wedding. It was so . . . stirring.*

"We could have had more. A day. A week. A moment. You have no idea how affecting one moment can be."

Yes, I do, George. Lord Castleton kissed me. The most thrilling and terrifying event of her life. He had disproved her assertion that a single kiss meant nothing.

"*I am a man, you are a woman, we deal well together. . . .*" Could he be . . . attracted? No. The thought was too ridiculous. He must have been joking.

But he kissed me.

"*He must feel some attraction to have done such a thing.*" Portia would have believed that about any other man kissing any other woman. But it couldn't be true for herself. No one wanted her that way anymore. No one.

She dwelled on it for the entire journey. His hand on her hip, his lean form pressed close against hers, his lips both hard and soft at the same time— such a thrilling paradox. And the feelings—the wild excitement that had built in her breast and the heat of parts below. Even if Castleton was not attracted, his kiss certainly affected Portia as if it had been "real."

How could she face him again? How could she attend one word he said, when they issued from a mouth that had known hers intimately for a span of time?

Could they remain friends, when what he did— whatever his reason—haunted her restless slumber that night? As much as she'd resisted it, Portia was attached to the idea of Castleton as her friend. She didn't want that bond to break, no matter what the Mr. Cheevers of the world thought.

But how could Portia remain his friend when she was now so supremely aware of him as a man?

7

PORTIA WENT NOWHERE for a sennight.

On the fifth day of her self-imposed confinement, Castleton called, but she sent down word she was "not at home." She cowered behind the curtains of an upper window to watch his retreat.

His stride was powerful, and he cut the heads off the daffodils in her neighbor's windowbox with one stroke of his walking stick. Portia nearly threw up the sash to call him back, but even from this angle the lines of his figure recalled dizzying memories of his embrace.

On the sixth day, her aunt Charlotte put her foot down.

"I don't know what ails you of late, Portia, and I'm not sure I wish to know," Charlotte said. "But I will certainly blame you if we spend our summer in London's dust. I won't send our apologies to the Barkers, and I will not excuse you. If you are unhappy with our arrangement, go live with James and Maria."

Portia nodded her reluctant assent and went upstairs to don her walking dress. *Perhaps some fresh air will help*, she thought.

Her quick clip took her straight to the park green where Arthur Ponsby exercised Bright Promise most mornings. Today Frederick held the reins under Ponsby's careful supervision.

Ponsby left his pupil to greet Portia's arrival. "Miss Kirby," Ponsby said, bowing to her, "I'm so glad to see you. You haven't been by in several days. Are you well?"

"I'm fine," Portia replied. "But how kind of you to notice. Especially when you are so occupied."

Ponsby smiled in Frederick's direction. "The training proceeds better than expected. Bright Promise responds well."

"As does Mr. Christopher," Portia replied, amused.

Ponsby smiled back. "He asked if he could practice until his uncle arrives," he said.

Portia's chest tightened. "Lord Castleton is coming here?"

"Frederick said he wanted to see how we were progressing," Ponsby replied. His tone softened. "Miss Christopher might come, too, if her appointment with the dressmaker ends soon enough." His brow creased with concern. "Are you sure you're all right, ma'am? You look so pale of a sudden."

"You mentioned the dressmaker," Portia lied with a quivering laugh. "I forgot I also have an appointment today. I think I have just enough time to hurry home and call for a carriage."

Ponsby bowed to her again. "Will I see you at the Barker's cotillion?" he asked.

"Yes," she replied, glancing around quickly lest a rider on a black horse gallop toward them unawares. "My aunt is pinning her hopes on them for a summer invitation. She insists I attend."

"I'll speak to you there," Ponsby said. "I've been remiss of late—"

"I really must go," Portia said, cutting him off. Were those hoof beats bearing down on them? "I will speak to you later."

Portia rushed away—no, ran away—as fast as was seemly.

By evening she was still uncertain how she would face Castleton. His presence at the Barkers seemed inevitable.

The litany of his kiss still sang in her thoughts, just as the sensation of his touch haunted her dreams. Even an afternoon nap to freshen for the trying night ahead was interrupted by his intense blue eyes and his phantom embrace.

Portia frowned at the circles under her eyes as she dressed her hair. She turned at the clearing of a throat near the door.

Her maid Lydia bobbed a curtsey. "Excuse me, miss, but Mark says there's a gentleman downstairs begging to see you."

"Did he say who it was?" Portia asked, suddenly finding it more difficult to breathe.

"No, miss," Lydia replied.

Portia shut her eyes. *Better to face him privately, perhaps*. But she wasn't ready. She wasn't sure she'd ever be.

"I'll be down presently," she said. She carefully smoothed her hair down and adjusted the tiny curls on her forehead. Despite her efforts, she looked no better than always.

She pressed her hand into her diaphragm and stalked to the drawing room as if on her way to the chopping block.

But it was Ponsby, his evening clothes too tight and his complexion red as he wore a steady path in the floral rug.

"Miss Kirby," he said, "I have come to lend you escort to the Barkers this evening."

"To what do I owe this honor?" Portia asked, pleased despite his trepidation.

"To my thoughtlessness," he told her. "To my total lack of intuition. I should have known when you left so quickly this morning, but I was absorbed by my own interests. And the only solution I could determine is to lend my arm to support you. . . ."

"Arthur, you aren't making sense," Portia interjected.

"Lord Castleton," he said. "You've quarreled with him, haven't you?"

Portia's cheeks reddened. "I would not call it a quarrel precisely," she said.

"That's what he said," Ponsby said. "A misunderstanding. But you fled this morning to avoid him. He's sought you everywhere, which would explain your absence in society of late. . . ."

"Sought me?" Portia asked faintly.

"That's what Frederick said after he left us. His

uncle's been all over town. Three to four parties a night. Because of you. Frederick was sure of that because his mother said so. Whatever happened, she blames you."

Portia shut her eyes.

"I told him you would be at the Barkers before I realized something was amiss," Ponsby confessed.

"If he attends three or four parties a night, he would have found me anyway," Portia soothed. "I feared you were he, in fact."

"Was it something very bad, ma'am?"

The kiss ran through her head again. The taste of Castleton, the texture of his mouth—Portia's stomach tightened.

"No, it wasn't . . . bad," she murmured.

"Then it can be mended."

"I don't know," Portia said, anguished. "But I would be very glad of your arm. At least through the front door."

"It is yours, ma'am," Ponsby said, squaring his shoulders.

If their unexpected ride to the Barkers in Ponsby's hired carriage surprised Portia's aunt, the widow didn't show it. After her profuse greetings to their hosts, Charlotte retreated to the cardroom, leaving Portia clinging to Ponsby's elbow.

Luckily, Ponsby was strong about the arms and shoulders. When Portia caught sight of Castleton, she squeezed so hard a lesser man would have flinched in pain.

Castleton conversed with acquaintances but

not intently enough to miss her entrance. His blue eyes pierced her from across the room. Portia knew as soon as he could extricate himself he would bear down on her. Panic hammered in her chest. She wanted to run. But she couldn't. Not this time.

"Miss Kirby?" Ponsby whispered. "Miss Kirby, what do you want to do? We can slip into the refreshment room. He may not notice. . . ."

"He already has," she replied, as Castleton bowed over the laughing dowager's hand and straighten in Portia's direction.

He wore black. Like the wicked villain in one of Mrs. Radcliffe's books. Only Portia'd never envisioned such men with irresistibly attractive features and kissable lips. A part of her—a wild, wanton part—wished Castleton would draw her back into his arms and kiss her again.

His gaze pinned her to the spot, commanding her to receive him as he advanced ever nearer.

Portia stood perfectly still, gripping Ponsby's arm to keep from buckling at the knees.

I can't, she thought. *I can't do this.*

"Dear Miss Kirby," Serina Applegate exclaimed, dancing up to her in a gauzy gown of the palest blue. "I've been waiting for you. I must speak to you at once."

Serina seized Portia's hand and dragged her toward the withdrawing room door. Portia glanced back at Castleton over her shoulder and breathed a silent prayer of thanksgiving as another acquaintance claimed his attention also.

Portia held so fast to Ponsby's arm she drew him along with her in Serina's wake. At the door of the withdrawing room, he dug his heels into the carpet.

"Perhaps I'd better. . . ." he stammered.

"Oh." Serina stopped. She turned and smiled at Ponsby as she never had before. "Please forgive me, Mr. Ponsby. How rude of me. We won't go in. I just wished a quieter corner."

"What is it?" Portia asked, shaken from her own disquiet by Serina's demeanor. Though radiantly lovely, she usually did not glow like this. Her friendly ease had Ponsby dazzled.

"Mama doesn't wish anyone to know until the announcement appears tomorrow," Serina said, lowering her voice to a whisper. "But I had to tell you, ma'am. Mr. Dodd and I are to marry!"

"Oh. Oh, congratulations!" Portia impulsively hugged her.

Serina laughed and hugged her back. "Mama wanted me to refuse him at first. But Nicholas came home from Epsom Downs last night and had a long talk with her. He thinks Mr. Dodd is perfectly suitable. If it can be arranged, we'll wed before the Season is over."

Portia suspected the state of Nicholas Applegate's pockets might have some bearing on his support. Despite that, Giles Dodd would be a wonderful match for Serina. Already the promise of marriage had unleashed the vital girl within the cool diamond.

"May I offer you felicitations and best wishes for

your future happiness, Miss Applegate?" Ponsby said in a soft voice.

"Thank you, Mr. Ponsby." Serina offered her hand to him, and he bowed over it. Serina flashed a beaming smile that encompassed them both as she said, "Now remember, not a word to anyone."

"As if her happiness wasn't clue enough...." Portia murmured as Serina floated away.

"She knew my name," Ponsby said in a dazed voice. "She's never addressed me so openly. She's ... very nice, isn't she?"

"Did her news upset you?" Portia asked.

"What? Oh, no. Not at all. I am very happy for her. I just can't believe Lord Castleton was so mistaken."

"I'm afraid I don't understand you."

"Lord Castleton made assumptions about Miss Applegate's nature based on her behavior," Ponsby explained. "But he was wrong. She is worthy of regard beyond appearances. And though I mistook that worthiness for something warmer in myself, I find my recognition of it gratifying. Do you think it's possible I know more about women than a leader of the ton?"

A staggering idea. But quite possibly true. Castleton had never actually pursued women. He didn't have to. His looks and his charm won over the average female as a matter of course.

Yet he had, in a fashion, pursued *her*, Portia realized. Sought out her company. Could Castleton have mistaken the growing good will between them for something warmer and stolen his kiss to see if there was more?

If so, her displeasure *must* have dispelled the notion.

Portia smiled warmly at Ponsby. "I do," she said.

"What are you agreeing to now, Miss Kirby?" Castleton inquired from scarce feet away.

Suddenly all fear was gone. He'd made a mistake. Whatever his reasons, Castleton regretted what he'd done. Portia could see it in his posture, in his uncharacteristic uncertainty.

"Ma'am?" Ponsby whispered, stepping close to her shoulder.

"It's all right," she said. "Thank you for your escort."

Ponsby glanced between them and withdrew with a bow.

Castleton stepped closer to Portia. Her heart beat faster, but she decided to ignore it. His friendship was too dear to throw away on a shallow animal attraction that had, in honesty, been there before his kiss.

"Shall I go down on my knees to grovel on your slippers, or should I return home to don the traditional sackcloth and ashes?"

"Don't be ridiculous," Portia said, and she smiled at him.

Relief nearly overwhelmed Castleton. He clasped his hands behind his back to keep from reaching for her. "I'm forgiven, then?"

"You are."

"And we are still friends?"

A rosy glow tinted her pale features. "Yes. We are friends."

She stressed the last word.

Castleton smiled anyway. He offered her his hand and, after a brief hesitation, Portia took it. He tucked her fingers into the crook of his arm.

Portia found it disquieting to stand so close to him. But she took solace that his touch, though unnerving, was impersonal.

They had much to discuss. The on-dits of the past week, the state of her health (her fabricated excuse for not appearing in public sooner), the weather. Castleton attempted to draw Portia out about Serina's manic joy. She kept her promise but laughed much at his efforts. After multiple circuits of the room, she was feeling easy in his company again.

Then the orchestra struck up a waltz.

"I think I'm ready," Castleton announced as the music began.

"Ready for what?"

"To try my luck on the dance floor."

"Ah." Portia glanced around. "Whom will you ask?"

"Whom do you think?" Castleton arched his brow at her.

Portia stiffened. "Are you serious?"

"I could trip up, or my leg give way. I need a partner who will forgive my missteps or allow me to lean on her, if necessary. Who else can I apply to, save . . . a good friend?"

A logical line of reasoning. Portia placed her hand in his. Castleton drew her into his arms and launched them into the couples already revolving around the room.

He kept his touch light. It felt good to hold her again.

Though her size was aesthetically unfashionable, he thought her physically ideal. Her head, had she'd chosen so, could rest comfortably on his shoulder, while the curve of her waist required no adjustment for his hand to guide her through the steps.

And should Castleton prevail—woo her and win her—he could look into Portia's face when reclined, and see what pained and pleased her. He could apply soft kisses to her lips and cheeks, and whisper the extent of his love in her ear to ease what he imagined would be an overpowering passion.

Something of Castleton's warm thoughts must have shown in his expression. Portia ducked her head away from him, not speaking to him or looking at him for half the set.

She was, in fact, in turmoil. She wanted Castleton to pull her closer. And her senses played a cruel trick—they said he wanted that as well. If his touch unbalanced her this way, there would never be ease between them.

Portia should relinquish their tie for her sanity's sake. The dance proved he was healed. He would return to his old life and she.... Well, she would go nowhere, but....

"How are they doing?" he asked.

"Excuse me?" Portia hazarded a glance at his face. That strange light was in his eyes again, mingled with good-humor.

"My feet," Castleton said. "They appear in working order to me, but you've studied them so intently...."

"I'm sorry. I'm a bit awkward," she replied.

"Not as a dance partner," Castleton corrected, "nor as a companion. And you performed both tasks together with pleasant results for Frederick."

"He was very nervous. I did my best to put him at his ease."

"And yet, for me...?" Castleton pressed.

"I confess, with you I feel the inferior."

"Inferior? Not in my mind."

"Nonetheless," Portia shut her eyes, "we are from different spheres."

"Different spheres of the same world," Castleton corrected.

"I'm not so sure of that."

Castleton frowned. "What are you saying?"

"I think, while we are friends now, it's not likely we can continue much longer."

"You told me my friendship was not easily given. Perhaps you don't realize that, once given, it is never taken away."

"You are too kind." Portia spoke so softly, Castleton had to drop his head to catch the words. "But there is no need...."

"No need to what? Seek you out? Enjoy your company? Do you wish me gone, Portia?"

She looked up, surprised at his deliberate use of her intimate name. "Perhaps it would be best. I'm happy I was able to divert your mind while your leg was healing," she began.

"But now I am healed, you want nothing more to do with me."

"I didn't say that."

"You implied it." Castleton halted abruptly, then drew Portia off the dance floor out onto the terrace. He placed his hand on her shoulder and tilted her face to look into his.

"Are you sure you are my friend? Do you care for me at all?" Castleton asked, inwardly hoping he hadn't given her too wide an opening to be rid of him.

Portia's jaw dropped. "I've enjoyed our talks these past few weeks. But it was just diversion."

"Then you haven't been attending me," Castleton replied, hardening his tone.

"I only meant, now that you are completely recovered, you will return to your former activities."

"Yes," he said. "But why should that put a period to us?"

"We move in different circles," she repeated.

"Ah, but we can choose to do otherwise," Castleton replied. "For instance, you could attend the races at Ascot this year with me and my family. There is more attention given to the crowd than the horses, so I know you will enjoy it. I can renew my invitation to the theater. Or we could attend a lecture by that Godwall fellow. . . ."

"Godwin," Portia corrected.

"When your aunt will not. I daresay his views on 'free love' will divert us both, don't you?"

"You really would not wish to do that."

"I would to keep a friend of you," Castleton returned. "Do you wish to remain my friend?"

"Yes," Portia whispered.

"Good," he said. "Then all is settled. Which play should we attend? I hear Keane is very good in *The Merchant of Venice*—a play that must hold some interest since you were named for its most radiant character. Or we can see this new drama at the Lyceum, which I understand is dreadful, but may afford us more amusement by virtue of its flaws. What do you say, Portia?"

"I think ... I will leave the choice to you," she said, meeting his gaze with effort.

Castleton wore a victor's smile for the rest of the evening.

Margaret dissolved that smile at breakfast the next morning. "A theater party on a Wednesday during the Season? Are you mad?!"

"It was the only day we were mutually free," Castleton explained as he buttered his toast.

"You may be free, but I am not," Margaret said in a reedy voice. "I am taking Sarah to Almack's."

"You can take Sarah to Almack's any Wednesday."

"I will take Sarah to Almack's *every* Wednesday." Margaret's tea cup trembled as she raised it to her lips. "You may take as cavalier an attitude about her future as you do your own—"

"Excuse me?"

"—but I intend to see my daughter is properly launched and eventually marries a man who is *worthy* of her regard."

"Portia is worthy," Castleton said, keeping his tone even.

"She abandoned my child—"

"To me...."

"To go off with a man of questionable character—"

"Who is a close relative...."

"And that," Margaret said stiffly, "is hardly a mark in her favor."

"Margaret, please...."

"You may plead all you want, and try to wheedle me with those amiable smiles, but I will not alter my plans to suit Miss Kirby. My resolve is fixed."

Castleton fell silent. But without the presence of another female in his party, his evening at the theater with Portia would be tantamount to a declaration.

He would be damned if he would cancel his hard-won assignation. There had to be another solution.

He removed to his study and took pen in hand.

It's a good thing, he thought as he scratched a note on his crested stationery, *Sarah did not report her encounter with Mahew to her mother.* Margaret seemed disposed to dislike Portia, and that act would put his beloved in her black books forever.

* * * * *

SARAH HAD FINALLY come to observe the training of Bright Promise. And, she admitted, while the reins had been in Arthur Ponsby's competent hands, the work had proved fascinating.

He was an agreeable young man. Not particularly handsome, but amiable. He seemed his most assured when engaged in physical activity, and he had a special affinity with the bay horse.

And with Frederick. Ponsby was incredibly patient with her brother, even if he might ruin all of Ponsby's hard work.

Ponsby repeatedly demonstrated the correct way to hold the reins and guide Bright Promise around the park green. Each time Frederick nodded and diligently followed instructions. But his enthusiasm inevitably led to another error Ponsby had to correct.

Sarah sighed. Ponsby's forbearance might be infinite, but hers was not. She wished she'd brought her maid, or that Vivian could have come.

But Mr. Barstow had taken Viv to Brighton for the week—those rare hours the widower could devote to his only child were considered sacred engagements in the Barstow household.

Sarah must wait for Frederick to escort her home.

She looked around. This section of the park was largely deserted. The flat green lawn, ideal for exercising a horse, had no outstanding foliage to distract her for an hour. There were some benches along the path a little distance from her brother. At least there she could wait in some comfort.

But as she strolled toward them, another figure crossed the green and seated itself.

Sarah hesitated. It was Miss Kirby's cousin, George Mahew. Sarah remembered her mother's anger on learning Miss Kirby had departed in his company. By tacit agreement, no one mentioned Mahew had spoken to her and to Vivian. From her mother's outburst, Sarah learned George Mahew was a notorious womanizer.

He didn't look like a villain. Sarah could sense only the deep, deep sorrow within him and remember his eyes—brilliant green and full of warmth. He'd been polite and considerate at that one meeting—caring for her reputation, not sullying it. His bleak expression was evident even from a distance.

Though she knew it was wrong, she closed the distance between them. "Excuse me."

Mahew looked up at her. His pupils dilated in surprised recognition. He rose and sketched her a graceful bow. "Miss Christopher. How can I assist you?"

"You can't . . . I mean. . . ." Sarah didn't know what she meant. He looked so sad. "You seem distressed, sir," she said. "You appeared so at Kew, also. I only wondered . . . if you were well."

Mahew blinked. A slow, dimpled smile brightened his face a moment but quickly faded again. "I have lost a dear friend."

"I am so sorry." Sarah took a seat on the bench. She brushed her hand along the surface to indicate he should join her.

Mahew sat again, keeping an arm's length between them.

"I've never lost anyone I was dearly close to, except my father. But I was too young to really understand that. And shortly after it happened, my uncle arrived to take care of us. He holds a father's place in my heart."

"Your uncle would not like this, Miss Christopher."

"What?"

"Conversing with a man of dubious reputation unchaperoned."

"Do you intend to make love to me, sir?" Sarah asked.

Mahew laughed. "I would never have spoken to you at all, ma'am, had you not approached me."

Sarah nodded toward her brother, who once again threaded the reins through his fingers. Ponsby shook his head and readjusted them with exaggerated slowness. Frederick nodded and tried again, this time earning Ponsby's approbation.

She sighed. "Frederick's driving lessons are very tedious. I wonder Mr. Ponsby can bear to have him work with that horse."

"A good horse must respond to any man who drives him."

"But this is not a good horse. Or so I'm told."

"It will take patience to bring him around, but Ponsby appears to have an abundance of that quality," Mahew replied. "I have a bet at White's he will succeed."

"You bet on him?" Sarah exclaimed.

"The odds are irresistibly against. Ponsby is not well-known, and his public persona is unrefined, to say the least. Most men are wont to judge by appearances."

"But you don't."

"In general, I let Portia be my guide in matters of character. She thinks quite highly of Mr. Ponsby."

"She is also very fond of you, sir," Sarah replied, remembering the concern on Miss Kirby's face and the tender way she'd embraced Mahew to soothe his pain.

"That's despite my defects, believe me, ma'am." Mahew rose. "She would be very put out if I sat beside you any longer."

Sarah rose, as well. "Then I should leave. 'Twas I who intruded on your solitude."

"Thank you," he said. "You have been ... most kind."

"Good day to you, Mr. Mahew." Sarah offered him her hand.

After a brief hesitation, Mahew bowed over it. He took one last look into her face—*How could a man who radiated such a friendly air be considered dangerous*? He tipped his hat and set it back on his curling locks at just the right angle.

It appeared to Sarah his broad shoulders were set a little straighter as he walked away, and that the change in his demeanor could be due to the notice she'd taken of him.

I will come again, she thought. *And if he is here, I*

will speak to him. Surely it could not be improper to hold a civil conversation with any man in so public a place?

Sarah did not realize Arthur Ponsby had turned to look at her—as he often did—and had observed the entire exchange in tableau. Ponsby kept his frown of concern from her as she wandered back toward them. As much as he wished it, Sarah's honor was not his province.

But he wondered what dealings Sarah could have with George Mahew. And, more distressing, what intercourse George Mahew could have with her.

8

PORTIA FOUND HERSELF questioning Castleton's invitation to accompany him to the theater. Once absolved of his earlier error, he hadn't backed away from further intimacies in the least. The civil contacts—taking her arm without leave, the dance—could be excused. But hustling her to the terrace, tilting her face to his, and the use of her Christian name....

And, since she'd been too shocked to deny him this familiarity, it appeared Castleton would continue to call her Portia. Like a brother. Or a lover.

Stop it, she told herself. *He likes informality. He calls every matron of his acquaintance by her given name. It's an endorsement of his friendship. You're nervous because you are not used to it. Given time, it will mean as little to you as it most likely means to him.*

Besides, Castleton's invitation placed a more realistic burden on her. She could not appear in his box wearing the same green gown of the past six weeks.

She'd never relished the refurbishment of her

wardrobe. During the Season there was such a long wait to gain her dressmaker's attention to obtain a style of clothing that would never flatter Portia, no matter how elegantly composed.

The sooner she faced the unpleasantness the better. Consequently, she forwent her usual morning walk and ordered a carriage. She decided to take Lydia with her, and so waited until the girl's usual chores were completed before setting out.

Even at nine a.m. Madame Claire's shop was abuzz with activity. Portia guided Lydia to one of the back counters to inspect fabric swatches and perused the first of what she suspected would be an hour's worth of fashion plates.

"Mademoiselle Kirby, what a delightful surprise."

Startled, Portia discovered Madame at her elbow. The little Frenchwoman beamed as if the sentiment were genuine and directed her to one of the better chairs. Even more astonishing, the lady whom Madame had been aiding when Portia entered the establishment smiled as she meekly accepted the assistance of an underling.

"How may we serve you today?" Madame asked in her lightly accented voice.

"I need an evening dress for a theatrical engagement."

"Lord Castleton's party?" Madame guessed.

"Why . . . yes."

Madame nodded. She beckoned to one of her workers.

"I have just the dress to suit you." Madame paged through her sketchbook handed to her and turned to a rather grand drawing.

Portia wasn't sure which bothered her more: that the dress, elegant but simple, was daringly cut for a spinster of thirty, or that the woman in the drawing resembled her—her figure, her hair; the face was even round.

"It's not what I'm used to," Portia said in a faint voice.

"No," Madame agreed. "But when one sits where one is seen, one should look their best, *ne c'est pas*? I thought verte, to flatter your eyes. And Marie designed the headdress. She can instruct your girl in the arrangement of your hair."

"I don't want to take so much time," Portia said. "I know how busy you must be. . . ."

"Tut, mademoiselle, you are a customer of long standing," Madame replied. "And we must be sure Lord Castleton is thought fortunate in his . . . friends, mustn't we?"

Portia iced up inside, but nodded to her obediently.

Although she'd been a customer of the dress-maker's since her come out, she'd never clashed with her opinion so much. Portia wanted a more sober color than the emerald-green satin Madame unfurled for her inspection. She wanted a higher neckline and a lower headdress.

And Lydia offered no support, having declared the drawing lovely. The maid added her voice to the chorus of Madame and her assistant not to change one detail.

Madame won out on the cloth, but Portia refused to yield on the other matters. She knew her own wishes were secondary to appearing at the theater in a spectacular gown of the modiste's making. The modiste's attitude brought to bear the impact of Castleton's regard.

Portia had received an increase of invitations as a direct result of her new friendship. There'd also been more calls on her. People spoke to her now or solicited her opinion.

"... *we must be sure Lord Castleton is thought fortunate in his ... friends, mustn't we?*" Madame's hesitation to term her Castleton's friend worried Portia. She remembered Mr. Cheever's erroneous assumption. And that had been before the kiss. Before Castleton had waltzed with her and invited her to be his guest for an evening. Did Madame think what Mr. Cheever had thought?

Whatever she's thinking, she's wrong, Portia said inwardly as she paced her bedroom floor on Wednesday.

She credited the scheduled last-minute delivery of her gown on a conspiracy to undermine her confidence. She was ready to surrender to her misgivings and send her regrets to Castleton and his family. The headdress had arrived earlier in the day, and had been modified to something less ostentatious. But Lydia had still been able to dress her hair to Mademoiselle Marie's design.

"It's here, Miss." Lydia swept into the room with the green satin creation carefully draped over her arm. "It arrived twenty minutes ago, but I wanted to press out the creases ... we don't have much time."

"No, we don't," Portia replied, casting off her wrapper and allowing Lydia to toss the shimmering material over her head. Lydia quickly fastened and buttoned. Portia gazed down at the sweep of the cloth around her waist, legs and. . . .

"Oh, no." Portia twitched away from Lydia's grasp to turn toward her looking glass. She gasped.

The stiff material lent a neater line to her soft figure, and the wideness of the facing below her breast hinted at the slenderness of her waist. But the artful satin drapes of the bodice barely concealed the nipples of her full bosom. She hadn't worn a dress cut this low since. . . .

"You look so elegant, Miss Portia," Lydia exclaimed.

"A tucker," Portia gasped. "Some lace. . . ."

"Oh, no, miss, you don't need it. You look ever so nice."

"Get me something *now*," Portia insisted, pushing Lydia toward her wardrobe. The maid curtseyed and rummaged through Portia's accessories looking for something suitable as Portia vainly tugged the material higher.

Charlotte entered after lightly tapping on the door. "Lord Castleton has arrived—my word!" Her sharp eyes swept over Portia's dress. "You look *very* well, Portia."

"It's too low," Portia insisted, yanking a strip of lace from Lydia's hand and tucking it around her neckline.

"It's fine," Charlotte said. "You ruin the effect with that."

Lydia agreed, her voice full of disappointment. She'd been dressing Miss Portia for five years, and this gown was the first inkling the her plain look could be raised to something alluring. In truth, she looked more beddable than beautiful, but there was nothing vulgar about the gown. Madame had only brought to light the gifts the Good Lord had blessed Portia with.

Charlotte shook her head and sighed. "Lord Castleton is here," she repeated.

Portia sat down at her dressing table and handed Lydia the headdress. "I will be down presently," she said.

Charlotte nodded and withdrew.

CASTLETON PACED CHARLOTTE Andrews's small sitting room. He prayed Lucy's flippant response to his invitation was assent. If he arrived at the theater with Portia, and she was not in his box, he would be sunk.

Charlotte returned with a troubled frown on her face to explain Portia was "not satisfied with her gown and wished to make an alteration." She sat down in a chair near the fireplace, and Castleton had no choice but to follow suit.

Without the pacing to dissipate it, nervous energy built like a weight in his chest.

"Will Mrs. Christopher meet you at the theater?" Charlotte asked. Her tone suggested she was only making conversation.

He shook his head. "She is taking Sarah to Almack's. But I've invited the Duke and Duchess of Wallace to join us."

"Oh." Charlotte's brown eyes sharpened. It was the first time Castleton could recall her full attention on him.

"Are you a fair hand at cards, Lord Castleton?" she asked.

"I hold my own," he said.

"What is your game? Whist? Piquet?"

Castleton shrugged, perplexed.

"You must favor me with a hand some day soon," Charlotte declared, "so I may test your mettle."

"I would be happy to oblige you, ma'am," he replied with a slow smile of understanding. She had discovered him. And wished to test his worth by her own unique scale.

"Here is Portia," Charlotte announced, recognizing the footfall in the hallway.

Castleton rose as Portia entered. He sucked in his breath.

Her figure was better than he'd imagined. The stiff emerald satin smoothed over the swell of her hips and deepened the color of her eyes. A veritable froth of tendrils cascaded from a demure band of gold and paste jewels accentuating the bones of her full cheeks. And her shoulders sloped over the most impressive. . . .

Castleton frowned. The lace tucked in the hollow between her breasts did not belong. Its awkward placement drew the eye to what Portia endeavored to conceal. An image awoke in his memory.

He laughed.

Portia heated to a blistering red. She turned on her heel, intent on fleeing, but he stepped forward and caught her arm.

"I'm sorry," he said, though bubbles of mirth punctuated his words. "I have, at last, remembered our first encounter. And it may flatter you a little to know half my study of Louisa was to keep my gaze from lingering on those damned roses."

Portia thought it impossible to redden further. She drew her shawl up around her shoulders.

Castleton shook his head at her. "Your strategy is all wrong, my dear," he said. "Better to distract than conceal. Remove it."

"My lord, really. . . ."

"It's tawdry, Portia," he said plainly.

She turned her back a moment, then faced him with her impressive bosom bared and her color high.

"You look magnificent," he said.

"You are very kind, but. . . ."

"You are not comfortable," he finished. Castleton consulted his pocket watch. "We can remedy that if we hurry."

He bowed to Charlotte, who beamed at him,

and offered Portia his arm. After delivering her to the waiting carriage, Castleton spoke briefly to his driver, then took the seat opposite.

Portia had drawn her gauzy shawl up around her shoulders again. Castleton did nothing to dissuade her, though he found it highly comical that it took an expanse of bosom to recall their initial meeting.

No wonder he did not recall her—he doubted Portia had raised her eyes to his from the moment they were thrown together. The fashion then had tended toward sheer, clinging cloth. Her present gown was modest compared to the dress she'd worn that night.

To add to her discomfort, the room had been cool. As they'd taken the floor, Castleton had noticed the hard points in the India muslin. And those roses, nestled so invitingly between the full, firm globes, had tempted one to pluck them out until only flesh remained. At the time he'd thought it a clumsy attempt to call attention to a woman's only outstanding feature.

Portia's hazel eyes flickered up to his face, then out the window. She straightened in surprise, the shawl slipping slightly down her back.

"We're on Bond Street," she said.

"I have a stop to make," Castleton replied. "It will take but a minute."

He made Portia wait in the carriage. When he returned a quarter-hour later he held a jewelry case in his hand.

"What is that?" she asked in a voice full of trepidation.

"A diversionary tactic." He opened the box.

Portia gasped at the large emerald pendant nestled in the white velvet lining. "I cannot accept such a gift," she said.

"I knew you would feel that way," Castleton replied wryly. "I've only hired it for the evening. Or, rather, you have. So remiss of them to have misplaced your order. Since I had no idea what arrangements you'd made, I told them to send the bill to my steward to sort out later."

He offered the necklace to her. The disquiet in her face was almost painful.

Castleton sighed. "You can't spend the evening swathed like an Egyptian corpse," he said. "Think about it, Portia. What will they look at with this about your throat?"

She unfurled the shawl and took the necklace from him. The clasp gave her some problems, most likely because her hands shook badly.

Castleton transferred to her side. He brushed the curls off her neck, fastened the ends of the chain for her, then smoothed its line over her shoulders. He didn't know what soap she used, but she smelled wonderful. It took all his willpower not to press a kiss at the base of her neck. He turned her toward him, saying, "Let's have a look."

The stone sparkled wildly to the rhythm of her rapid breath. Castleton was mesmerized. What would she do if he kissed her now?

He sternly told himself he could not risk it and returned to his side of the carriage.

"I should have nipped a glass while I was about it, shouldn't I? No matter." He reached into his pocket. "These *are* a gift, but if you could see your reflection you would understand. Don't put them on unless you can be comfortable about it. I swear I will never tell a living soul where they came from."

Portia opened the second box which contained a dainty pair of emerald earrings set in gold filigree. In her mind's eye she realized they would suit her outfit better than the pearls she now wore.

It was too intimate a gift; she knew that in her heart. But his efforts to secure her comfort were too compelling. Without a word, she took the pearls from her ears and replaced them with the emeralds, storing the other earrings in the box and the box in her reticule.

Castleton smiled. "Perfection," he declared.

Portia almost believed it when the word came from his lips.

LUCY, DUCHESS OF Wallace, wondered if she'd made an error. She should be at Almack's seeing her son dance with his share of debutantes; though, at nineteen, Vane was far too young to marry. Because the Who's Who of Society danced on King Street, the theater was light of company, the pit filled by the boisterous middle classes.

And Castleton was late. Perhaps he had not

prevailed upon Miss Kirby to accompany him. It was highly irregular. But if any man could convince a proper lady to attend the theater as his escort without the security of a duenna it was David Carlyle.

They arrived just as the curtain rose. Castleton whispered apologies as he settled Portia in the chair beside Lucy then took a seat behind them next to Wallace.

Lucy flashed Portia a smile. The poor woman looked half-frazzled. But so elegant. For the first time she appeared a future baroness. The necklace was particularly lovely. And most likely hired, the way Portia assured herself of its existence every few minutes.

The farce was not amusing. Lucy found her attention more on the couple in her box than on the stage. Could Castleton's attentions really be serious?

Portia was nothing above the common. Her face was pleasant enough but nothing pretty or exotic. The gown suggested a voluptuous figure—many men found that sort of ripeness desirable. But she lacked the bold manner necessary to capitalize on such bounty.

And yet, Castleton was clearly besotted. His eyes lingered on Portia with proprietary concern.

He leaned forward in his chair and whispered a comment in her ear. Portia's lips twitched in response—she was more appealing with a smile on her face, Lucy owned. Castleton glanced toward the stage and made another intimate remark to his companion. This time Portia was sufficiently diverted to suppress a trill of laughter.

She leaned back, her eyes large and sparkling in the dim theater lighting, and made a comment of her own.

Castleton laughed.

It surprised Lucy. She'd heard him laugh before. Or thought she had. There was a heartiness in the sound new to her ear.

The first interval arrived to tepid applause. Castleton tapped Lucy's shoulder, an apologetic smile on his lips.

"Are you wishing me to perdition?" he asked. "Late for my own party, and then the farce is hardly farcical."

"It was inferior. But, I was surprised to actually hear the lines," Lucy admitted. "I look forward to the drama."

"So do I," Portia said. She turned toward Wallace. "What about you, Your Grace?"

Wallace started from his comfortable doze, sat his brawny figure upright, and cleared his throat. "Theater's not my passion," he admitted. "Like a good duel, though."

"I can understand how that would appeal to a man of action like yourself," Portia said. "You enjoy a good hunt, don't you?"

"Do you hunt, Miss Kirby?" Lucy asked in surprise.

"I'm afraid I don't even ride," she said. She smiled warmly at Wallace. "But my friend Arthur

Ponsby admired your mount the other day. He said he looked a prime fencer."

"Oh, he is, ma'am." And to Lucy's amazement her normally taciturn husband leaned forward and regaled them with tales of his most memorable hunts.

Portia not only nodded at the appropriate times but asked questions that indicated she actually listened with interest to what Wallace had to say.

Castleton flashed Lucy a proud smile.

There is, Lucy thought, *definitely more to her than one would suppose.*

The melodrama more than made up for the earlier performance. It was simply enthralling, though Lucy thought the young "virgin" stretched the point. When the sword play of the first act began, Lucy glanced at Wallace to see if he was awake.

He was. But his attention was not on the stage. He gazed at Portia. So did Castleton, but Lucy expected that. She turned to look at Miss Kirby.

Totally absorbed by the performance, Portia's hazel eyes were glued to the stage. But her hand made a lazy circuit around the contours of the pendant—back and forth, back and forth—with tantalizing slowness over her full breasts. A clearly unconscious yet totally agitating motion. Lucy felt her own face warm, and she wasn't even male.

Though she deplored chatter during a good play, she leaned toward Portia and whispered: "Do you think that's the natural color of her hair?"

Portia started and turned toward Lucy. Her

hand, thankfully, dropped to her lap. "I don't see how it could be," she whispered back. "That yellow is nearly green."

"It's so disconcerting," Lucy said. "I'm having a difficult time believing in her innocence because she's colored her hair. Virgins don't do that."

"Elderly ones do," Portia replied. "I can think of one who would do better to let her hair go grey as nature intended...."

"Harriet Bascombe," they said in chorus. Then both giggled loudly enough to cause a fat woman in the pit to hiss up at them.

Miss Kirby would do very well for Castleton, Lucy decided. She would do everything in her power to encourage the match.

At last, the acting troupe deserted the stage to thunderous applause. There was little time to discuss the performance, however. A steady stream of visitors invaded their box. Coming for a closer look at Castleton's future bride, Lucy thought, though she doubted Portia realized it.

But any attention seemed to make Portia nervous. Her hand stole back to the necklace—its presence offering her comfort, though her stroking drew notice to her impressive dimensions.

Lucy did what she could to ease Portia's discomfort, deflecting questions and guiding the conversation so its stream flowed more generally than a focus on Portia herself. She was inwardly congratulating her success when Millicent Lynde—a portly bore of a woman—entered with her sour-faced husband.

Millicent was a distant cousin, though neither of them acknowledged the relationship overmuch. Lucy disliked Millicent's piety and judgmental air of superiority, while Millicent had openly declared Lucy flighty and frivolous. Lucy marveled that she'd come to the theater at all, let alone to their box, although she greeted the Lyndes with cool civility.

She was about to make introductions, when Millicent seized Portia by the shoulders and pressed a cheek to hers—as close a gesture of affection as Lucy had ever seen from the woman.

"I could hardly credit my eyes to see you here, my dear," Millicent said, as she examined Portia's dress. "And without your aunt. What would Avery say?"

"I suppose he would be quite shocked," Portia said. "For I thought the play very good. And such a moral ending, ma'am."

"True." Millicent sighed. "Though one must bear witness to the degradation of the characters before the conclusion."

"Like the revels of Sodom and Gomorrah before the Lord smote them," Castleton interjected in a bland voice.

"Do you know Lord Castleton, Mrs. Lynde?" Portia asked, her voice trembling.

Millicent acknowledged Castleton as he gravely bowed.

"We cannot linger," Millicent told them. "We do not intend to stay for the next portion of the program. Kate Leigh is to appear in it, and we do not approve of her."

"We must thank the Lord for adding Miss Leigh in the program," Lucy replied when they departed. "Remind me at services on Sunday, Wallace."

"Who is Avery?" Castleton asked.

"Millicent's late brother. A bore if ever there was one. His every utterance was guaranteed to set your teeth on edge."

"And his relation to you, Portia?" Castleton asked.

Portia turned a fiery red. "We were engaged."

"Oh, my dear, I am so dreadfully sorry," Lucy exclaimed. "I had no idea."

"It was never formal," Portia replied. "He asked if he might speak to my father when he returned to London that last time, and I assented. There was no announcement."

"But to have trod on his memory in your hearing is quite unpardonable."

"You only spoke the truth," Portia replied. "I confess, I dreaded the looming Sundays I would have to sit in clear sight of all and listen intently."

"What happened to him?" Castleton asked.

"Typhus," Lucy said. "It felled a good portion of his parish before he arrived and carried him off within a fortnight of exposure. That must have been, what, seven years ago?"

"Nearer nine," Portia said.

"He must have been a man of some perception," Castleton murmured. Lucy started at this pronouncement but could not respond to it. She had no idea how attached Portia had been, though she suspected the engagement was simply to secure a husband rather than an inclination for Avery Greenwood's company.

Portia was fortunate to have remained a spinster. She appeared to be a woman of some sensitivity, possessing a quiet but well-developed sense of humor.

If the Angel of the Lord had appeared at Avery's deathbed and offered him longevity in exchange for one honest laugh, he would have died just the same, Lucy thought as she greeted the Refferts and invited them to sit beside her.

For her part, Portia wished the next performance would begin. She'd felt a moment's trepidation when they first arrived, and she realized this was not the family party she'd expected. But the Wallaces were good company, and the play held a touch of magic. Portia enjoyed herself when it was just the four of them.

But then people drifted in, staring at her unfamiliar plumage and her borrowed jewelry. Sitting in the thick of society was not nearly so entertaining as observing it from afar.

Then she'd had to acknowledge her past relationship with Millicent Lynde—she'd sensed Duchess Wallace's distaste before Millicent had addressed her. What must they think of her engagement? Pity? Disgust? Obviously, she'd entertained Avery's suit out of desperation. And at his death she'd lost her only chance to marry—poor, pathetic Portia.

Castleton's mind reeled. A suitor who had won

her. What had this Avery possessed that he did not? Though Portia conceded a dislike for his style of oratory, she knew exterior behavior often masked the person underneath.

How much had she loved this man? Castleton wanted to ask more, but dare not stir the memory further. At this uncertain phase, he had no desire to compete with a ghost.

A hand touched his shoulder. Castleton looked up and froze.

"Fitzhugh!" he said in too loud a voice.

Portia met his eye.

Castleton immediately broke contact, but the brightness to his smile was not entirely born of pleasure at meeting an old acquaintance. His gaze traveled Fitzhugh's torso but resolutely fixed at last on the major's dark mustache. "How do you do?"

"I'm very well, very well...." Fitzhugh tapped his cane lightly on the floor. "Still a hitch in the step, but I will live. I hear you were limping about yourself awhile."

"A temporary infirmity." Castleton glanced toward Portia. She was pointedly *not* looking at them. He must introduce her. Fitzhugh was indirectly responsible for their relationship. He rose and took Fitzhugh's arm. "Come meet a friend of mine."

Portia peeped from a steady regard of her twined fingers to acknowledge the introduction with an over-bright smile. She coyly lowered her eyes. And then her hand crept up to the necklace....

Castleton couldn't blame Fitzhugh's warmer

thoughts. As she'd caressed that jewel throughout the play he'd had more than a few warm thoughts himself. Her languid, lingering caress—imagining the softness of the skin beneath her stroking fingers. He'd looked. Wallace had looked. The motion had mesmerized.

Lucy uttered a hushed gasp. Then the couple sitting across from her whispered.

Castleton refused to actually look. He tugged Fitzhugh's arm to turn him, and asked after the major's mother in the blandest voice he could muster.

Lucy gasped, and Portia looked up. Castleton tried to spin the major but not in time. Mrs. Trent and Mrs. Cray had been correct ... and this time it had been she. . . .

9

OH, THE TALK! Portia should have removed this abominable dress and donned her customary gown. She could feel blood staining her too-visible flesh crimson bright.

"Miss Kirby," Duke Wallace gained his feet with surprising dexterity and stepped between her and the major. "Would you care to stroll about the gallery with me for a while?"

"Yes," she answered gratefully. "Yes, I would."

The duke made no push to engage Portia in conversation as he led her from the box. When hailed by others in the gallery, he acknowledged them with a brief nod or smile, but continued forward, not requiring Portia to rise above her acute embarrassment. He didn't even offer her refreshment until the corridor lightened of company.

"No, thank you," Portia said. Although dreading it, she added: "We should go back."

"The play will proceed whether we're there or not," Wallace replied. "You mustn't worry. Lucy and Castleton can marshal an army between them. Mr. and Mrs. Reffert will say nothing."

"You are too kind," Portia murmured, feeling her face pucker tearfully despite her best efforts.

Wallace patted her hand. "Now, now...." he soothed. "Poor Fitzhugh. It must be galling to no longer conceal those inklings of desire Nature plagues us all with. I'm sure he is no more culpable than I. Or Castleton, I daresay."

Portia's eyes widened. "I beg your pardon?"

Wallace beamed at her in an innocuous fashion.

"A friend of mine fancies himself a man of science. Was telling him about one of my bitches.... Not much to look at, but when she's in heat, I have to sequester her. The boys fight over her like she's the Queen of Sheba. My friend asked me about her pups, and I have to say they're glorious. Have requests for them all over Derbyshire.

"He says this French fellow has a theory. Couldn't make it all out—you know the French— but it had something to do with Nature passing on the best traits of the parents to their offspring in order to propagate a strong and healthy breed."

"That's very interesting," Portia replied politely.

"Underneath our rags and robes we're only animals, Miss Kirby," Wallace told her. "The good Lord's given us a little control over Nature, but it still exerts its pull from time to time. Have you never found yourself woolgathering about some buck your head says you'd never give the time of day?"

"Well...." Portia flushed. "I suppose I must say ... yes."

"Brush of fancy," Wallace said. "That's all it is. A

man sees something about a woman—flash of ankle, stroke of a hand over a piece of jewelry...."

Portia's hand flew to the necklace, and Wallace nodded. She dropped it to her side again, stained as red as the rest of her.

Wallace smiled. "Nature says there's more to you than meets the eye, ma'am. But an evening in your company affirms the same, in a more civilized fashion."

He led her back to the box without another word.

As the performance had already begun, Portia was able to slip into her chair without having to speak to Castleton or the duchess. They both acknowledged her arrival with encouraging looks, but made no comment either.

Portia clasped her hands tightly in her lap to keep them from straying and fixed her eyes on the stage. But her mind was full of Wallace's words.

The duke had as good as told her he'd experienced an attraction to her, an attraction that made him sympathize with Fitzhugh's unfortunate disorder. Fitzhugh's reaction had been observed by everyone in the box. If two strange men could harbor such feelings for her, she had to lend it credence.

She possessed something...sexual. In a way, she'd always known it. She'd hated that dress—the one she'd first danced with Castleton in—but her mother had insisted she wear it. Mama said Portia may as well show a man what little she had to offer.

She was allowed to adopt only a modest style

when Avery began to court her. It wouldn't do for the future wife of a clergyman to expose her breasts to the whole of Christendom.

Although he'd only kissed her once, Portia knew she stirred a lustful inclination in Avery. Instead of attending Miss Leigh's performance, she examined the proof of his regard in her memory.

At times, she'd reduce his bulk in her mind to glimpse a handsomer man beneath. But even good looks couldn't have offset his self-absorbed pomposity. He knew everything, or so he believed. A life with him meant burying her opinions beneath a resentful silence for the rest of Portia's days.

But with her parents ill and her brother newly engaged, he'd seemed her only viable future. So she agreed to let Avery speak to her father.

His kiss had been almost as surprising as Castleton's. Portia shuddered at the remembered fleshiness of his lips.

Despite his profession, there'd been nothing chaste about the embrace. His large hands had slipped off her shoulders to bear down on her buttocks, pressing Portia hard against his bulk as his lips sawed at hers with what she assumed was passion. There was no answer of that emotion within her. In fact, it took all her willpower not to thrust him off her, because she'd just given herself to him. Tolerance would be her lot in life.

"Too bad God was not as kind to James as he was to you. I had hoped Providence would intervene again, but. . . ."

The sweeter memory of her second kiss crowded out the repugnant reverie of her first.

Her brother's wedding guests had returned to her father's house after the ceremony in deference to his fragile health. Portia overheard Maria vocally remaking the decoration to her liking and lamenting the only mar on her happiness—being stuck with James's cow of a sister until her dying day.

To hide her distress from her father, Portia had fled to the garden, only to find George there before her, determinedly emptying the last dregs from a champagne bottle he'd drunk by himself. In gesturing her to a seat with his glass, he spilled its contents on his pantaloons.

Portia laughed as he swore an oath. On the morrow she would say it served him right. But at that moment she'd been too grateful for his comforting presence to scold him.

"Have you been banished, too?" he asked.

"More like driven out," Portia replied, taking the glass from his lax fingers and stealing a sip for herself.

"Too bad God was not as kind to James as he was to you. I had hoped Providence would intervene again, but. . . ."

"George! That isn't kind."

"Not kind," he agreed, grinning wickedly. "But true. Lord, that woman is a shrew. And so cold! Poor James. I'd rather drown myself in the old pond than be trapped in a passionless match."

"How do you conclude Maria is passionless?"

Portia asked. "She certainly argues with great fervor."

"It's the way she kisses."

"You've kissed her?!" Portia exclaimed with mock horror.

"God, no." George looked as if all the champagne in his stomach had soured. "The way she kisses James. Like a halibut. Lips splayed out but shut back at the teeth. And there's nothing inviting in her manner. She'll be one of those women who 'submits' until her martyred manner drives James from her bed. And, knowing James, he won't turn elsewhere. . . ."

"Is monogamy so wrong, George?" Portia inquired primly.

"I've found it near impossible," Mahew replied, arching his brow. She slapped his arm. "And I do think it's wrong when its enforcement causes someone unbearable loneliness. I see no good for James in this marriage."

"Neither do I," Portia said. "And yet. . . ."

"What?"

"I think I'd rather know a fictional state of matrimony for a time than face a life alone . . . as I probably will now."

Then George leaned forward and kissed her. Softly, sweetly—nothing coarse at all.

Portia drew back. "George!"

His eyes gauged her a moment before his dimples flashed.

"You kiss like a courtesan, Portia," he informed

her with a laugh. "Open-mouthed and inviting. And
you have a lover's figure. I'd wager you could make
quite a name for yourself as a Cyprian if you shed
your missish airs."

"Don't tease, George. I'm nothing to look at."

"You're no freak, either, no matter what your
mother said. You have animation and passion on
your side, along with the ability to listen. That and
your body attired in charming deshabille would take
you farther than you ever dreamed."

"I don't want a life like that."

"No. You want love. And I wish it were in my
power to give it to you. But in lieu of it, I offer my
best advice."

"The advise that gets you banished from respectable society?"

"The advice that gains me entree into respectable society despite my reputation," he replied.
"Accept who you are. If no one else will love you,
love yourself—the way a lover would, flaws and all.
And above all, never forget . . . you've been kissed by
a rake."

"George!" And she'd laughed, even as she boxed
his ears.

She'd clutched at that idea at times in her life.
But she'd discounted George's words and behavior
as the follies of drink. Because his kiss, though nice,
had roused nothing in her, either. Not like. . . .

Portia glanced back at Castleton and found his
gaze on her. He smiled. So supportive. Portia looked
toward the stage.

The Frenchman's theory certainly applied to him. Women of all ages fluttered when Castleton was about. But he didn't like that kind of attention. In fact, a woman who expressed her desire to know him intimately would most likely drive him away.

I should have tried that a month ago, Portia thought.

But she knew why she had not. It hit too close to the mark. And considering how she suddenly roused male interest after years as a social non-entity, a man of science might suggest the heating of her own blood had produced this startling effect.

The bitch is in heat, she realized with dread. *And it's all his fault.*

"Miss Kirby!" Lucy hissed as if for the third time. Portia turned toward the duchess, startled out of her reverie. "We thought we might forgo the last part of the program for a quiet supper at Gunter's. Is that agreeable?"

"I suppose so," Portia replied, though the idea of returning home held more appeal.

Now that she acknowledged her base allure she could see interest in her figure from every passing male glance. Even at the restaurant, the young waiter's eyes drifted into her cleavage as he poured a glass of wine for her.

And Castleton? His every glance was suspect.

"I thought the performances got better as the evening progressed," he said. "Miss Leigh was particularly talented. Mrs. Lynde denies herself a treat by shunning her."

"Mrs. Lynde is a prude and a hypocrite," Lucy declared, then glanced in Portia's direction. "I'm sorry, my dear, but whatever transgressions she believes Miss Leigh has committed, they are likely no worse than those of any other woman in her position."

"You don't have to defend your feelings for Mrs. Lynde to me, ma'am," Portia said, taking a liberal sip from her glass.

"What was your favorite part of the program, Miss Kirby?" Wallace asked.

"I enjoyed the melodrama best," Portia said. "Green-haired virgins not withstanding."

Lucy laughed. "I admit I forgot my prejudice at the reunion of the young lovers. I found their embrace most affecting."

"That's because they are lovers offstage as well," Castleton told her, before he popped a sweetmeat into his mouth.

"And how would you know that, sir?" Lucy asked.

"The Ladies Cats, of course," Castleton replied, after chewing and swallowing his mouthful. "Those two old women know everything about everyone. If they'd worked for Napoleon we would have lost the war in year one. Don't you agree, Portia?"

"They will probably speak of us on the morrow," she said, but her tone was more worrisome than light. She drained her glass.

The waiter immediately refilled it, taking another look down the front of her gown. Castleton warned him away with a glance. Lucy set her fork aside and squeezed Portia's hand.

"If they do, they will say you looked magnificent and we had the most marvelous time. That is the truth, isn't it?"

"I suppose," Portia replied.

But the idea of talk pressed heavily on her.

She took refuge in her meal and her wine glass, letting the others carry the conversation without her. Even if Fitzhugh's reaction to her attire went unreported, there must be talk. She had spent the evening as Castleton's companion. Not a member of his party or a mutual guest. She'd worn a dress that drew attention to her, and jewelry the world must know she could never afford. How could they not talk?

And if Castleton truly felt some attraction for her....

"Portia?"

She looked up at him in surprise. She knew by his expression that they had been striving for her attention for some time.

Even so, she found it difficult to concentrate. Portia set her empty glass down and pressed a hand to her forehead. The room was far too warm. "I'm sorry," she said. "I think...."

"I think it is time to conclude this evening," Lucy finished. She gestured to her nodding husband, who rose and held her chair. "You will see her safely home, Castleton?"

"Of course," he said, rising to bow to the duchess.

Portia's senses swam as Lucy leaned forward and pressed her cheek to hers.

"We must do this again some time," Lucy said. "Don't you agree, Wallace?"

"A most pleasant evening," Wallace replied, bowing over Portia's hand. "Good night, Miss Kirby."

"Yes, good night," she replied, watching their retreat in confusion. She was alone. With Castleton. Who smiled at her. Again.

"Shall we go?" he asked, holding a hand out to her.

Portia stood. The room swayed beneath her feet. Castleton's hand shot out to steady her, connecting with the skin above her glove. Every inch of her body hardened with goose flesh.

"Portia?"

"Too much wine," she murmured. "I am not used to it."

"There's a garden," Castleton whispered, his breath tickling at her ear. "Perhaps a walk would revive?"

She obediently responded to the pressure of his cupped hand under her elbow. She could not walk unsupported. She leaned on him all the way to the garden terrace.

And all the while Portia was aware of his hold on her, of his body close to her own. Her addled wits could even twist the solicitous look on his face to something tender.

Strolling was beyond her. Castleton guided her to a stone bench. When he seated himself beside her, he twined a supportive arm around her waist.

"I feel very foolish," she said.

"I have seen men in far worse condition," he replied with some amusement. "Women, too, if truth be told. You are but one sheet to the wind, not two."

A breeze lifted the curls off her forehead, cooling her a little. This was actually very pleasant: sitting beside him, his arm about her. She shut her eyes and let the haze wash over her.

"I can see the lure of habitual drunkenness."

"You will feel quite differently tomorrow, I'm sure."

"It's so strange." Portia struggled to keep her head high.

Castleton smoothed the blowing tendril off her face, and his hand rested lightly on her cheek. She looked at him. Even in darkness his eyes glowed with some intrinsic light. She had an overwhelming sense—or was it a desire?—he would kiss her.

Portia leaned toward him, everything inside her willing it to happen. Then Good Sense shoved its way through her cloudy thoughts. Another kiss would be the end of everything. Castleton would know she had strong feelings for him. Feelings beyond the bounds of propriety.

Portia stood abruptly, and the terrace whirled around her.

"Portia!"

He was on his feet, holding her. Portia turned her face from him, lest it reveal how his touch affected her. It was bad enough she had such ridiculous thoughts. To have him discover them. . . .

"Perhaps you should take me home," she whispered.

Castleton reseated her on the bench. "I will summon the carriage. Wait here for me."

She nodded. He re-entered the restaurant through the terrace door, and Portia buried her face in her hands.

The whole ride home she was silent, inwardly chiding herself for her continuing folly. Because the idea of a kiss—any kiss—preyed on her mind. Her practical side said it was impossible, but her baser nature whispered hope.

Castleton *might* have kissed her because he found her attractive. And if he found her attractive now, when she knew she was attractive because other men had indicated it was so.... But that was an illusion cast by the dress. She wasn't attractive. If Castleton didn't kiss her—and Portia didn't think he would—she would know for sure.

The carriage pulled to a halt before her aunt's house. Portia did not wait for the driver to alight, but thrust the coach door open. She stumbled to the curb, but Castleton was right beside her. His hand made negligible contact with her shoulder as he adjusted the slipping shawl around her back.

"You must allow me to see you inside," he said.

"That isn't necessary."

"Yes, it is." He kept her hand imprisoned in his own until they reached the door. Portia fumbled with the latch. A solitary candle burned on the table at the bottom of the entry staircase, but no more.

"Have they all gone to bed?" Castleton asked.

"Most likely." She forced a smile to her lips. "Thank you for the pleasant evening. I'm so sorry I embarrassed you."

"Embarrassed?! You mean, the drink?"

Portia nodded sheepishly.

He laughed. "Portia, whatever transgressions you think you've committed are a figment of your imagination. I had a delightful time."

"Did you?"

He nodded. Portia thought the warmth in his eyes would buoy her clear up the staircase.

She put an automatic hand to her throat. "Oh," she said, the hard stone reminding her of its presence. "You must take this with you."

She turned her back to him. The weight of the emerald lifted away from her so quickly she overbalanced backwards at its loss. Something solid kept her upright, though. She tipped her head back to find Castleton's face hovering above hers.

She was leaning on him. It was too familiar. But it didn't feel wrong. It didn't feel wrong at all.

She shut her eyes. The light brush against her lips could have been anything. His chin. His fingertips. But she imagined it was his mouth, answering the unremitting summons within her head.

"Sweet dreams," he whispered.

Then Portia was alone, gripping the rail of the staircase. Wondering if that last had been proof of some tangible regard, or a drunken spinster's vain imagining.

10

"MISS PORTIA!"

Portia groaned and turned on the bed. The throb of her head was less now than it had been an hour previously when she decided rising wasn't worth the effort. Her stomach gurgled in protest. She pushed Lydia's hand off her shoulder.

"You must get up, miss," Lydia persisted, pushing the bed curtains wide. "Mr. Mahew is downstairs."

"Tell him I'm not well." Portia tossed the covers back over her head. If she had her way, she would never rise again.

How could she ever face Castleton? *If* he had kissed her, it was only because she had wantonly offered herself to him. And so light a touch. She imagined it more a kind rebuff than any answer of passion within him.

She'd made such a spectacle of herself. Enough to draw George to her door, it seemed.

"I tried to send him off, but he's in such a state," Lydia told Portia. "He says you'd best come down before he wastes the last of his reputation to fetch you."

Portia slipped her feet out of the side of the coverlet and rolled to a sitting position. She wished she could think of some remedy to quell her churning stomach, but the thought of ingesting anything made her bilious. She rubbed her temple.

"Get me a dress," she said. "Anything will do. Once he's gone, I'm returning to bed."

She coiled and pinned her night braid, but offered no other toilet. Let George know he'd roused her from a state of misery.

"It's about time," he snapped as she entered the sitting room.

"Please don't yell. I had a very bad night."

"It can be no worse than my morning," he replied. "Why weren't you in the park today?"

"I went to the theater with Lord Castleton last night," she said. "And supper afterward."

"Well, I hope you enjoyed *some* of it, since he will never speak to you again."

"Why?" Portia sank into the nearest chair and pressed her fingers to her forehead, massaging the space between her eyes.

Had she been that bad? Oh, she must have been if Castleton had publicly announced some disgust of her. She should never have worn that dress. She would burn it before the day was done.

"I am in such trouble," Mahew said. He sank into a chair himself. "What could I do? I couldn't leave her hanging there, could I?"

"Her?"

"Sarah Christopher."

Portia sat up straight and stared at him.

"She wandered away from her brother and your friend this morning to play heroine to some miserable brat's kite," Mahew said. "She climbed a tree and over-balanced while knocking it down. By the time I arrived the wretched boy had run off, leaving Miss Christopher dangling from a branch."

"Oh dear God," Portia whispered.

"I could barely reach her," he continued. "I gripped her ankles, and she slid down. She shook like a blancmange. I doubt she could have stood unassisted if I'd released her."

"Someone saw you together," Portia guessed.

"Yes," he replied, springing to his feet to pace the floor. "And only the embrace; I'm sure of it."

"Who was the witness?"

"Miss Melinda Trent and groom."

"Oh, God!" Portia groaned. "As soon as Melinda tells her mother, it will be all over Town!"

"Don't you think I know that?" Mahew snapped. "But it's worse. Miss Christopher slid down through my arms. After Miss Trent galloped away I realized her hem was caught on the buttons of my sleeve. Her skirt was raised to the waist behind."

"George!"

"Don't 'George' me," he retorted. "I wasted a full hour looking for you afterward. I'm expecting pistols at dawn from Castleton and so must flee to the Continent, because I'm no match for him. I won't risk my skin when it was *not* my fault. . . ."

"Shut up!"

He fell silent. Portia waved off his astonished stare.

"Let me think," she said, gripping her temple. "There has to be some way to fix this."

They sat silent. Portia held her hands over her eyes.

This scandal eclipsed anything that could be said about her this morning, but the thought offered little consolation. Sarah was as good as ruined. George, too. His amours with fast widows and lonely wives were tolerable, but not the seduction of an innocent. Even with a reasonable explanation, his reputation was bad enough to condemn them both simply for being alone together.

"If only you had been there," he muttered through clenched teeth.

Portia stilled, peering out through her splayed fingers.

"Who's to say I wasn't?" she replied in a soft voice.

She rose and tore the pins from her hair. "Give me ten minutes to make myself presentable."

"I knew I could depend on you, cousin."

Portia barely heard him in her haste to exit the room.

CASTLETON'S EVENING WITH Portia left too much to be desired. Their public appearance made her nervous. The Fitzhugh incident had been embarrassing. And, while drink lent a sultry droop to her eyes that drove him half-mad with desire, he doubted it was wise to allow her to imbibe so much when despondent.

Castleton wanted some chance to win her before the gossips sunk his chances. If only he could spend time with Portia alone.

A letter from his steward in the morning post was like an answer from Providence.

"I must go to Welton on business," he informed Margaret at the breakfast table.

"Do you?" She smiled in relief. "The time away will do you good, I'm sure."

"Why don't we make a family party of it?" Castleton asked. "Nothing long. A fortnight, perhaps. We could ask a few people to join us."

"A few people?"

"Miss Barstow and Mr. Ponsby to keep the children company. You could ask the Ballingers. Maybe the Wallaces would like a change of pace...."

"And let's not forget Miss Kirby," Margaret replied stiffly.

"Well," Castleton said. "If you'd like to extend her an invitation...."

"Don't humbug me, sir. This scheme is for her benefit."

"Would you like to read Mr. Tyler's letter?" Castleton asked, waving the missive in her direction.

"If your business is so urgent, you'd best tend to it without us," Margaret said. "I'm sure we'll manage without you."

The noisy arrival of Frederick and Sarah

prevented his reply. Some escapade was in the wind. Sarah's dress was rumpled and rent, her bonnet askew on her head. Yet her posture was defensively proud, while Frederick looked extremely irate.

"You needn't treat me like a child," Sarah said as she crossed the threshold, shrugging off her brother's hold. "I've done nothing to be ashamed of."

"Then *you* tell them," Frederick shouted. "Of all the hoydenish, stupid females. . . ."

"What is going on?" Margaret demanded.

"I didn't do anything wrong!" Sarah replied.

But as the story spilled from her lips, even Castleton saw her ruin before him. All those years of playing Society's game gone for naught. Margaret swooned where she sat, and he was obliged to ring for her maid to fetch her hartshorn.

"I would have fallen if Mr. Mahew hadn't come to my aid, Uncle David. He only helped me down. Surely anyone with sense would understand that."

"Mr. Mahew shouldn't *have had* to help you down in the first place," Castleton replied, waving the malodorous concoction under Margaret's nose. "If rescuing the kite was so important, you should have fetched your brother."

"Excuse me?!" Sarah retorted. "I didn't need a ladder to save *me* in the apple orchard."

"I was only ten," Frederick muttered.

"Well, I was six, and well able to climb up and down by myself."

"And now you are sixteen, and the idea of climbing a tree should be unthinkable," Castleton retorted. "You're sure Miss Trent did not see your predicament?"

"I don't think she could. There is a bend in the road just there surrounded by thick trees," Sarah said.

"All right," Castleton said. "Go change."

"I didn't do anything wrong," Sarah persisted.

"We know," Castleton said calmly. "But convincing the rest of the world may prove a challenge."

"Oh, my God, Castleton," Margaret wailed when the children departed. "She'll be ostracized. We all will."

"Let's see what can be done before we ship her off to a cloister."

But it looked very bad. A sixteen-year-old girl alone in the arms of a womanizer, his hands thrust up her gown. And Castleton couldn't fault Mahew. He would prefer Sarah rescued but disgraced than borne home with a broken neck.

He went to his club, where word of Sarah's folly had not yet spread, though his evening with Portia engendered some interest.

"So what's going on there, Castleton?" one lord asked with a wry look. "Dressing the old bird before you stuff it?"

Castleton quelled the urge to shove his teeth back down his throat. He smiled instead. "Made you sorry you view the world with blinders on, didn't she, Morrow? But nothing more than a pleasant evening in good company.

"I had to abandon the house today. Margaret's in a dither. It seems Sarah decided to climb a tree in Hyde Park this morning. Perhaps she should have made her debut next year. There's still so much of the child in her."

Morrow and others assured Castleton they thought no less of Sarah for this unladylike activity. He encouraged their goodwill, knowing their opinions might discourage their wives from condemning Sarah once the entire story was told.

He casually mentioned his impending trip to Hampshire, then read two journals. It was vital he show no panic or concern.

The first gossip arrived at St. James Street around noon. Cheever whispered something to Lord Morrow, and both fixed Castleton with speculative looks. Castleton ignored them, reading the journal in his hand a second time before taking his leave.

After arranging transportation at the livery for his journey, he decided to visit Leicester Square. Mahew's social life was on the line, as well as Sarah's. Portia might be inclined to help. He could use her calm support to carry him through Margaret's certain hysteria.

The butler told Castleton Portia had left the house some time ago and was not expected to return for luncheon. Since this was a more involved answer than she was "not at home," Castleton chose to believe it.

He returned to Curzon Street to discover his house turned upside down. The hallway was stacked with trunks and boxes; servants rushed everywhere. Margaret darted down the stairway, her normally tidy hair sticking out of a much-adjusted cap.

"There you are," she said. "Have you arranged the carriages? I wrote to Welton to apprise Mrs. Adams of our arrival, and have canceled all our engagements. We can depart within the hour...."

"Margaret," Castleton said. "We can't leave yet. At the least, we must put in an appearance at the Evertons' tonight."

"No! I won't subject Sarah to that." Margaret trembled. "The whispers. The shunning. They may turn her away at the door. I couldn't bear for that to happen, David."

He mounted the stairs to embrace her. Margaret sobbed on his shoulder. He led her to the drawing room, shutting the door on curious servants, then let her cry herself out before speaking.

"Listen to me," he said. "If we sneak off in the night, we're as good as admitting a seduction. We must support Sarah's story. That means we do not approve of her climbing the tree, and we do not blame Mahew for aiding her."

"You expect me to be glad a man like George Mahew had his hands on my daughter?!"

"Inasmuch as it saved her from possible injury... yes. I won't lie to you, Margaret. I expect a most unpleasant evening. But we must be seen in public and let Sarah face censure for her behavior. It's the only way she can salvage her social position."

Still, it felt as if he led a funeral procession

toward the Evertons' drawing room. They arrived late, Castleton hoping to endure one gasping silence from the whole room instead of jolt upon jolt of disapproval. But no one in the reception line looked at or spoke to them. There were noticeable whispers in the small group waiting on the stair.

Margaret held her trembling head high. Frederick was clearly uncomfortable. Sarah looked near to tears. Since all but Sarah's misery were usual, Castleton's stricture to behave normally was being three-quarters met.

The motherly embrace Lady Everton bestowed on his startled niece was not the greeting Castleton had expected.

"Sarah, my dear," she said. "How brave of you to come tonight! Such an ordeal! I imagined you prostrate from Miss Kirby's report."

"Miss Kirby?" Margaret asked stiffly, her face cherry red.

"Now you mustn't be too severe on her, Margaret," Lady Everton said. "She feels perfectly dreadful about the incident."

"What makes her...?" Margaret began, but stilled as Castleton squeezed her arm.

"Did Miss Kirby tell you everything, Nora?"

"I hope there is no more!" Lady Everton exclaimed. "That poor woman. She's so terribly upset. She never would have left Sarah alone if she'd known her cousin was anywhere nearby."

"But...," Frederick also fell silent as Castleton's foot caught on the instep of his shoe.

"Where is Miss Kirby now?" Castleton asked her.

Lady Everton gestured through the room. Castleton's heart swelled. For once, Portia was not stuck in some corner. She sat between Mrs. Cray and Mrs. Trent, the center of attention, holding the majority of the Evertons' guests in thrall. Words poured from her mouth in rapid succession, and her features shone with penitent animation.

She didn't notice their arrival. Castleton caught some of the folderol saving Sarah's character.

"... we had quite a time tracking the boy down because I hadn't seen him clearly, and Sarah was in no condition to give me a detailed account of him. I sent her home with her brother, poor child. George and I spent the next hour searching...."

"I saw your cousin darting through the park in an agitated state not much before nine," Phoebe Ballinger exclaimed. "If only I had known!"

"Were you able to find the boy, Portia?" Mrs. Cray asked.

"We did," Portia exclaimed with exaggerated pride. "He was reluctant to confess the abandonment at first, but at last related the whole to us and to his mother. She wrote Lord Castleton an apology then and there, and I hope it offered Mrs. Christopher some measure of solace."

"What did the note say, Margaret?" Phoebe asked, noticing her friend nearby.

Portia met Castleton's eye, and she popped to her feet, her face as red as Margaret's. "Lord

Castleton, Mrs. Christopher ... did Lord Sefton deliver my message?"

"He did not," Sefton said, coming upon them rapidly. "I was detained this afternoon, and this is the first I've seen of them."

Sefton reached into the breast pocket of his jacket and pulled out a ragged scrap of paper. He handed it to Castleton as he flashed Sarah a smile. "You had quite an adventure, Sarah. This will teach you to leave the heroics to the young men in future."

Castleton glanced quickly at the page, which he recognized as coming from Portia's sketchbook. A pencilled note asked him to "forgive Johnny for abandening your nice in the tree." He passed the note to Margaret. After sharing it with Phoebe and other curious onlookers, she clutched the tangible proof of Sarah's story to her breast.

"I explained how this wouldn't have happened if I'd been a more vigilant chaperon." Portia spoke in a rush, her hazel eyes beseeching them to support her. "I was too far from Sarah to stop her from climbing up. When she slipped and the boy ran ... I am ashamed at how I panicked. I swear I was only gone long enough to fetch Mr. Christopher and Mr. Ponsby. But I was so incoherent, they couldn't make out a word I said. Right, Mr. Christopher?"

Frederick blinked. His mouth opened, but no sound came out.

"You were quite agitated when you approached, ma'am," Arthur Ponsby corroborated from the edge of the crowd. The young man wore a sober look, but met Castleton's gaze squarely. Castleton nodded thanks to him. Ponsby nodded back, but turned quickly away.

Portia took Sarah's hand in her own. "Can you ever forgive me for leaving you?"

"Miss Kirby...." A tear slipped down Sarah's cheek. "You mustn't do this. What happened was entirely my fault."

"Oh, no, you mustn't blame yourself." Portia gave her a little hug. "Everyone knows what a good-hearted girl you are. You were only trying to help a distressed child."

"Yes, you mustn't blame yourself," Mrs. Trent echoed. "When Melinda said she saw you in George Mahew's arms, I told her there must be more to the story."

"Mr. Mahew rescued me," Sarah said emphatically.

"Yes, yes...it's good to know he has some honor," Mrs. Trent said. "Though in future you would do well to stay closer to those who supervise you. And stay out of trees."

Sarah gazed helplessly at Castleton. He arched his brow.

"You are right, ma'am," she relented in a chastened voice.

"Well, that boy should be whipped," Mrs. Cray declared.

"His mother chastised him soundly," Sefton said. "I felt sorry for the lad. The kite was damaged in the incident, and his family didn't appear to have the blunt for many luxuries."

"You met the boy?" Castleton asked, trying to determine if Sefton was a party to this conspiracy.

"George and I had split up to search for him. I found the boy, but was afraid to confront him without support," Portia said. "Lord Sefton happened to be riding by, and was so kind to lend his aid when I explained the whole."

In other words, "no," Castleton thought, marveling at her cunning. While her connection to the principals might foster doubt, Sefton's validation cast the story as inviolate truth.

"You went to quite a lot of trouble, ma'am," Castleton let his eyes tell Portia what he could not say aloud.

She did not falter. "After letting you down so terribly it was the least I could do," she said.

"What do you think of that, Margaret?" Castleton asked, turning to his sister-in-law. "Has Miss Kirby let us down?"

Margaret's eyes shimmered. "No," she said. "Not at all."

She threw her arms around Portia's neck. Portia's brow rose in alarm over Margaret's shoulder. *She is quite right*, Castleton thought. A fit of vapors might quash everything.

He gently detached Margaret's hold. "Well, now," he said. "All is forgiven, and we can leave the rest of the evening's entertainment to our hosts."

The room laughed. Portia slipped her hand-kerchief into Margaret's hand, earning a trembling smile.

"There is one more thing," Margaret declared. "Castleton's been called to the country, and the family's going with him. Would you accompany us, Miss Kirby?"

"Mrs. Christopher, that's not necessary," Portia stammered.

"Please?" Margaret asked. Sarah echoed the word.

Portia looked around. Every eye in the room was upon her. Every ear waited for her response.

"If you're sure you want me," Portia said at last.

Castleton beamed. Equally satisfied, the company broke down to small pockets of conversation. The tempest was but a shower.

Castleton took hold of Portia's arm and led her to the nearest corner. "You are magnificent," he whispered.

"I'm sorry you weren't warned. I thought Lord Sefton would report the morning's activities to you long before this."

"I came looking for you today to enlist your help, little dreaming you were out on your own making all well."

"They would have damned them both for nothing," Portia said. "I couldn't let that happen."

"We are eternally grateful to you," Castleton said. He took her hand and brushed her knuckle with his mouth.

A jolt surged through Portia. It *had* been lips. And if his eyes had glowed this way last night, there was nothing indifferent about it. A strange exhilaration coursed through her.

"Then I may tell George you won't be calling him out?" Portia asked him, lowering her eyes to lighten the intensity of emotion flowing between them.

"I had no quarrel with him regardless of this outcome," Castleton said. "This scrape was entirely of Sarah's making. She tends to act first and think afterwards. I must break her of it."

"Must you?" Portia asked, still breathless. She glanced toward Sarah, surrounded by a group of her young friends. "I think a good heart serves as a better guide in the long run."

"Do you think I could refuse you any request at this moment?" he asked with a light laugh.

"I don't know. Will you ask your sister-in-law to rescind her invitation? It was hardly warranted."

"On the contrary," Castleton replied. "I thought it added an affecting conclusion to the whole. The penitent sinner welcomed home with open arms. Miss Leigh could not have played it better."

"So you *can* refuse me something," Portia said.

"Leave it to you to expose my selfish inclinations. But I vow you'll not regret my holding you to your word."

Portia crossed her arms and shivered. She'd fully intending on shunning him when she woke this morning, and now she would be sequestered in his company for two full weeks.

Meanwhile, the young ladies were more than a little curious about Sarah's adventure.

"What is he really like, Sarah?" Melinda Trent

whispered so her mother could not hear her. "I've never been that close to him."

"I have," another young lady declared with a sigh. "He's ravishingly handsome."

"And you were in his arms," another young woman exclaimed. "Did you swoon? Just the thought of being held by George Mahew makes my knees quiver."

"It wasn't like that," Sarah told them, over-whelmed. She'd been truly unconcerned until they'd stepped through the Evertons' front door and she'd discovered her innocence didn't matter.

If it hadn't been for Miss Kirby, every person here would think her ruined. Yet, now the girls acted as if she'd made some magnificent conquest. And Sarah was afraid to tell the truth—she considered George Mahew her friend.

"He was very kind to me," she said in a faltering voice.

"That's the rake's method, Sarah," Melinda replied in superior tones. "They gain your confi-dence with honeyed words and smiles. Then, when your guard is down, they pounce."

"Yes, I'm sure George Mahew expected to find Sarah hanging from that branch and ripe for the plucking," Vivian Barstow said in withering tones. She must have only just arrived. "How like you, Melinda, to twist an act of gallantry to something sordid."

Vivian drew Sarah away from the bristling Miss Trent.

Sarah clutched her friend's supportive arm. "Vivian," she whispered when she was sure no one could hear her. "Miss Kirby wasn't there."

"It doesn't matter," Vivian whispered back. "She made the truth known. It was good of your mother to reward her with a trip to Welton. She's asked me to come, too. Did you know?"

"No," Sarah exclaimed. "But I'm so glad. You are coming?"

"Of course," Vivian replied. "But Mr. Ponsby seems reluctant to accept his invitation. He says he's at a critical point in the training of that horse, but I don't think that's the reason."

Sarah glanced over at Ponsby, who shook his head emphatically in response to her brother's entreaties. When he noted Sarah's regard, the young man flushed and looked pointedly away. Confusion rushed back into her heart.

"He lied for me," she realized.

"Did he? I didn't think him capable of it."

"Do you think if I asked him…?" But as Ponsby continued to avoid her with his eyes, Sarah knew it wouldn't help. One person in the room still condemned her, and it pained Sarah that it was her brother's friend.

"Miss Kirby intends to speak to him," Vivian assured Sarah as she noticed Portia draw closer to Ponsby. "I have perfect confidence she'll bring him around."

Portia was relieved to learn she wouldn't be the only guest at Welton. The Ballingers and the

Wallaces would arrive a week after the family. That meant Vivian Barstow and Arthur Ponsby must keep attention off her for the first sennight. Vivian was too much a family fixture to offer much distraction, however.

Learning Ponsby had declined his invitation, Portia asked if she might speak with him alone.

"Thank you for supporting my story," she said.

"I didn't lie, precisely." Ponsby flushed. "You *were* upset when you approached me in the park this morning. It was two hours after the incident in question, but...."

"She told the truth, Arthur," Portia said. His disquiet suggested he still found something sordid in the morning's activities. Although she'd explained her intention at the park, Ponsby hadn't supported her actions as she'd expected. And his habitual glance toward Sarah bore more disappointment than ardor.

"I know," Ponsby replied. He looked as if he might speak further, but shut his jaw resolutely.

Portia sighed. "Can't you bring Bright Promise with you? I'm told there are acres of parkland at Welton. It might be safer to hitch him to a carriage in the country than here in Town."

"I cannot go, ma'am."

"Even if I begged you?" She let some of her own disquiet show in her face. "Lord Castleton and I...I'm not entirely comfortable with him. And I barely know the rest of the family. Your presence would ease my mind greatly."

"Miss Kirby. . . ." Ponsby mustered a smile. "You have been the kindest friend, and not just to me. How could I not support you?"

"Well?" Castleton asked as he joined them.

"Miss Kirby has talked me around, sir," Ponsby said. "If I drive the bay on a gig, and lead Bright Promise behind, I can continue his training on your grounds, if you'll allow."

"It sounds like a fine idea," Castleton replied.

As Ponsby sought Frederick to inform him of his decision, Castleton leaned close to Portia. His lips hovered close to her ear. "Your powers of persuasion are remarkable, Portia. I believe you could talk anyone into whatever you wished."

Portia did not believe him. If that were true, she could talk herself out of this strange feeling she'd fallen into a snare she wasn't sure she wished to escape.

11

PORTIA MET WITH George in the park the next morning. She related the night's events and informed him of her impending departure in consequence, scheduled for early the next morning.

"Whatever would I do without you? Or will I do without you? I'll fear to get into mischief with you gone," George said.

"See you don't," Portia said. "My nerves were on fire last night. I was fully prepared to share my experience with Major Fitzhugh to divert them if need be."

"And you say Castleton wasn't angry?"

"He knew you were innocent of any impropriety."

George's soft smile did not quite reach his eyes. Portia felt momentary unease. But his next statement distracted from it.

"And now Castleton's taking you to Welton. . . ."

"I'm going as Mrs. Christopher's guest," she corrected. "And I'm very nervous about it."

"Nervous? Whatever for?"

"I think it very likely . . . though I cannot

conceive why...." Portia gazed at the grass beneath her feet. "Lord Castleton is flirting with me."

She took a deep breath and related the whole of it. The kiss. The waltz. The restaurant garden. The small intimacies that had her trembling with trepidation at the thought of spending weeks alone, or nearly alone, in his company.

"Do you like him?" George interjected.

"Very much," Portia said. "He's become a good friend. But I don't know what he means by acting so."

Mahew had a very good idea what Castleton meant. Castleton would never presume upon a woman in Portia's circumstances unless his intentions were honorable. He meant to marry her.

A pang gripped Mahew's heart. He had no idea what this change of status would mean to his own relationship with his cousin. But if anyone deserved love, happiness, and an elevated station in life it was Portia. He must encourage her toward the match.

"He probably means nothing," he lied. "The fact he pays you such attentions is a testament to your bond. A man must trust the women he flirts with. The chance of rebuff is far too great."

"Not for Castleton!" Portia scoffed. "Can you imagine any woman rejecting him?"

"You seem eager to."

"Not ... so eager," Portia confessed.

George turned. "Ah, here's the crux of it," he said. "You are not upset because Castleton flirts, but because you like it."

"Yes, but I don't *understand* it."

"Then don't try," Mahew said. They strolled onward. "Don't let your imagination hamper what could be a pleasurable experience. A little flirting never hurt anyone. You'll be leagues from Town, so you needn't worry what anyone will say. Just enjoy it."

"But. . . ."

"No buts." George placed a light finger on her lips to silence further protest. "From this moment on, you play an extended game of pretend. You were the champion when we were children. You might even try flirting back. That would shock Castleton to no end, I'll wager."

Portia laughed. "You're right," she replied, suddenly aglow with high spirits. "It's only a game. If I put my mind to it, I might even rout him."

Mahew flashed his dimples at her. If Castleton wasn't already vanquished, he expected to hear of Portia's victory and the inevitable engagement on her return.

THE TRAVELING COACH pulled into a road lined with ancient oaks, and Portia felt a moment's trepidation. She glanced out the window, trying to see down the secluded passage.

"It's still a half-mile to the house," Margaret offered helpfully. She had been all kindness in the two days of their easy journey. Portia's preservation of Sarah's good name had dissolved any stiffness or reserve.

"We're closer than I imagined when we set off from the inn this morning," Portia responded. "We might well have completed the journey last night."

"I think Castleton wished to give Mrs. Adams ample time to prepare," Margaret replied. Her hands fluttered over her pelisse, smoothing out imaginary creases. "You mustn't let Mrs. Adams unnerve you, Miss Kirby. She may seem ... formidable, but she's an excellent housekeeper. Though we come here seldom, everything is always in perfect order."

Portia wondered if the formidable housekeeper explained the pall over Castleton's high spirits.

She had followed Mahew's advice and accepted without reservation whatever sally or remark fell from his mouth. A few quips of her own had drawn the most breathtaking smiles from him. Margaret's over-solicitousness and the girls' exclusive whispers had diverted much of Portia's attention out the window to Castleton riding beside.

But as he'd handed her into the carriage this morning, he seemed preoccupied. And his expression now, when she hazarded a peep out at him, was most decidedly glum.

"I hope Frederick and Mr. Ponsby drive on through instead of stopping," Vivian said, looking out the window with excited curiosity. "It seemed so strange to pass them by yesterday."

"Mr. Ponsby will do anything for his horses," Sarah responded shortly.

They had paused on the road to converse with the two young men, who were taking the journey in shorter segments to spare Ponsby's bays. Ponsby had continued to treat Sarah with terse civility. By the time travel continued, Sarah's own attitude had become defensively stiff and formal.

Portia sighed. She would have to take Ponsby aside and discover the reason for his frosty manner if they wished a peaceful fortnight.

But the awkwardness between Ponsby and Sarah was not an immediate concern.

The roadway changed to fine gravel, and the tree line gave way to a broad, manicured lawn. Portia gasped in delight at the clean lines of the manor house, with its double stone staircase set between two wings of tall windows. Servants in full livery lined one set of steps, watching their approach. At the top of the portico, a tall woman in black stood sentinel. *The dreaded Mrs. Adams*, Portia thought.

A boy at the bottom of the stairs rushed toward Castleton and bowed before taking Caesar's reins. Castleton dismounted. The smile on his face did not reach his eyes.

"Welcome to Welton," Castleton said, as he opened the door to their carriage. His voice was curiously devoid of emotion.

Portia allowed him to hand her out. Feeling Mahew's phantom prompt from seventy miles away, she smiled warmly.

"It's beautiful," she said. "The painting above your mantel doesn't do it justice."

A momentary spark kindled in him. "That's the southern view of the house," he explained, as he helped Margaret, Sarah, and Vivian alight. "After luncheon, we can view that aspect from the formal garden. I daresay you'll find a walk refreshing after a few days in a coach."

"I daresay I will," Portia replied.

Castleton glanced toward the waiting servants and sighed. "I wish they would not lie in wait for me like some abandoned regiment. They must have better things to do than queue up for my inspection."

"If it makes you uncomfortable, ask them not to do it," Portia said, tucking her hand under his proffered arm.

"Unfortunately it's tradition," he said, bestowing curt nods as they breached the gauntlet. "The lord of the manor returns."

Portia frowned at his bitter tone.

Mrs. Adams was a thin woman with superior posture. Her dark eyes were devoid of emotion as she dropped them a curtsey, accompanied by a rustle of stiff silk and the jangle of keys at her waist.

"Welcome, my lord," she said in a rich, low-toned voice. "We trust your journey was a comfortable one."

"Well enough," Castleton responded.

"On behalf of the staff, may I say. . . ."

"Must you?" he interjected, astonishing Portia. For a man famous in Town for his ability to get along with anyone, he was being deplorably rude.

He waved the servants on the stair toward the house. The confused maids, footmen, gardeners, and grooms glanced toward Mrs. Adams. She released them with a nod, and they scampered in all directions. Heat flickered in the housekeeper's dark eyes. Her mouth, the most prominent feature on a chiseled face, tightened to a hard line.

Castleton introduced Portia and Vivian and explained Frederick's delay to the housekeeper as they walked into a vaulted hall with a checkerboard marble floor and deep walnut paneling from floor to ceiling. The massive room had two fireplaces flanking an ornately carved archway, which led to an airy salon. Portraits of Queen Elizabeth and a gentleman with a pointed beard and twinkling eyes topped each of the mantels. The first Baron Castleton, Portia guessed.

"I've prepared rooms in the family wing for those arriving with you, my lord," Mrs. Adams said. "We'll house the guests arriving later in the west wing. Mr. Tyler asked me to excuse his absence. He would have been here to greet you but the problem in the south pasture...."

"I'm sure everything is fine," Castleton said impatiently.

Really, Portia wondered, as she crossed to examine the baron's portrait, *what is wrong with him*? If she were Mrs. Adams, she'd be irate, too. Snapping at the housekeeper for doing her job. And doing it well despite a lack of encouragement or praise.

"You'll want to withdraw upstairs and settle in." Castleton stood at her elbow. Portia was about to ask how one got upstairs, but Mrs. Adams displaced a door in the paneling to reveal a smaller marble hall to their right with a railed stair running up and around it. Portia glanced carefully at the left wall and noted another door there, also. She would never have guessed their presence if Mrs. Adams hadn't opened one.

"May we see the house first?" Portia asked.

Castleton drew back at the intensity of her sudden question.

"Instead of the garden," Portia persisted. "I should like to tour the house."

He gazed at Margaret helplessly.

"I'm afraid I'm not familiar enough with the house to do it justice," Margaret responded.

"Nor am I," Castleton admitted. "But if you're worried about getting lost, you needn't be. Just remember the bedchambers run in the east/west wings and the common rooms run between them. And the family wing is the closest to the staircase—"

"Mrs. Adams?" Portia asked, cutting into his explanation.

The housekeeper turned toward her. Her frown was formidable.

"I know you must be very busy," Portia said. "But I should hate to have come to such a marvelous place and miss any of its delights."

Happily, Mrs. Adams's smile was just as delightful as her frown was forbidding. "I should be honored to show you the house, ma'am," she said.

"May we accompany you?" Sarah asked her,

stripping the bonnet from her dark curls. "I've always wondered about some of the portraits. Specifically the shepherdess in the green gown. . . ."

"Miss Honoria?" Mrs. Adams unbent further. "A lovely young lady, wasn't she? I'm told she was the most beautiful girl in five counties."

Castleton laughed. "That depends on whether you met her at twenty-one or ninety-one, Mrs. Adams. All I recall of her were those black teeth and her twig-like hands reaching out to draw me close for a loathsome kiss."

Mrs. Adams laughed, as well. "You took refuge in my lady's skirt and would not leave her side all day, sir. But I'm surprised you remember Miss Honoria. You were all of four years old when she passed on."

"Some memories are just too vivid," he murmured. He glanced around the hall, and something melancholy descended on him again.

They made a quick plan to refresh for a half-hour, eat luncheon, then return to the hall for Mrs. Adams's tour.

Portia found the attentiveness of Castleton and his family amusing. Apparently, many of the anecdotes Mrs. Adams related as she led them from room to room were as new to them as they were to Portia. Almost as if the house belonged to someone else. Castleton had obviously made no alterations since inheriting the property. Thirteen years ago, by Portia's reckoning.

Poor Mrs. Adams. Curator to a museum no one ever visits.

And yet, Portia could not term Castleton indifferent. Any time the previous occupants of the house were mentioned, he launched into anecdotes of his own.

"Why does a curtain hang over the door between the drawing room and the dining room?" Portia asked. "To keep off a draft?"

"That was Lesley's stage curtain," Castleton answered. "My cousin fancied himself the next Garrick. My uncle feared he might run off to try his luck on the boards. He let Lesley organize some of us in the neighborhood into his own amateur troupe."

"Father was quite an actor, according to Uncle David," Sarah said. "He lived here in Hampshire when he was a boy."

"With me and my father," Castleton explained. "His Christopher relatives made a push to gain custody of him after our mother died, but my uncle Castleton intervened. He had strong feelings about blood relations remaining together. William lived with us until he was sixteen, then moved to Kent to learn the administration of his estate. But he would return for holidays, always expecting to second Lesley."

"A visit to Welton was not a visit to Welton without one of Lesley's plays," Margaret agreed.

"We all looked forward to Mr. William's visits," Mrs. Adams said. Portia could swear tears shone in her dark eyes. "Shall we move along to the gallery?"

As they strolled along the hallway lined with ancestral portraits, Castleton wandered away. Portia left Mrs. Adams' informative commentary behind to follow.

He fixed his attention on a ruddy-faced man with the Castleton twinkle in his eyes. The man sat on the lawn before Welton with a graceful lady leaning on his shoulder and five healthy children gathered around them.

"Is that your uncle?" Portia asked.

"Yes," he said. "And Aunt Alice, Lesley, Douglas, Amelia, Celeste, and Dorothy." He pointed to each, letting his fingertip graze along their faces. A mischievous smile suddenly lit his face. "I'm in there, too."

"You are?" Portia scanned the portrait carefully, at last discovering three tiny figures on a distant hill—a man and two boys so far away they were only blobs of paint on the canvas. Portia laughed, drawing the others to her.

"Miss?"

"I'm just admiring Lord Castleton's portrait. How old were you, sir? I can't quite tell from this vantage."

"I was six," he said. "And when my uncle unveiled this picture I was very annoyed. It was supposed to be a family portrait, and weren't we all family? Uncle brought the painter back to remedy his error, and, to make the return journey worth Mr. Johnson's while, commissioned another portrait of Father, William, and me with figures of my uncle's family driving behind us in a barouche."

"That portrait hangs at our house in Kent," Margaret said.

"My uncle insisted I take it with me when my father died. To remember my Welton family. As if I would ever forget them," Castleton said in a low voice.

Tears pricked Portia's eyes as the heart of the matter came clear to her. It was the piece of him she could never decipher, most likely because he would never display it in London's glittering environs. It made everything about him abundantly clear. And so achingly dear.

"Which one is Honoria?" she asked, looking around at the other pictures to hide her emotions.

Sarah took her hand and guided her up to a charming portrait of Late Restoration beauty. Honoria's dainty ankles were crossed beneath a beribboned gown too ornate for a real shepherdess, and she leaned coquettishly on her staff, a patch set in the corner of her provocative mouth.

"They say she had her choice of a dozen suitors and had a score more languishing for her favor," Mrs. Adams said.

"Can you imagine wearing such a dress?" Vivian asked with a giggle. "So tight at the waist, and with hips so wide you'd have to turn sideways to enter a room?"

"Not to mention the wig," Sarah added.

"That dress is above stairs, isn't it?" Castleton asked Mrs. Adams.

"Is it?" Sarah exclaimed.

"Can we see it?" Vivian asked.

"I'm not sure I could lay hands on it," Mrs.

Adams replied. "You children tossed things about so up there."

"Props," Castleton informed Portia. "And costumes. Though not originally."

"Ah," she said.

"Can we go look anyway?" Sarah asked.

So Mrs. Adams led them to the attics, where treasured attire abounded. It took her three attempts to find the right trunk with Honoria's dress in it. There were so many portmanteaus and boxes packed with rich brocades, heavy satins, and quilted petticoats.

The dress, when at last found, looked a trifle threadbare, but Sarah found another gown that took her young breath away.

"I think this should fit me if I had a proper corset," she said, holding the deep blue frock up for inspection.

"There are corsets and hoops about," Mrs. Adams said. "Wigs too, though I should shake them well. I found some mice nesting in one a few years back."

"This one's full of gentlemen's coats," Vivian exclaimed as she opened another trunk. She held up a garish brocade suit with heavily cuffed sleeves and reached for the ruffled shirt beneath. "Do you think we could persuade Frederick to model this?"

Castleton gazed at the coat thoughtfully.

"What are you thinking, sir?" Sarah asked.

"I'm thinking *She Stoops to Conquer* or something by Molière."

"A play?!" Sarah exclaimed. "Oh, won't that be wonderful!"

"Not for me," Margaret replied. "I shall read lines from a chair if need be, but please don't ask me to perform. It's far too exhausting."

"Portia?" Castleton turned to her.

Portia picked a fan out of the nearest open trunk and unfurled it with a snap. "La, sir," she said, fluttering the fan provocatively. "That's Mrs. Hardcastle to you."

A SUMMONS FROM below stairs interrupted their search for costumes and accessories.

"Beg pardon, Mrs. Adams," a maid said with a timid curtsey. "Mr. Wilkes and his family have come calling. They've been shown to the salon, but Mrs. Wilkes is insisting they come up to you. . . ."

"Tell them we'll be right down," Castleton said. "And tell Mrs. Wilkes she'll be thankful when she sees the state of our attire."

"We are a mess," Margaret agreed, brushing dust from the skirt of Sarah's muslin gown. "Should we change?"

"And keep Alvenia waiting?" Castleton replied. "Are you that brave, Margaret?"

"No," she said, shaking her dress out and twisting to be sure her skirts weren't badly soiled in the back. Portia wiped the worst spot away for her, earning a grateful smile.

"The second trial upon us," Margaret whispered

as she linked Portia's arm. "Though Mrs. Adams has been remarkably pleasant. I suppose it would be too much to expect the same from Alvenia."

Apparently so. Alvenia Wilkes was an amazon of a woman with jet-black hair and flinty blue eyes. She paced the salon, a thundercloud of purple and puce, while two raven-haired girls chased after a sturdy toddler and Geoff Wilkes looked out on the formal garden, his back turned to the tumult his family kicked up behind him.

"It's about time!" Alvenia exclaimed as she descended on Castleton. She turned her cheek to him pointedly. Portia smothered a grin as he dutifully gave her a peck.

Geoff's handshake with Castleton evolved into a hearty embrace.

Castleton introduced Portia to them.

"Never mind that," Alvenia said, beckoning behind them. "There is someone here *you* must meet, Castleton. Up, up, Juliet."

A mousy girl of fifteen obediently rose from a chair by the door and dropped them all a curtsey. She wore a fashionable walking dress two sizes too large for her. Something cut down from Mrs. Wilkes's wardrobe for this occasion, Portia guessed.

"This is my sister's girl, Juliet Robertson. She's staying with us until summer. You mustn't tease her over much," Alvenia remarked with brittle gaiety. "Though she looks quite the sophisticate, she is not yet out."

"I promise I will not oppress her," Castleton

remarked, as he bowed over Miss Robertson's hand. The girl gazed at him, her expression one of dumb-struck terror.

"Shall we all sit down?" Margaret invited.

Alvenia pushed Castleton toward a seat beside Juliet on the divan. *Mrs. Wilkes must have windmills in her head*, Portia thought even as she felt sorry for Miss Robertson, who looked more uncomfortable about the situation than Castleton. He must have sensed the child's disquiet, for he was kinder to her than he normally was in these matchmaking situations. But his marked politeness had Alvenia in obvious transports.

I do not wish to witness this, Portia thought. Mrs. Wilkes and her imperious manner reminded her too much of Maria. It was not Portia's pleasure to dance to a shrew's tune. *And since I'm a guest . . . I don't have to*, she realized.

She marched over to the black-haired children now clustered quietly behind their father's chair. "And who are these young ladies?" she asked.

"Those are my girls," Alvenia responded in a withering voice. "And my little Evan. Come here, precious. Come make your bow to Lord Castleton."

Evan toddled into his mother's outstretched arms.

"Rebecca and Eustacia," Geoff Wilkes murmured in a low voice to Portia. Portia curtseyed to them and they curtseyed back, eyeing her suspiciously.

"Do you know any games?" Portia asked.

"Do you?" Rebecca countered. She was the elder

of the two. About nine years old. Eustacia looked about six.

"I know a few," Portia said. "Card games, mostly."

"We don't have any cards," Eustacia said.

"Perhaps Lord Castleton does." Portia cut off Alvenia's entreaty for Castleton to lead Juliet's first dance when she made her debut next Season to ask if he had playing cards about.

"I'll inquire," he said with a brash smile.

Mrs. Adams brought two decks of playing cards along with refreshments. Portia had the table set up far away from the adults in the room as she motioned Sarah and Vivian to join her.

"We're going to play a game called Steal the Bundle. It isn't difficult but you can assist the young ladies in the strategy," Portia said. She leaned back in her chair and called, "Miss Robertson, would you care to join us?"

"Miss Robertson is fine where she is," Alvenia snapped.

"I'm sorry, ma'am. I only thought she might appreciate the society of people her own age," Portia responded sweetly. "If she's to make her debut next year, she might find the young ladies' experiences enlightening. And we require a fourth."

"I should like to play," Juliet said, popping to her feet. "Though I should warn you, ma'am, I'm not very good at cards."

"We're all new to this game," Sarah said, making room for her at the table. "I'm sure we'll all be dreadful."

Thank you, Portia, Castleton thought, noting how much easier Miss Robertson was now that she was not compelled to sit beside him. Unfortunately, her departure from their sphere did not stop Alvenia from extolling her virtues. Geoff gave him a wicked smile as he drew Evan into his lap and chatted easily with Margaret.

From time to time an outburst of feminine laughter from the card table would shatter everyone's concentration. Castleton glanced over, and Portia smirked at him.

Baggage, he thought, revoking his earlier gratitude. Rescue Miss Robertson but leave him dangling beside Alvenia Wilkes. And he would warrant their afternoon trailing Mrs. Adams about the house had been a nothing more than a ploy to put the housekeeper in a better frame of mind.

A ploy that worked very well, he owned. For once the phantoms of the past had smoothed his way instead of snarling it. He had to stop his jaw from dropping the first time Mrs. Adams smiled. He couldn't remember the last time he'd seen her teeth. And while she directed the responses almost exclusively to Portia, she had answered all their inquiries with good grace. Who knew Mrs. Adams had any good grace in her?

Miss Rebecca Wilkes provided his own rescue. She threw her cards down and stomped into their midst, an indignant parody of her mother. "Mama, you must come play with us," she insisted. "That old Miss Kirby is winning all the cards for her and Stacie."

"Isn't that the object of the game, Becky?" her father asked in a weary voice.

"If mama played, she'd let me win," Becky exclaimed with a stomp of her foot.

"Miss Wilkes," Castleton gasped. "That would do you a grave disservice. Far better to learn the rules and beat your opponent outright than to rely on their charity. Napoleon would never 'let us win,' would he?"

"Do you know how to win, sir?" Becky asked, cocking her head at him speculatively.

"I don't even know the game," he said, rising. "But I'm willing to learn if you are."

Portia raised a brow as he approached the table.

"My partner and I wish to rejoin the game," he said.

"Shall I have Miss Robertson relinquish her chair, Lord Castleton?" Portia asked in an arch voice.

"No, she must help me, too," Castleton replied with a smile for Juliet's benefit. "I do not know the rules, and need all the help I can get. Miss Wilkes intends to coach me."

"Then I can search the library for our play," Sarah said, relinquishing her seat to her uncle. When Vivian expressed a desire to join her, Geoff passed Evan to his mother and stepped in to help Miss Eustacia. Portia smiled at both gentlemen, shuffling the cards with practiced ease.

The game was a variation of cassino with the objective to steal the pile in front of another player with a card of equal value. Portia was a skilled and ruthless player, not above stealing Geoff's cards to keep Castleton or Juliet from claiming them. Inevitably the game came down to either Castleton or Portia, with one prevailing first, then the other.

Even Margaret and Alvenia gave up their conversation to watch them battle, with Alvenia shouting out instructions to everyone at the table in turn. No one realized how late it had become until Mrs. Adams entered the room to light the candles on the mantel.

"Good Lord," Castleton said, glancing out at the twilight sky, tinged at the shrub line with streaks of orange. "We'd best do something about seeing your brood fed, Geoff."

Mrs. Adams cleared her throat. "If your lordship will allow," she said. "I've set up a cold collation in the dining room. I thought it would be easier to serve the children and would last the evening should the young gentlemen still arrive."

"Excellent, Mrs. Adams," Castleton exclaimed, rising. He offered his arm to Alvenia. "Shall we dine, Mrs. Wilkes?"

"Oh, Castleton," Alvenia tittered. "You should offer your arm to a younger lady."

"That's why the Good Lord gave me two, ma'am," he said, obliging her by offering his other arm to Miss Robertson. Geoff followed his lead, taking both Margaret and Portia in with him. Sarah and Vivian were in the dining room before them, Sarah studying the text of a play with absorbed concentration.

"Have it all worked out?" Castleton asked.

"We require males," Sarah informed him.

"A typical young lady's lament," Geoff quipped.

"What will you perform?" Alvenia asked. "Is there a place in it for Juliet? What part do you play, Castleton?"

"Pater Hardcastle," he responded.

"Then she could play your bride," Mrs. Wilkes exclaimed.

"No offense to Miss Robertson, but the audience might find it hard to believe she is Sarah's mother. . . ."

"Vivian's mother, sir," Sarah corrected. "She will play Miss Hardcastle to Frederick's Mr. Marlow. I will play Miss Neville. And I'm afraid, ma'am, Miss Kirby has already agreed to the role of Mrs. Hardcastle. But there's the part of a maid to fill if you would like it, Miss Robertson. . . ."

"Oh, yes," Juliet said. "I have never been in a play. I think a small part would suit me best."

"And we hope to prevail upon Mr. Ponsby to take a part, but we are left without a Sir Charles Marlow. . . ."

"Consider that role taken," Wilkes said.

"Oh, thank you, sir," Sarah exclaimed.

"But there's still a major gentleman's role, depending on which one Mr. Ponsby decides to take," Vivian said.

"If he decides to take any," Sarah replied.

"I'm sure we can persuade him," Portia said.

"I'm sure *you* can persuade him," Castleton corrected.

Portia smiled at him.

The ladies withdrew to the salon with the children, while Castleton and Wilkes shared a decanter of port.

"Thank you for your kindness to Juliet," Wilkes said. "Alvenia is so delighted at your attentiveness, I am loath to open her eyes to the truth."

"Which is?"

"You are *aux anges* over Miss Kirby."

Castleton grinned. "I appreciate your discretion," he said.

"It's more for Miss Kirby's sake than anything else," Wilkes said. "Am I mistaken, or is she totally unaware of your intent?"

"Just as long as she continues to respond to my attentions," Castleton replied. He rubbed his hands in satisfaction. "Only a day at Welton, and I've already made great strides."

"Congratulations," Wilkes replied in a bland voice.

"What?"

"Forgive me, David, but do you really think that woman would refuse you? Forget that you are remarkably well-formed and agreeable. You're a baron with a large estate and a sizable income. She's a woman alone in the world, well past the age when most women expect to be made an offer. It seems if you really want her, all you'd have to do is ask."

Castleton gaped at him.

Wilkes laughed. "That's never even occurred to you, has it?"

"No." But he was discomfited at the thought. He fumbled to explain it. But, as usual, Geoff already understood.

"You'll settle for nothing less than a love match. And I can hardly blame you with my own example before you. I remind myself too often that, if I'm in hell, it's a hell of my own making."

"I'm sorry," Castleton said, placing his hand on Geoff's shoulder.

Wilkes mustered a smile. "It's not half so bad since we stopped sharing a bed."

Castleton's shock must have been plain.

Wilkes laughed. "Why do you think we coddle Evan to excess? Neither of us wants to go through the struggle of begetting another son. And Evan's welfare finally gives us a common interest. But I think I should have been a happier man if I'd approached marriage your way."

"Geoff...."

"Don't worry about me, Lord Castleton. But don't let whatever game you're playing now blind you to the truth. As things stand, there's no reason Miss Kirby wouldn't have you."

When they rejoined the ladies, Geoff insisted his family take their leave over Alvenia's loud protests.

"Evan is asleep, my dear, and the girls are becoming fractious," Wilkes said, gathering his slumbering son off the divan. "We've given Castleton and company no time to settle in."

"It cannot signify when we are practically like

family. . . ." Alvenia replied, accepting her wraps with a glower.

"Perhaps Miss Robertson would be kind enough to return on the morrow?" Castleton asked as all escorted the Wilkeses to the portico. The twin raising of brows Portia and Wilkes directed at him was almost comical. "We have barely a fortnight to prepare for our performance."

Alvenia beamed. "Of course, I will bring her back first thing in the morning."

"Not too early, ma'am," Castleton said gravely. "Miss Kirby is a heavy sleeper and does not rise before noon. I would not wish to discomfit a guest to suit my own inclinations."

Portia choked. Mrs. Wilkes frowned.

"I'm sorry," Portia stammered. "The night air. . . ."

"Yes, it wreaks havoc with your lungs, doesn't it?" Castleton replied solicitously. Portia's hazel eyes danced in the moonlight before she ducked her head and nodded. Alvenia sighed, then directed Wilkes in the careful dispersal of Evan in their waiting carriage. The children had just settled in the wide seat of the barouche when a small equipage and rider appeared at the end of the drive.

"See, we can't leave now," Alvenia exclaimed. "Here is Frederick and his friend. I'm sure Juliet will want to be known to them."

Frederick rode ahead, and bowed to the Wilkeses as he dismounted. "We are sorry to be so late, sir," he told Castleton after introductions were made. "But. . . ."

He gestured toward Ponsby's gig, which had two horses tethered to its rear instead of the expected one. Bright Promise's total change of demeanor over the past month was more apparent when compared to the sorry roan beside him. Ponsby relinquished his reins to Stubbins, who nodded a greeting to him. He dusted off his modestly caped coat and strode toward Castleton with a resolved expression on his round face.

"Our delay was entirely my fault," he explained. "And I hope it will not inconvenience you, sir, if I beg another stall. I rescued this poor girl from a hard-handed master."

"Oh, poor, poor creature," Juliet exclaimed, rushing past them all to stroke the mare's nose. The horse shook away from her as her hand moved down its cheek. "Her mouth's been sawed most cruelly."

"Not to mention the liberal use of the whip on her," Ponsby replied.

Juliet's eyes scanned Bright Promise as she softly caressed the roan. "He's a splendid fellow. Is he lame?"

"He's not quite broken to the harness yet. He'll receive his first tryout on the gig once he's rested up from our drive."

"Oh," Juliet exclaimed. "I should like to see that, sir. We don't have such horses in Blythe."

"No," Ponsby agreed, amused. "You have to travel inland twenty miles or so."

"Do you come from the North?"

"I do."

"And are you acquainted with the Ponsbys of Morpeth?"

"I am a Ponsby of Morpeth."

"Oh, how famous," Juliet exclaimed. "Wait until I write my brother Tom. He'll be positively green. He's been after father for an age to see your stock, although, as Pa says, your horses are above our touch. Even I can see that now. . . ."

"Juliet!" Alvenia intoned in a seething voice. "You keep us waiting with your chatter."

"Oh." Juliet fell silent, crestfallen.

"Perhaps, ma'am, you would do me the favor of coming to croon again over poor Miss Roan," Ponsby asked Juliet in a low voice as he led her to the carriage. "Kindness is the medicine she requires most at present."

Juliet smiled tremulously at him as she nodded. Alvenia directed a particularly black look at Ponsby. Castleton contained his laughter only until the departing carriage hit the tree line. Portia's bubbled forth in ready response as the others gazed at them in perplexity.

"Have I done something untoward?" Ponsby asked.

"Only exposed the key aspect of Miss Robertson's nature," Castleton replied, clapping him on the shoulder. "And you shall earn my undying gratitude should you decide to press your obvious advantage. But for the moment, just know that you are heartily welcome here, Mr. Ponsby. You and every horse in the county."

12

CASTLETON RODE OUT with his steward early the next morning. Flooding in the southern pasture had disrupted grazing and displaced a half-dozen tenant farmers from their homes. Castleton assured Tyler, an earnest young man, that his plan to improve irrigation after the fields were drained met with his whole-hearted approval. He left Tyler compiling a list of materials needed to repair the damaged farmhouses and rode back toward Welton, slowing as he noticed a figure strolling in the park.

Portia, apparently, had not waited for a tour of the formal garden, and had risen early enough herself to pass out of its massive walks to the wilder lawns and trees beyond.

Castleton tried to imagine the scene with her romantic eyes. The slight roll of the grassland, the groves of trees, the glimmer of the pond to the east. And Welton—its soft, pale brick aglow in the early slant of filtered sunshine, its garden gate wide and inviting, beckoning one from Nature's beauties to nature tamed in an impressive array of color and form.

This was his favorite approach—far more welcoming than the stiff formality of the northern aspect. He would tug on his father's hand at this point in their stroll from their own house—urging him to hurry because who knew what they had missed in the hours between supper and his morning lessons at Welton.

Now the lure was Portia's smile of pleasure as she noticed him on the slope above her.

"It's a fine morning, isn't it?" she said when he reined in beside her. "Please don't tell Mrs. Wilkes, but I've been up for nearly an hour just exploring. . . ."

"Have you discovered the villa?" he asked.

"The villa?"

"A folly set on the southern side of the rise," he explained, gesturing toward the long slope of land where he could discern the roof of the little building amidst the trees.

"Oh," Portia said, her enthusiasm dampened by the obvious distance. "Perhaps when we leave the carriage could drive in that direction. . . ."

"Pudding heart," Castleton chided. "It's but twenty minutes' ride at a brisk trot."

"I don't ride," Portia said. "It might provide motivation for a long afternoon's walk."

He snorted. "Put your foot on my boot."

Portia stared up at him.

"Come on," he urged. "There is no one about. We can be back before breakfast."

She studied Caesar's dimensions and shook her head.

Castleton leaned down toward her. "There's no need to be afraid," he said. "I would not ride you ragged nor let you fall. It's worth the risk. I promise." He held out his hand to her. "Trust me, Portia."

She slowly placed her fingers in his palm. He clasped them, tugging up with steady insistence. Portia gathered up her skirt long enough to free her leg, stepped hard on the upper of his boot, and then she was before him, legs dangling against Caesar's flank, secured between Castleton's arms. A major victory. But to savor it would be a costly error.

He urged Caesar forward with a flick of the reins. Castleton kept his gait to a walk until Portia gradually relaxed.

"All right?" he asked.

"Yes," she said, looking around with interest despite her convulsive clutch of the saddle. "That smoke isn't coming from your 'villa,' is it?"

"No," he said. There's another house beyond."

"Part of your property?"

"Most definitely," he replied. "I'm going faster. Hold tight."

Her hands were red from clenching when he dismounted and helped her from the horse.

"You can wear my gloves on the way back," he said, as he tied Caesar to a post.

Portia danced away, surveying the scene with shining eyes.

"It doesn't matter," she said. "How wonderful!" She glanced back at Welton. "This is the vantage used to paint the landscape. And the villa is charming.

Such a cunning little room with its tiled roof and the portico with its own stone table and benches."

"My aunt and uncle honeymooned in Italy. He had this built for her as a surprise on their return," Castleton said. "She would ride out here to read sometimes, and we'd all meet here for picnics on the slope. It upset Douglas to no end that I was two years his junior but could always beat him in a race down. I had more practice. I made the journey nearly every day."

Portia looked at the other house situated about a quarter-mile away down the other slope. It was too large to call a farmhouse, but too small to consider a manor. Her own childhood home was two bays larger. The architecture was solid Georgian, nowhere near as grand as Welton.

And yet Castleton's eyes reflected a deeper affection than on their arrival at the Tudor house. He pointed to the upmost window on the right.

"That was my room," he said. "I could see the villa from my window. It fueled many dreams of journeys to far-off lands."

"Over land," she added.

"Oh, most definitely," he replied. "Though somehow I survived that voyage to India and back. Don't ask me how." He shuddered comically, and she laughed.

"It looks a fine place to have been a boy," she said.

"It was," he replied, something shimmering on the surface of his eyes.

Portia's own eyes misted. "I understand," she said.

"Understand what?"

"Why you cannot play Lord Castleton here as you do in London. It means something here. Something you are uncomfortable with because you are just David Carlyle, who belongs on the other side of the rise."

"Your witchery can be very disconcerting at times, Portia," he replied in a soft voice.

"I wish I'd known you when you were just Captain Carlyle."

"Lieutenant Carlyle," he corrected. "I was Castleton before I was a captain. And I'm not really all that different, except I suffer fools more easily now."

He glanced toward the great house, nestled in picturesque landscaping.

"We'd just trudged through miles of hot, muggy jungle—the mud was so deep it made the march feel twice as long. I was exhausted. . . . You would have thought a letter from home would be the most wonderful surprise.

"I hit the first man who congratulated me on ascending to the peerage. No one understood the terrible loss it entailed. My uncle was a truly noble man. He looked out for us—for William—because he was a part of us. Every man, woman, and child connected to this estate was family in his mind.

"My aunt was a quiet, golden presence who liberally bestowed hugs on little boys who had no mother of their own. Lesley and Douglas were my playmates, and the girls . . . Amelia was newly wed. She might still be alive if she hadn't rushed home to support her family in the crisis. Celeste had just become engaged. And while Dorothy was only twelve when I left for India, she was already in a fair way to casting old Honoria in the shade. . . ."

He gestured toward the smaller house.

"That was the only part of Welton I ever aspired to. I wanted to retire from a long military career and warm my aching feet on that hearth. And know that on 'the other side of the rise,' as you put it, a family waited for me, always ready to welcome me with open arms."

He stripped his gloves off and scrubbed at his face. He grimaced when he looked at her, then brushed a tear from her cheek with a feather-light touch. "I think that's enough wallowing in ancient misery for one morning."

"Who lives in your house now?" Portia asked, swiping the other side of her face.

"The Misses Burnley. Spinster sisters who lost their father about the same time I lost mine. My uncle established them in the house when I went to live with William. He didn't like the idea of its sitting empty."

"He would be appalled to see Welton deserted, wouldn't he?"

Castleton sighed. "It wasn't practical to establish myself here. I was used to the house in Kent. I'd lived there nearly as many years as here. And I wanted the children to grow up in familiar surroundings."

"And what will your excuse be when Frederick marries and takes control of his property?"

"I don't know," he said. "But I'm sure I'll think of something. You must have noticed the household dreads my coming as much as I dread being here."

"I didn't notice anything of the kind."

"Is your sixth sense failing you?"

"Not at all," Portia said. "It's your own ability to read a situation that's gone awry. They are not upset because you come, but because you come too seldom. Mrs. Adams was aching to tell you everything she'd done to make the visit pleasant, and you cut her off. What a novelty to have someone to serve, if only for a fortnight. . . ."

"You make a point," he replied.

"And you're wrong about something else," Portia continued. She gestured toward the Georgian house with its cozy little flower beds and smoke curling from its chimneys. "You don't belong over there. Not in Mrs. Adams's eyes. She remembers you as a part of Welton's history—clinging to your aunt, one of Lesley's players—you are one of the children to her. I'm sure that's why your disinterest irritates her so much."

"I'm not disinterested," he exclaimed. "I just . . . don't know how to be Lord Castleton. Not the way my uncle was, at any rate."

"Then just be Lord Castleton in a way you know," Portia said. "Not that I'd suggest you play a farce with them, but—good heavens—you can hold a conversation with Addison Cheever, and you detest him! Surely it can't be difficult to charm people who work so hard to preserve a place you care about."

"I suppose not. Anything else?"

"Since you ask," Portia said. "It's rather disturbing nothing's changed in thirteen years. Why don't you paint a wall a color you like or let Sarah rip up the flower beds?"

"That will thrill the gardener, I'm sure."

"It just might," Portia replied with a touch of asperity. "He may hate those shrubs and wish he could tear them down. . . . You don't know that any more than I."

"No, I don't," he admitted with a wry smile. "But I promise I will do my best to find out."

THE SUN WAS much higher but clouded over by the time they quit the villa.

"They'll all be up by now," Portia said in an uncertain voice as the house loomed closer.

"Most likely," Castleton said. "Shall we concoct a scenario to explain your presence in my saddle? Twisted ankle? I found you prostrate on the green, overcome by the heat?" He glanced at the faint glow in the cloud bank. "You wilt very easily."

Portia laughed. "Why don't we say you offered me a ride and I accepted?" she suggested.

"The truth?! Portia, how bold of you."

"I know. I don't understand it myself. It must be something in the air."

A groom rushed out to take hold of Caesar's head as they walked into the stable yard. Castleton dismounted, then reached up for her.

For one long moment after her feet touched the ground, her hands remained on his shoulders as he held her by the waist. Portia smiled, her eyes loamy soft. She gently pushed away from him and swept him a curtsey.

"Thank you for the ride, Lord Castleton."

"I live to serve you, ma'am," Castleton said, bestowing a quick kiss on the knuckle of his own glove, which was far too large for her hand.

Laughing, Portia slipped out of it, leaving only leather in his grasp. She tossed him the other glove then walked toward the house, each step filled with a light and graceful energy.

Castleton followed the groom toward the stable just as Ponsby came out the door, leading the bay to his waiting gig for a morning of exercise.

"Ponsby," Castleton acknowledged in passing.

"Are your intentions honorable, sir?" the young man asked.

Castleton stopped cold. He turned back, eyeing Ponsby's grave face, full of concern for a friend. A sudden burst of affection for the young man filled his breast.

"Yes," he replied.

Ponsby smiled and nodded. Castleton swore he heard him humming as he hitched the bay to the gig.

* * * * *

SINCE THE YOUNG men had arrived so late the previous night and Ponsby had spent his entire morning in the stables, Sarah had to wait until nearly luncheon to broach the subject of the play.

Frederick was more than amenable to the idea. She knew he would be. It was one of the few activities they mutually enjoyed. Playing opposite Vivian made the idea agreeable as well.

He also had a solution for their lack of a cast member. "Vane's supposed to accompany his parents. I'm sure he'd be game, but we might have to shorten his lines," Frederick said.

"We'll have to shorten everyone's lines," Sarah said. "We have only one copy of the play to share amongst us. Although, if we sent a message to Town, Lord Vane could study his role a bit beforehand. Which part should we give him?"

"Hastings, I think. Ponsby has more of the Tony Lumpkin look about him."

"I don't think. . . ." Ponsby stammered, as Vivian handed him the book. He shut his eyes. "I've never been any good at dissembling," he finished.

"If you're not comfortable playing Tony outright, you can read his part from a chair," Sarah said.

Ponsby paged through the play. He frowned. "This character seems. . . ."

"It's a comedic role, but an important part," Frederick explained. "Tony's a trickster, of sorts. He keeps the action going. You see his mother wants him to marry his cousin, Miss Neville . . . that's the character Sarah will play. . . ."

Ponsby thrust the book back into Vivian's hands. "No, thank you," he said.

"But we need you," Vivian exclaimed.

Sarah's eyes shimmered. "If you think something in the part will contradict your sensibilities you needn't worry. Your character hates my character, too."

Sarah rushed out of the salon into the formal garden. It was so . . . insupportable. She'd never dealt with such censure in her life. She shouldn't care. She didn't know why she did.

"Are you all right, Sarah?" Vivian asked. Sarah threw her arms around her friend's neck and sobbed on her shoulder. Vivian soothed her for but a moment, then stiffened. Sarah looked up.

Ponsby had followed, also. His face was as red as a lobster, but his brown eyes were resolute. "I do not hate you, Miss Christopher," he stated.

"You think I did something wicked," she exclaimed, brushing at her face angrily. How dare he witness her distress?

"No," he said. "But you are not entirely blameless in the matter of George Mahew, either. Are you?"

Sarah stilled.

"Whatever do you mean?" Vivian asked.

"She was looking for him that day," Ponsby asserted.

Vivian laughed. "How on earth did you conceive such a ridiculous notion? She's met the man all of twice in her life. . . ."

"Six times," he corrected, his eyes locked on Sarah's.

"What?!"

"Six that I know of," Ponsby replied. The bitterness returned to his voice. "Though I suppose there could be more."

"Seven," Sarah whispered, avoiding Vivian's shocked gaze. "But it's not what you think. Nothing improper happened between us. We were only talking."

"Sarah!" Vivian gasped.

"Yes, you only talked," Ponsby agreed. "And since you always approached him, I cannot suppose he oppressed you in any way. But if your actions bear no impropriety, why does Miss Barstow gape at me like a codfish? You didn't even confide the liaison to your closest friend."

"You don't understand," Sarah said in an exasperated voice.

"And I'm not sure I want to," he retorted. "But if you were my sister, I'd advise my father to ship you off to the strictest boarding school he could find. Now, if you'll excuse me. . . ."

He stalked away to the refuge of his precious stables, leaving Sarah to contend with Vivian's obvious horror.

"You haven't really been meeting with George Mahew," she whispered.

"They weren't meetings, precisely. He walks in the park some mornings, and I have spoken to him on a few occasions."

"Sarah!"

"Will you stop?!" Sarah stomped along the

garden path. "You're as bad as Mr. Ponsby. There was nothing improper. Simple conversation, Vivian."

"Then you won't mind if I apprise your uncle of it," Vivian replied stiffly.

"You wouldn't!"

"No," Vivian said. "I will not tell him. You have my word. But if the horror of your uncle's finding out does not give you an understanding of Mr. Ponsby's attitude, perhaps my own disappointment will show you how very wrong you are."

Vivian turned on her heel and walked back into the house, leaving Sarah to weep among the roses.

LUNCHEON WAS UNCOMFORTABLE. Only Margaret, Portia, Frederick, Alvenia Wilkes, and Juliet Robertson attended. Castleton had returned to the southern pasture, Ponsby remained cloistered in the stable, and both Sarah and Vivian had retired to their rooms complaining of headaches.

"The city air has damaged them," Alvenia exclaimed as she made room on her already-laden plate for the next course. "You can depend on it, Margaret. Two weeks in the country is not nearly long enough."

"And yet, you seem eager to thrust your niece into such a poisonous atmosphere, ma'am," Portia remarked, as she cut her meat into tiny pieces.

Alvenia glared at her. "One Season in London is all *most* young girls require to catch a husband," she replied frostily. "No doubt that point escapes a woman in your position."

"Yet you have no confidence in your niece's ability to do so," Portia replied. She smiled at the surprised Juliet. "Don't let her press you to a role you are not yet ready to play. I have every confidence you can find a man more to your liking than someone chosen by your less-astute relations."

"How dare you, madame!" Alvenia exclaimed.

"I dare because I was once in Miss Robertson's position," Portia declared. "Thrust at men I had no particular feeling for, just for the sake of being married. But I am not married, and I am perfectly happy. Perfect happiness might be beyond your ability to comprehend, Mrs. Wilkes." Margaret choked. Portia reached out to pat her on the back solicitously as she continued, "But I offer it as a truth to you, Miss Robertson. Marriage is not the be all and end all of the world."

"Sarah's just out of sorts because Ponsby has ruined our play," Frederick offered.

"We will have our play," Portia declared.

She stormed off to the stable after the last plate was cleared away. Ponsby and Castleton's groom Stubbins attended the roan mare. Portia didn't bother to excuse herself. She took Ponsby's arm and drew him out to the stable yard.

"There is more to Sarah's encounter with George than is readily know," she stated without preamble.

"Yes," he replied. "She. . . ."

Portia lifted her hand to stave his words. "Don't

tell me," she said. "You feel justified in your censure, and that is all that matters at present.

"Once, in the beginning of our acquaintance, you alluded to an error in judgment on your part of which you are still heartily ashamed. Do you remember that?"

Ponsby flushed and hung his head. "Yes."

"How does Sarah's behavior compare to yours in that particular incident?"

His head snapped up, and he regarded her with an owlish gaze.

"It isn't even close, ma'am," he replied without hesitation.

"And how old were you again when you did this thing?"

"Eighteen."

"Sarah is but sixteen. And a young sixteen at that," Portia replied. "Now, bearing in mind her age and your unfortunate experience, do you really have a right to judge her so severely?"

"No," he said, "but...."

"Arthur," Portia took his hand, "I know you care for her. And you feel helpless to protect her from her own behavior. But we learn our lessons best when we learn them on our own. And you are wasting a golden opportunity for Sarah to know you better by holding on to anger for something that is past."

He stared at her.

"We're rehearsing for that play in a half-hour," Portia said. "It's the only way we'll get Mrs. Wilkes to quit the premises. Perhaps you can use that time to consider your decision. Remembering, of course, that you promised me support."

"Miss Kirby," he said in astonished voice. "You make my head swim."

"We are only here a fortnight," she declared. "I don't know about you, but I intend to have a pleasant time."

THE AIR WAS scented with faint bread and stronger beef, and filled with the buzz of gossipy conversation.

"Did she actually say that?!"

"Aye. Shocked the life out of me, it did. . . ."

"Mrs. Chris looked near to splittin'. Had to whisk the plates away meself to keep from shoutin' out a laugh."

"Well it serves her right for sayin' such a wicked thing," a dark-haired maid declared.

"Shh," Mrs. Adams hissed, and all eyes turned as Castleton crept farther into the kitchen with his muddy boots in hand. He paused a moment, cowed by their silent regard. Even those servants who had made the trip to Hampshire from Town were staring as if he'd lost his mind.

What if Portia was mistaken? *Then I shall have an opportunity to prove myself right*, Castleton thought as he carefully disposed of his soiled footwear in a corner. He plastered a smile on his face.

"I'm sorry to interrupt your meal," he said. "I hoped to beg a tardy plate from you."

"Of course, my lord." Mrs. Adams gestured to a redheaded footman, who rose and grabbed for the coat hanging on the back of his chair.

Castleton waved the young man back to his place. "No," he said. "I'll not cheat you of your own meal. Just let me take a plate here, out of your way."

They filled him a plate, watching in awed silence as he took the lowest seat at the table and began to eat. Mrs. Adams snapped her fingers, and the staff returned attention to their own luncheon. But conversation ceased. That wouldn't suit Castleton's purpose at all. He glanced around at the downcast faces, noting a propensity of red hair spilling down foreheads, and peeking from beneath caps.

"Exactly how many Kellys do I employ?" he asked. Every red head bobbed up and fixed a pale blue eye on him.

"Five in the house, two in the gardens, and one in the stable," Mrs. Adams replied.

"And does your grandmother still make the best gingerbread in Hampshire?" Castleton asked.

"She does, me lord," the littlest redhead exclaimed. His nearest Kelly relation boxed his ear, but the boy remained adamant. "It's true, Mike. Ain't no cause ta sock me."

"He's quite right, Mike," Castleton agreed. Mike's face turned as red as his hair.

Castleton focused his attention farther down the table. The two maids nearest Mrs. Adams's seat were unfamiliar to him. Both had dark hair, but the one to the left was a French pastry of a girl wearing a gown he vaguely recalled seeing on Vivian Barstow last winter. The other had a sturdier look about her. She looked everywhere, trying to judge how she should react to his invasion of their luncheon by the attitude of the others.

"Do I know you?" he asked, startling her speechless.

"Lydia is Miss Kirby's maid," Mrs. Adams explained.

"Ah," he said. "Are you enjoying your trip to the country, Lydia?"

"Oh . . . oh, yes, my lord," Lydia stammered. "It's nice here. So green and pretty."

"And has everyone treated you well?"

"Yes, my lord. Everyone's so kind and polite."

"And yet, when I entered the room you were remarking that someone deserved a set down."

Lydia stared at him, swallowing hard. The others glanced down into their plates.

"Lydia was referring to Mrs. Wilkes," Mrs. Adams said.

"Is Mrs. Wilkes here?" he asked her with dread.

"Yes. She brought Miss Robertson for rehearsal, I believe, and arrived just in time for luncheon."

"Of course she did." Castleton sighed and shook his head. "What did she say?"

The servants all looked from one to another.

"You may as well tell me," Castleton said. "Visitor or not, I won't have guests insulted in my house."

"She made a remark to my mistress," Lydia said. "About her bein' . . . you know. . . ."

"An old maid," one of the footmen finished, earning a jab of the elbow from the housemaid seated next to him.

"But you needn't worry about it, my lord," Mrs. Adams interjected quickly. One of those bizarrely beautiful smiles lit her severe face. "Miss Kirby put her in her place quite neatly."

"Did she?" Castleton smiled. "Good for her."

The whole table relaxed. The tweeny cast eyes at the bowl before him, and Castleton offered it to her with a flourish, earning a blushing giggle.

"Miss Portia has her stubborn fits," Lydia confessed, buttering a slice of bread. "She gave me such a scold for packin' that green gown for her."

"The dress she wore to the theater?" Castleton asked.

"Aye. Now, you seen that dress, my lord. She looked a picture in it. And with a duchess comin' next week and that evil woman sayin' such things to her...."

"You did the right thing, Lydia," he assured her. "Let me rummage in my aunt's jewel box. I'm sure I can scare up some perfectly lovely bauble to disguise its defect."

"What is wrong with the dress?" Mrs. Adams asked.

Lydia exchanged a glance with Castleton. He scooped the breast of his riding jacket in illustration. The maid who had jabbed the footman tittered, giving him a chance to pay her back.

"I'll take a look at it," Mrs. Adams offered. "I've

not tried my hand at fine sewing in awhile, but I used to serve my lady well."

Castleton laughed. "How many times did you mend that russet frock before my uncle took Douglas to task for yanking so hard on his mama's skirts?"

Mrs. Adams smiled at him. "That boy was a disaster in shortcoats," she replied. "I remember when he stuck his head in the balustrade and they had to call the carpenter to set him free. I never heard such a yowling in all my days."

"That's because I told him they'd brought the saw to trim off his ears," Castleton confessed with a wicked grin, making the whole table laugh.

MARGARET POUNCED ON Castleton when he entered the salon. Alvenia sat by the window, her back ramrod straight, her head raised in haughty disdain. She even took no pleasure in Juliet's hushed but fluid conversation with Frederick across the room.

"You should have been at luncheon," Margaret whispered.

"Yes, I've heard. Where is Portia?"

"She's upstairs trying to persuade the girls to come down. I think they've had a quarrel. But Miss Kirby will get around them." Margaret's eyes danced. "She's made Alvenia so angry, I haven't had to speak a word to her for twenty minutes."

Castleton smothered his own grin, knowing this

had been no hardship, and patted her hand affectionately. He approached Alvenia with a contrite expression on his face.

"I'm so sorry to have kept you and Miss Robertson waiting," he said. "And I see the girls are late."

"It is most likely a ploy of that woman's to drive us away," Alvenia exclaimed. "I don't know why you brought her with you."

"She's Margaret's guest," he explained in a whisper. "If it had been my decision. . . ." He let the sentence dangle in the air.

Alvenia unbent. "You should have been there. She actually rejoiced in her single state and told Juliet that marriage was not the be all and end all of the world."

"No," Castleton exclaimed in an astonished voice. "I wonder that she dared."

"You should take her to task, Castleton. I am a guest here."

"You leave her to me, ma'am." He glanced in Portia's direction as she entered, shepherding two sullen young ladies before her. With a room's breadth between them, she still rolled her eyes and smiled at Castleton's theatrical expression. "I will do everything in my power to discredit that foul declaration."

Mrs. Wilkes returned to her pointed study of the garden as Portia approached him.

"It's a good thing you and I begin this play," she said. "It appears no one else is speaking to each other."

"Any idea to correct that? If we wish to correct that," he added as he glanced in Alvenia's direction.

Portia coughed a laugh in reply. "Just begin and hope for the best.

"All right." Castleton clapped his hands for attention. "Who has the book?" he asked.

"I do," Frederick replied, waving it above his head.

"Why bother?" Sarah asked in a gloomy voice. "Mr. Wilkes isn't here, and we are still short of players."

"I've acted in many a play with Mr. Wilkes. He's a quick study, I assure you," Castleton replied. "I'm sure Margaret will oblige us by reading any absent roles."

"Yes, of course," Margaret said.

"Since we will have to share the same book, I suggest we move the furniture closer together. Frederick?"

They moved chairs closer to the divan. Vivian seated herself between Frederick and Juliet, separating two who had been getting on a little too well, Castleton suspected, and likewise keeping Sarah at a distance. Castleton set his niece between himself and her mother. Portia took the seat next to him, leaving one chair between herself and Frederick open.

"I won't be joining you," Alvenia announced.

"Should I inform her that chair is for Mr. Ponsby?" Portia asked Castleton in a low voice.

"Is Ponsby coming?" he asked.

"No," Sarah and Vivian answered in chorus,

drowning out Portia's affirmative reply. The girls gave each other a hard look, then looked away from each other.

"He will be here," Portia assured Castleton.

He bit back a grin, and opened the play to the first page.

"We can omit the prologue," he said. "That makes the first speech yours, Mrs. Hardcastle."

Portia took the book from him. She studied the passage a moment, cleared her throat, and launched into a perfect parody of Alvenia Wilkes as, in character, she lamented her lot of being stuck out in the country while even the "two Misses Hoggs and our neighbour Mrs. Grigsby go to take a month's polishing every winter." Her parody was lost on no one save Alvenia, who continued to gaze out the window with disdain instead of affront.

Portia passed the book to Castleton, who delivered his first lines in a quivering voice and returned the book to her. Halfway through Portia's second speech, Vivian glanced in Sarah's direction, and the two girls giggled.

Alvenia herself laughed at the slurs to Mrs. Hardcastle's age as the scene progressed. "I can see now why they chose you for this part, Miss Kirby."

"Yes, it takes a woman of some maturity to understand the role," Castleton agreed. Even Juliet joined the shimmer of laughter as Mrs. Wilkes nodded satisfaction to him before continuing her garden vigil. Castleton winked at Portia, and she smiled as she continued her wicked lampoon.

But as the topic of the scene changed to Mrs. Hardcastle's son, Tony Lumpkin, Sarah grew very quiet again.

At last the cue for the uncast role was reached.

"O, there he goes—a very consumptive figure, truly," Castleton exclaimed. He passed the book to his sister-in-law. "Margaret. . . ."

"Of course," Margaret said.

"That won't be necessary, ma'am."

Portia smiled like the cat who'd emptied the cream pot as Ponsby slipped into the seat beside her and held his hand out to Margaret for the book. He looked at nothing save the page. Even so, Portia had to point out his speech.

"Might I read a bit to understand the role?" Ponsby asked.

"Take your time," Frederick said.

Ponsby flipped the page back to read the lines leading up to his entrance and then farther. He ran a hand through his dark hair and shook his head. "Well," he said, hazarding a look at them all. "Thank goodness it's a comedic role. I have a terrible feeling they'll be laughing at me any way."

"Give us a week," Castleton said. "We'll whip you into shape. Won't we, children?"

Sarah, Vivian, and Frederick nodded in unison. Ponsby began to read in a halting voice. By the time they reached the heart of the play, all were laughing and chatting easily.

When Juliet's little part was finished, Alvenia announced they would take their leave. Castleton saw them to the door with a profusion of thanks. Sarah shifted into the seat beside Vivian to make the reading of their scenes together easier.

Castleton leaned over Portia's chair to whisper in her ear.

"Are you ever wrong, Portia?"

"Very rarely," she whispered back. "Something you should always bear in mind."

"Oh," he replied, smiling down on her. "Believe me, I do."

13

L ATE THE NEXT morning, Frederick summoned them all to the main stairway on the front of the house.

"Do you intend to entertain us on the lawn?" Castleton asked.

"Not I, sir. Wait but a moment. . . ."

The wait was more than a few moments. Sarah glanced at Vivian. Matters were better between them since yesterday's rehearsal, but she couldn't say they were entirely well. They had held no private discourse. Sarah wasn't looking forward to it. There was a reason she hadn't told Vivian about her conversations with Mr. Mahew, though leave it to Ponsby twist her silence into something sordid.

At least he had relented about the play. Though his assessment of his acting ability had been painfully honest. Still, her uncle and Miss Kirby thought only a little coaching was necessary. Sarah would have to see it to believe it.

"Here he is!" Frederick exclaimed, gesturing toward the oak-lined drive. Something surged through Sarah's heart, wiping all resentment away as Bright Promise trotted out of the tree line and up the gravel drive. Ponsby reined him in smoothly.

"Congratulations, Arthur!" Portia said, clapping her hands together. The others followed suit, giving Ponsby a round of applause as Frederick darted down the stair to catch hold of the bridle. Ponsby alighted from his gig with a pleased smile on his face. He stripped off his glove to shake Frederick's hand.

"He's more than I dreamed," Ponsby said, caressing the horse. "Much steadier than his partner. I couldn't ask for better."

"If you need a carriage to try them out together, I'm sure we have something," Castleton said.

Ponsby shook his head. "He must accustom himself to the rig first. I won't chance them together for a few weeks. But if they cannot work together, Bright Promise can still bear a solitary load." He hugged the horse. "That is a major accomplishment."

"Yes, it is," Sarah exclaimed in excitement.

Ponsby's brown-eyed gaze touched her face. His features appreciably reddened as he approached the stair. "Would you care to drive out with me, Miss Christopher?" he asked, shocking her.

"I'm sure one of the others. . . ." Sarah stammered. "Frederick. . . ."

"I'll get my chance later," Frederick said. "You should go, Sarah. All those mornings you came out to watch us. . . ."

Sarah's own face warmed guiltily. She glanced at Vivian.

"Go on, Sarah," Vivian urged in a soft voice.

Sarah walked down the stone steps, and let Ponsby hand her into the gig. He climbed in beside her—uncomfortably close—and took the reins from Frederick. A light flick of Ponsby's wrist, and the gig lurched into motion. Sarah kept her attention on the horse, his powerful legs moving in a slow and easy rhythm.

"You can't even tell this is his first time," she offered finally, as they pulled out of Welton's drive to the country road beyond. "You've done a magnificent job."

"I know how to deal with horses. People, however. . . ."

She hazarded a glance to find him regarding her. He had soft eyes . . . like a deer. . . . His face scrunched into uncertain lines.

"I'm sorry," he said, his tone resolute. "I had no right say what I did yesterday. And certainly not before Miss Barstow. It was not my intention to cause discord between you."

"I don't know what to tell her," she confessed. "She'll be so hurt."

"*She'll* be hurt?" he asked, confused.

"That I turned to Mr. Mahew instead of her. It was just . . . he understood, you see, and she doesn't."

"I'm afraid I don't understand, either."

"I'm . . . odd," Sarah confessed. He frowned at her. "I don't fit in. They only think of gowns and conquests . . . 'Who called on you today? Did Mr. So-and-So send you flowers? Did he beg you to dance with him more than twice? And who do you think will make you an offer? The Season is half over. Where are your beaux?' When I mention a book I read they say I am too smart. But they laugh at my French and think it appalling I can't embroider a stitch. . . . They say I don't know anything."

He laughed, long and heartily. To a point where Sarah was discomfited she'd betrayed her private feelings to him. She clasped her hands tightly in her lap and turned away.

"I'm sorry," he stammered. "I should not laugh. I realize this disturbs you deeply. But surely you must realize that, if you are odd, then I am a total aberration."

Sarah turned back to him, blinking.

"They won't even speak to me," he said. "I took on Bright Promise's training to while away the time so my Season in London wasn't a total waste.

"But, strangely, the moment I concentrated on what I knew best, I attracted notice. Suddenly, I have a whole circle of friends and acquaintances. Can I ask you a personal question?"

Sarah nodded warily.

"Do you really wish to be wed by the end of the year?"

Sarah widened her eyes in horror. "No! I mean . . . there is no one I even *remotely* care for in that fashion. . . ."

"Then why worry about catching a husband through artificial means when you intend to let natural inclination guide you?"

It was Sarah's turn to laugh.

"What?" he asked, his features reddening again.

"You gave me sound advice, sir. Don't you think?"

"I hope so."

"Mr. Mahew said the exact same thing," she stated in satisfaction. "He said I was fortunate to have a choice in the matter and I shouldn't waste my time worrying about such *nonsense*—his word, Mr. Ponsby—when I am too young to be thinking of marriage anyway."

"Is that what he told you?"

"Yes. Moreover, he stated that French, embroidery, and the ability to dance had nothing to do with marriage—unless your intended was a French dancing master who expected you to take in sewing to supplement his income."

Ponsby smiled.

Encouraged, Sarah continued: "He said I had many admirable qualities and I shouldn't consider the suit of any *young* man—his word again, sir—unless he appreciated every one of them. Now . . . does that sound like he was making up to me in any way?"

"Only in his acknowledgment of your special qualities," he admitted.

"Oh, he thinks me the greatest nuisance. He told me to begone on more than one occasion. If our conversation grew protracted he would stand up in the middle of it and walk away. It was vastly annoying."

Ponsby sobered. "He does care for you," he asserted. "On more than one morning when you did not come to watch us, he lingered in the vicinity. I think he hoped to see you."

"Oh." Sarah sobered, too. "He's very lonely. His mistress died recently."

Ponsby gaped at her.

"He didn't tell me that," she said hastily. "It was the girls—Melinda Trent, specifically—who betrayed the nature of their relationship. You may think me wicked, but I'm glad they had each other for a time. She had a horrible life and he ... oh, if you could see the way his eyes and voice change when he speaks of her, you would know your fears are groundless. He loved her. He still loves her. He would not spoil her memory by taking up with a green girl like me."

They fell silent. Sarah thought about George Mahew. She'd been drawn to his loneliness, and yet, in the midst of such terrible pain, he'd given her support and understanding. It bespoke a generous nature. Sarah would miss him. Clearly, she could not take him her childish complaints anymore.

"Perhaps a time will come when you can openly claim him as a friend," Ponsby said, almost as if he could read her thoughts.

"I don't see how."

"When your uncle and Miss Kirby marry."

Sarah gaped at him. "My uncle means to marry Miss Kirby?" she asked. "Really?!"

"He told me so when I asked him," Ponsby replied.

"Oh! Oh, how marvelous!" She impulsively hugged his shoulder. Bright Promise shook in his harness at the unfamiliar tremble of the reins. The gig careened across the road. Sarah released Ponsby so he could set their course right again.

"I'm sorry," she said. "I didn't mean to fly at you. I just. . . . You asked?! How ever could you be so bold?"

"Miss Kirby is my friend. At one time, she was my only friend. I don't think she realizes how deep her feelings run, but your uncle plays on what is there so easily, I had to be sure."

"How good of you," Sarah said, "But you must know my uncle would never toy with a woman's affections. He deplores that type of behavior. How sly of him! I had absolutely no idea he was in love with her at all!"

She resisted the impulse to hug him again, but the good will flowing between them made her wondrously easy and light. "And there is the proof," she said, relaxing completely. "True love is worth waiting for."

"Yes," Ponsby agreed with a slow smile. "No matter how long it takes."

PONSBY WAS COMPLETELY besotted with Sarah again by their return to Welton. Castleton sighed. So much for hoping a mutual interest would sweep Miss Robertson out of his life.

Still, the young man offered a drive to Juliet

when he discovered her waiting on the front steps. His invitation and its eager assent annoyed Alvenia—that was all Castleton required. He had no wish any of the young people suffer on Mrs. Wilkes's account, though he hoped Ponsby understood a match with his niece would have Castleton's blessing only when he was certain Sarah returned the young man's regard. But the pair were on much friendlier terms when they pulled into the yard, and Sarah immediately drew Vivian off, which indicated all was mended.

Portia's open disdain of Alvenia continued to astonish him. And it appeared Portia won the battle of wills handily when Alvenia stopped accompanying Juliet to their rehearsals. Geoff came instead, his lines already learned, to cast a Halcyon glow on the next few days.

In the mornings Castleton and Tyler would see to the estate, more often than not coming upon Portia out for a morning walk. In the afternoons they would practice for their play, while the evenings were filled with music, laughter, and good conversation.

The Ballingers and Wallaces arrived far too soon.

"You may have to perform your little drama again when you return to London," Lucy told Castleton as he kissed her hand upon arrival. "Vane has spoken of nothing else for days. Though I must confide that he makes a better Marquess than a Hastings. I have drilled him every day to no avail."

"Let us take a crack at him," he replied. "Ponsby was similarly abysmal when he began, but he's coming around quite nicely. Portia missed her calling. She has a way of explaining a role that even a novice can understand."

"I thought Portia's calling was to be Lady Castleton," Lucy remarked in an arch voice.

"One thing at a time, my dear." Castleton patted her hand affectionately as he led her up the stone staircase. "One thing at a time."

PORTIA ENJOYED HER reunion with the Wallaces, who greeted her as if she were one of their close circle of friends.

Their son, the Marquess of Vane, was a pleasant young man who had inherited his mother's luxuriant chestnut hair and tawny eyes, and his father's affable temperament. Although but in short coats when Castleton returned to England, Vane could have been the model for his outward persona—his face was always wreathed in a smile, and he did his best to put everyone at their ease. But there was no underlying motive for his behavior. He was one of the most naturally friendly people Portia had ever met in her life; one could not help but like him.

But his memory left something to be desired.

"That's your line, Vane," Frederick prompted when they assembled in the drawing room to rehearse the first afternoon.

"Oh, yes, of course," Vane said. He shut his eyes

and rubbed the center of his forehead like some magic lantern. "Now let's see, that was . . . 'your unaccountable reserve.' No, wait, there was something before that. . . ."

"You have the idea of the line correct," Castleton said. "Don't worry if you can't remember it exactly. We've had to cut quite a bit of the text and are all trying to stick to the spirit of the play when memory fails us."

"Jolly good, then," Vane declared, beaming at them all. A long silence of expectation followed.

"Lord Vane?" Portia prompted.

"Oh . . . oh the line. . . ." Vane's brow clouded. "Can you say your piece again, Christopher?"

"Yes, of course," Frederick repeated his first line.

Again silence. Portia nodded to Vane in encouragement.

He snapped his fingers and rolled his eyes up toward the ceiling. "If your unaccountable reserve would have allowed us to . . . to . . ." he stopped, giving himself some internal coaching, then snapped his fingers again, "to make inquiries, Christoph . . . I mean, Marlow. . . ."

They all looked at Portia. She made eye contact with Castleton, then placed a smile on her lips. "Perhaps," she suggested, transferring the book from Juliet's hand to Lord Vane's, "you should read your part the first few times. Just until you are used to hearing the cues."

"Capital idea, ma'am," Vane said. He glanced at the book, then cleared his throat. "Oh, yes . . . I see now. And all, Marlow, from that unaccountable reserve of yours, that would not let us inquire more frequently along the way."

He gazed up at them all triumphantly. As Frederick delivered his next line, Castleton leaned close to Portia and whispered, "One down. . . ."

She smiled. She was always smiling now. Always laughing at something. She had never felt so carefree in all her days. She knew it was foolish of her, but she loved Welton. She spent hours prowling both inside the house and out of doors.

The only mar on her holiday had been the odious Mrs. Wilkes. But even there Portia derived a certain satisfaction that she hadn't given way to the matron's high-handedness. Portia's open challenge had earned her Alvenia's scorn, but no one else seemed to mind. Not even Margaret was disturbed by Mrs. Wilkes's scowls, since they also tended to be accompanied by her silences.

Portia returned to her bedchamber after rehearsal to change for dinner, and discovered Mrs. Adams sitting in the chair by the writing table, setting straight the last stitches attaching a gold-embroidered facing to the despised emerald gown. The housekeeper flushed and dropped Portia a flustered curtsey.

Lydia beamed. "Try it now, miss."

"Oh, Mrs. Adams. . . ." Portia gathered the dress in both hands, examining the alteration with delight. The two-inch strip enhanced the neckline of the gown and shortened its plunging depth to something comfortable. "However did you manage with all you've had to do this past week?"

"With the costumes to prepare, what was one more dress to alter?" she replied. Her beautiful smile warmed Portia's heart. "It was my great pleasure, Miss Kirby. But Lydia is correct. You should try the dress in case the border does not lie correctly."

But the gown was perfect. And a raid on the late Lady Castleton's jewel box of some jade pieces, and the aid of Miss Barstow's maid Constance, who happened to follow her mistress out of Vivian's door when Portia opened her own, and begged to change Miss Kirby's hair when she saw the dress. . . .

"You have such fine hair, mademoiselle," Constance exclaimed as she undid Lydia's handi-work before the looking glass. "It goes exactly where desired."

Even Portia had to acknowledge she looked well. Both Mr. Ballinger and the Duke of Wallace bowed over her hand when she entered the salon. And Castleton's blue eyes glowed with something so warming, Portia thought she might float up to the dining room. Since the Wilkeses had not yet arrived, Portia took a seat beside Lucy on the divan.

"You cast us all in the shade, Miss Kirby," Lucy declared.

Portia took in the duchess's trim figure, elegant gown, elaborate chocolate curls, and glittering diamonds. She laughed.

"You fib, Your Grace, but I do think the trim is an improvement."

The sound of weeping put an end to all discourse. Alvenia entered, pushing her niece before her. The girl clutched her paisley shawl tightly around her shoulders. Geoff Wilkes entered behind him, his square face scowling.

Margaret rose immediately and reached out a comforting hand to the young girl. "Miss Robertson, whatever has occurred?"

"Miss Robertson does not deserve your consideration," Alvenia announced to the room in seething tones. "Miss Robertson reveals her unworthiness to be taken for a lady by bolting into the stables in her evening dress. Just look what she has done!"

Alvenia wrenched the shawl loose. Juliet shut her eyes. but tears streamed from them regardless. A dark stain spread from breast to knee on what Portia suspected was another of Alvenia's gowns cut down.

"I went to see the roan," Juliet sobbed. She opened her eyes and sought out Ponsby, directing her explanation to his sympathetic face. "Mr. Stubbins was applying liniment, and I thought I could hold her. But she's still so tender. She shied and the bottle spilt."

"We are of a size, Miss Robertson," Sarah said, popping to her feet. "If you will come with me. . . ."

"No," Alvenia declared. "She will not hold up the meal further. She will not be excused, either. She shall have to endure her first public dinner in a stained gown."

She glared in Portia's direction, taking in her elegant attire. There was such enmity in her expression. *This is what comes of acting against my better nature*, Portia thought. She wondered guiltily what other censure Juliet had endured that rightly belonged to herself.

Something of her thoughts must have shown in her expression. Lucy squeezed her hand, her light brown eyes alight with curiosity and concern.

"This is my fault," Portia said in a low voice, as Sarah and Vivian lead Juliet to a corner chair, trying to ease her distress with their own natural behavior.

"How can you think that?" Lucy exclaimed. "What an odious woman. If she had one ounce of feeling for that girl...."

"It's something my mother would have done," Portia confessed. Lucy turned to stare at her. "I've picked at Mrs. Wilkes all week, which has kept her in a constant black humor. And now she's taking it out on that poor girl...."

"And that is just spiteful," Lucy whispered back. "Not to mention rude. She's ruining this evening for all of us, not just Miss Robertson."

Castleton bowed before Lucy. "You'd best let me take you up to supper before I give in to the temptation to do violence."

Seeing Castleton approach his wife, the duke bowed to Margaret and offered his arm. Portia tried to arrange them in her mind. Poor Mr. Ballinger, a dapper, balding fellow, would have the unpleasant task of leading Alvenia in to dinner. Wilkes would have to ask Phoebe, and Vane, by rights should ask Sarah as the daughter of the house. Frederick would take Vivian in, of course. That left Ponsby to Portia and poor Juliet to go alone. Portia would not stand for that. She would insist Ponsby escort Juliet.

But it appeared the others had their own ideas. Wilkes stalked over to Portia and bowed to her. "This is the best way I know to punish her at present, ma'am," he said. "We will both dine easier, knowing she'll be well away from us."

Portia rose and took his arm, earning herself another hard stare from Mrs. Wilkes. Vane looked about the room, truly torn. As the highest-ranking man without a partner he should ask the highest-ranking woman.

He hesitantly approached Mrs. Ballinger, but she laughed.

"Young man," she said. "You can't seriously desire my company when there are three pretty girls in need of a partner. Let's forgo etiquette for one evening." She turned her head in Alvenia's direction and sniffed. "Some of us have already."

Vane digested this comment thoughtfully. He turned to the young ladies, still clustered in the corner. As he bowed to them, his attention was clearly centered on Juliet's tear-stained face. "Miss Robertson, would you do me the great honor of sitting beside me at dinner?" he asked.

Sarah and Vivian both urged her to accept. Frederick offered his arm to Vivian, and Ponsby did the same to Sarah. But the meal was a stilted, uncomfortable affair. Vane acted the most natural among them, pouring such kindness and good will into every sentence he uttered that Juliet's tears were dried and forgotten by the last course.

I must mend my fences with Mrs. Wilkes, Portia thought as the ladies withdrew to the salon once more. But every glance in Alvenia's direction resulted in firm rebuff. There were only two ways to deal with bullies: stand up to them or withdraw. Having done the first too well, she decided to take the second course for the rest of her visit.

Since Portia seated herself in a remote corner, and Mrs. Ballinger and Mrs. Christopher were intent on excluding Mrs. Wilkes from their conversation, Lucy felt the time was ripe to bend Alvenia's ear. She took the seat beside the matron, studying her proud visage. Truly, she could have been a most attractive woman with her pitch-black hair and violet eyes. But her sour expression robbed her of the admiration her looks might have afforded her.

"You are being remarkably foolish," Lucy whispered. "Miss Kirby has tried to engage your notice several times. . . ."

"I want nothing to do with that woman," Alvenia hissed. "Look at her in her peacock regalia. Does she think that will endear her to anyone here?"

"She doesn't have to endear herself to anyone here," Lucy replied, astonished at Alvenia's density. "She's engaged Castleton's interest. That is all that signifies."

Alvenia turned a totally dumbfounded stare in her direction.

"Are you saying Castleton and that . . . that. . . ?"

"I am. So I suggest you stay on Miss Kirby's good side."

She rose to join Margaret and Phoebe Ballinger, satisfied her words had not fallen on deaf ears. Alvenia didn't approach Portia or offer any apology for her behavior, but her frown took on a more thoughtful cast. They were gifted with her reflective silence for the remainder of the evening, even after the gentlemen rejoined the ladies.

Vane, Frederick, and Ponsby swarmed around Miss Robertson. A little too much, in Lucy's opinion, though she intended to embrace her son heartily for his good-heartedness later. Wallace retreated to Portia's corner where they conversed with animation—Lucy must discover exactly how Portia did that. And while Castleton entertained the Ballingers, his gaze continually strayed toward Portia. A regard that was not lost on Mrs. Wilkes.

Lucy smirked in satisfaction, confident now there would be a wedding before the end of the season.

SINCE THE DINING parlor was to act as their dressing room, it was decided to hold the first performance of the Castleton Players in the afternoon, so all could be cleared away before supper. The ladies had repaired to their rooms right after luncheon, Juliet reporting it had taken them a good half hour to lace Vivian in her corset.

The maid's wardrobe consisted of an old

homespun gown and cap, so she was in the dining parlor when Castleton arrived in his so-casual-he-could-be-mistaken-for-an-innkeeper attire. Ponsby followed on his heels, wearing a wig dyed black to give him a queue, and an open shirt and knee breeches that actually lent his sturdy figure a roguish appeal. Frederick and Vane adjusted their elaborate long coats with heavy cuffs and powdered wigs in decidedly different fashions as they entered.

"I feel like a girl in all this frippery," Frederick complained. He shoved the lace cuff of his shirt back up his coat sleeve.

"Makes you wish for a short, tailed coat and a bit of crisp linen, don't it?" Vane agreed, even as he admired the lay of his long coat in the looking glass set in the corner.

"Look at my good fortune," Wilkes exclaimed as he arrived with both Sarah and Vivian clinging to his fulsome sleeves.

Sarah's sweet face was framed by powdered curls. The blue brocade gown hugged her slim figure to the waist then flared out dramatically.

Vivian's gown had been chosen for its ability to be transformed to something simpler, since she would have to change costumes throughout the play. Her white underskirt and cherry-striped gown enhanced the bolder Miss Hardcastle. Her simple wig was easy to remove for those scenes when she would go without. Her maid followed with her brushes and combs, ready to style her mistress's hair between appearances.

"Ladies," Castleton exclaimed, waving his hand with a flourish before bowing from the waist. "I am in awe."

"Uncle David!" Sarah giggled. "Please be serious."

"Oh, he is serious, Miss Christopher," Vane exclaimed. "Your comeliness shall distract me from getting the lines right."

"It's fortunate you'll be reading them, then." Castleton said, winking at Sarah.

"Oh, that's right ... I'll be looking at the book," Vane said. "You'd best give me leave to stare now, ma'am."

"Doing it too brown, Vane," Frederick said.

"Don't you think we look well, Mr. Christopher?" Vivian asked.

"I ... I ... Why, yes, but. . . ."

"What he's saying is that you always look well, Miss Barstow, so there is no need for Vane to act as if your beauty is some great revelation," Ponsby said in an amused voice.

"Mr. Ponsby!" Vivian fluttered her lashes at him. "Perhaps you play the wrong role."

"Frederick is perfectly tongue-tied," Geoff said with a laugh. "And so is Marlow. It's up to you to inspire eloquence, Miss Hardcastle."

Frederick flushed, avoiding Vivian's arch study of him.

Margaret opened the door between the dining parlor and the drawing room, carefully drawing the curtain shut behind her. "We hear your chatter in the other room," she warned them in a whisper. "Are we almost ready to begin?"

"We're still a player short," Castleton said.

"Here I am," Portia exclaimed from behind him.

He turned. *She was born in the wrong era*, he thought, glancing around at the astonished delight in all their faces as they gazed at Portia's splendor.

The green and white brocade gown nipped neatly at her tiny waist, while the hooped skirt's flare totally concealed the broadness of her hips. The high wig, along with the subtle application of a pink to her cheeks, made her face appear more oval. A heart-shaped patch nestled in the hollow of her cheek gave the illusion of a dimple; her well-formed mouth seemed most provocative in consequence. She wore a diamond collar borrowed from his late aunt's coffers for the occasion, and glittering jewels hung from her ears.

She snapped her ivory fan open, cooling herself with rapid, energetic strokes.

"Madame," Castleton said, bowing to her as he had the young ladies. "You are truly a vision."

"La, sir," Portia replied, her eyes dancing. "You shall put me to blush."

"I think we are ready now," Castleton told Margaret. She nodded and returned to the drawing room, where she loudly announced the performance was about to begin.

Castleton drew Portia's hand in his own and squeezed it.

"Nervous?" he whispered.

"Surprisingly, no," she replied, giving him a warm smile. The tiny heart set in the corner of her lips stirred him to the core. He smiled back and led her through the curtain to the drawing room where their little audience awaited.

The play went off with only a few minor mishaps. Vane got caught in the curtain on his first entrance because he gazed too intently on the play book. Vivian had trouble donning the wig again and missed a cue, but Castleton covered for her with an impromptu monologue that would have had Mr. Goldsmith laughing.

Ponsby was astonishingly good. Portia had given him one instruction that enabled him to treat Sarah with the right mixture of horrified disdain blended with friendly affection. "Pretend she is your sister Jane." When the performance was over all agreed he had stolen the show, although Portia had come a close second when she fell to her knees to beg Castleton, mistaken for a highwayman, to spare her mischief-making son.

While she'd waited for her cue, she'd removed the diamond collar and tipped her wig to one side. With outflung hands and martyrish demeanor, she drew such a shout of laughter from their audience Castleton had trouble keeping his expression sober.

They received a resounding ovation, and two curtain calls from the Ballingers, the Wallaces, and Margaret. Alvenia even applauded with enthusiasm at the performance's immediate conclusion. She was less enthralled when Castleton led Portia over to chat with the Wallaces, while the children and Wilkes rushed upstairs to change.

"She's still upset with me," Portia murmured when she at last withdrew on Castleton's arm.

"Alvenia has never been one to forgive or forget, I'm afraid. Can you bear it?"

"For two more days?" She laughed. "It shall be difficult, but I will try."

"I was thinking of the future," he remarked.

Portia stopped. She looked at him.

God, he hoped, *let Geoff be right*. "I thought, perhaps, you might like to stay here this summer. Your aunt, too, of course."

"Oh," Portia's eyes softened. "It's very hard to refuse you, but I fear I must. There is too little society for Aunt here, and even could I win over Mrs. Wilkes, she's abominable at cards."

"I'd forgotten cards were part of the bargain," he said. "But you must promise me you will come back here some day."

Portia nodded. Her loose wig tipped down her forehead in consequence, and they both laughed.

"Let me," Castleton said, dragging the wig free and extracting what pins still held it to the falling strands of light brown hair. She shook her head to let the rest of the pins fly, and her hair tumbled down. She reached out for the wig, but Castleton shook his head and set it on a table behind them.

"Someone will take care of it," he assured her.

"Thank you," she said, the patch setting off her grateful smile. In a gown that enhanced her figure, with her hair hanging down and such a smile, he could honestly term her ravishing.

"A husband's duty," Castleton responded. "It's a pity I cannot reap a husband's reward."

Her eyes darkened. She stepped toward him, put her hands on his shoulders, and lightly brushed her lips across his. It was all she intended. She was pulling back again before his shock had time to register.

He could not let her withdraw after she'd finally approached him. He placed his arm around her waist and drew her tightly to him. His mouth covered hers, drawing deeply on its sweetness. Portia curled her arm around his neck, stroking up through his own wig to clutch at the nape. Her lips parted.

Sensation washed over him like a dam breaking. He drowned himself in kisses, tasting her, teasing her ... and her uninhibited response robbed him of all control. It took a little mew of discomfort to bring him back to reality.

He'd pinned her tight against the table, his thigh lodged betwixt her legs, cushioned by her heavy skirts. Castleton stepped back, breathless. Portia gripped the table hard, her breasts rising and falling with panting breaths. Her eyes glowed.

"We'd best retire, ma'am," he said, "before curiosity gets the better of us."

Portia nodded, but still clung to the furniture. She wasn't sure she could stand upright. Or walk. She'd unleashed something that had totally overwhelmed her. It was he who bowed and withdrew, retreating to his chamber at a near dash.

She took two steps after him, before she realized her own room was in the other direction. She was so befuddled she couldn't even think straight. This was more than flirtation. This seemed like. . . .

"You shameless, brazen. . . ." a voice hissed beyond her. Alvenia glared at her from the other end of the corridor. "How dare you pursue your illicit relations in so public a manner. There are innocents on the premises."

"It wasn't what it appeared," Portia stammered, feeling a flush like no other suffuse her.

"Don't play the virgin with me, ma'am," Alvenia sniffed. "If I weren't already aware that you are Castleton's mistress. . . ."

"Excuse me?!"

"That embrace left no room for doubt," Alvenia continued. "No man would kiss a woman he had honorable feelings for in that fashion. Shame on you, Miss Kirby."

Alvenia continued down the corridor to rap on the door of Sarah's room, where her niece quickly admitted her. Portia stumbled to her own room, with those censorious words ringing in her ears.

14

BOTH MRS. ADAMS and Lydia waited to assist Portia in the removal of her gown. She stood quietly as they unfastened and unhooked hoops, skirts, and petticoats.

"There's but an hour before supper, Miss," Lydia exclaimed. "Would you like to dress now?"

"No." Portia drew her wrapper tight about her. "After the excitement of the afternoon, I'm feeling ... queer."

"A rest will do you good then," Mrs. Adams declared as she took Lydia by the arm. "We will see you are not disturbed."

"Thank you, Mrs. Adams."

Portia sank down in the chair before her dressing table, staring in the looking glass. She plucked the patch from her mouth with a trembling hand. His mistress. She thought Portia was his mistress.

"That wouldn't be so very bad, would it?" she whispered to the owl-eyed stranger before her. When she was not struck dead for such a wicked thought, Portia allowed herself to dwell on it. Her ruin began pleasantly enough. His passionate kiss repeated and expanded. The press of him against her. Unclothed. No, even that enthralled. Yes, she could do it. She could give herself to him and be content. . . .

Until he tired of her.

He would tire of her some day, she thought staring at her image. She had nothing to hold him beyond the power to amuse. She did not discount that one desirable attribute, but how long could its allure last? A month? A year? What would become of her when he moved on to other lovers? Or took a wife?

The inevitable wife particularly pained her. Marriage would put a period to their friendship whether she lay with him or not. Not necessarily because Castleton would want it, but because she could not bear the thought of standing by while another woman assumed the role she suddenly realized she desired herself.

"You have dreamed too far," she told the woman in the mirror. "And now it's time to wake up."

She did not go down to supper. When Margaret came to check on her, she feigned sleep, which never did come as the night progressed. Pale and shadow-eyed, she knew she looked ill when she came down to breakfast and claimed a fear of sickness coming on. She begged a place in the Wallaces' carriage back to Town when they declared their intention to depart at noon.

"You should return to your room and rest," Castleton said with halting concern. "We can delay our return journey until you are recovered."

She could not meet his eye. "I think it best I go," she whispered. "I know I'll feel better when I am home again."

What could Castleton do? Obviously, that kiss had been too much. Its intensity had nearly over-powered *him,* and he had some experience in these matters. So while his niece and Vivian cajoled, and Margaret weighted Portia's departure in her present state with nervous foreboding, he insisted Portia must do what she thought best.

After a perfunctory leave-taking he watched Ponsby hand Portia into the Wallaces' coach from the top of the portico. He stared down the tree-lined drive long after she'd departed and the others filed back into the house.

He did not realize Mrs. Adams was standing beside him until she cleared her throat to gain his attention.

"It was Mrs. Wilkes," she said.

Castleton frowned at her.

"She witnessed your embrace and remarked on it to Miss Kirby. I couldn't discern the words, but her tone was particularly venomous."

"And you know this because. . . ?"

"I saw you kiss her, too," Mrs. Adams responded in a placid voice. "What's more, I saw Miss Kirby's face directly after you left her. She was discomposed, but not unpleasantly so. Not until Mrs. Wilkes spoke to her."

"I see," Castleton replied. "Thank you, Mrs. Adams."

The housekeeper nodded to him, her dark eyes shining with encouragement before she stepped back indoors.

God bless you, he thought, breathing a little easier. He didn't bother to confirm the story. Alvenia was perfectly capable of inflicting cutting wounds with her barbed tongue. And Portia tended to withdraw when she felt cornered.

On their return to Town, Portia remained elusive. She kindly received a call from Margaret and the girls, but would not commit to one engagement for the forthcoming week, declaring she was still pulled from her journey home. She no longer came to the park, Ponsby reported, although she also received him, informing him she'd been far too busy to indulge herself in a morning walk.

Lucy came to Curzon Street demanding to know exactly what Castleton had done. She'd sent two invitations to Miss Kirby to further their acquaintance and had received only polite notes declining the honor in response.

"I'll have a devil of a time flushing her out," Castleton said, after explaining the whole to the duchess.

"That odious woman," Lucy declared. "To speak disparagingly to Miss Kirby after I made your feelings plain to her."

"Obviously Alvenia has decided, in her typically high-handed manner, that we do not suit, and convinced Portia of the same."

"Then you must convince Portia otherwise."

"Impossible without some form of contact. I think it's time to resort to desperate measures."

"Will you storm the citadel and carry her off to Gretna Green?" Lucy asked with a sparkling eye.

Castleton shook his head, eyes twinkling. "My plan is far more insidious."

AFTER READING THE same page twice without comprehending a word, Portia cast her novel aside and rested her head on the window pane of the sitting room. Sunshine and brisk foot traffic beckoned to her, but she resisted their enticement.

She had no idea where Castleton lay in wait for her. Any activity would be reported back by his myriad friends who had thus far tried to draw her from her aunt's house. As long as she remained here, she could keep him at bay.

He had not come himself. That disturbed her. But she did not mistake his neglect as disinterest. He would act eventually. That was his nature. She was marshaling her energies to resist whatever inducement he would offer.

And he must have known that too. So he did not cast his lure to her at all.

"A card party," Charlotte exclaimed, waving an invitation above her head. "A card party at Lord Castleton's home. The very thing to raise you from these doldrums."

"I'm not sure I can go," Portia replied, her face warming as she read Castleton's charming note.

The cad. Amidst his flowery words, his intent rang through. Though extended to her aunt, Mrs. Andrews' invitation was dependent on Portia's accompanying her.

"Of course you can go," Charlotte said, frowning. "You've declined every other invitation we've received for the next fortnight. Lord Castleton is right. 'A quiet evening of cards and conversation' is just the thing to ease you back into a more social routine."

"Perhaps I've grown away from social routine. I have not visited James and Maria in some time...."

"What utter nonsense! Look me in the eye and tell me you would prefer Maria's company over Lord Castleton's."

Despite the knowledge that a withdrawal from Town was the only safe course of action, Portia could not do it.

Charlotte's lined features softened. "Have you quarreled with him, Portia?"

"No."

"Then why are you avoiding him this way?"

"I ... I have made myself too familiar," she said lamely.

"Not in his estimation," Charlotte said, holding up the invitation again. "He has a care of you. The whole of London knows it. If you held some dislike of him I might rip this up, but I know that is not the case.

"I happen to think his friendship has been good for you. And for me, in consequence. I've already accepted this. Flee to Surrey, if you must. But if you go, don't bother to return. You cannot evade the man forever, and I refuse to share your exile."

Charlotte turned on her heel and quit the room, leaving Portia feeling shaken to the core.

SARAH WOULD NOT have approached George Mahew again if she hadn't witnessed his intense conversation with Miss Kirby as Arthur Ponsby drove her through Hyde Park that morning.

"In a week, I'll give Bright Promise a try with his partner," Ponsby was saying, as they sped past the couple on the bench.

Sarah could have brought Portia and Mahew to his attention—now that Ponsby was privy to the particulars of her friendship, he might oblige her by stopping as long as Portia sat beside her cousin. But Portia was the topic Sarah wished to discuss, and admittedly, one last private conversation to explain why they must not meet again seemed appropriate.

So, Sarah said nothing. Or rather, she remembered a promised outing with Vivian. Ponsby dropped her at her doorstep a quarter-hour later. Sarah didn't even enter the house. She walked all the way back to the park as fast as her feet would carry her.

She arrived at the spot she'd seen Mahew in time to observe Portia's departure through the gate. Sarah scurried through the park, looking in all directions. Fortunately, Mahew was walking very slowly, his broad shoulders less upright than normal as he thoughtfully ambled a secluded walk.

"Mr. Mahew!" Sarah called out.

Mahew's head snapped around instantly, and his green eyes rolled in exasperation. "Miss Christopher," he said. "I thought you'd learned your lesson. . . ." He looked around them, frowning. "Who are you here with?"

"No one. I just wanted. . . ."

"Not even a maid?! Have you taken leave of your senses?"

"Oh, for heaven's sake!" Sarah rolled her own eyes. "I know I have naught to fear from you, sir."

"Do you think young girls are counseled on the dangers of venturing out unescorted to ward me off exclusively?" Mahew said in an angry voice. "When I think of the tongues that cannot wait to report some indiscretion on either of our parts. . . ."

He took her arm and started back down the path at a clip. "Portia was just here. If we're quick, perhaps we can catch her."

"No." Sarah dug her heels in. "I wish to speak to you about Miss Kirby. What happened? She isn't ill. I know she isn't. Did we do something to offend her?"

Mahew's green eyes softened. "Portia is quite well," he said. "A little agitated. Your uncle has maneuvered her into a social engagement."

"He did?" Sarah nearly crumpled in relief. "I was afraid he'd given up."

Mahew's dimples flashed. "Then a match between them would meet with your approval."

"Oh, yes," Sarah said, falling into step beside him. "I like her ever so much. Though I confess, I had no idea what was in the wind until Mr. Ponsby informed me."

"Ponsby?"

"I know. I've underestimated him greatly, despite what you said. Congratulations. You can expect to win your bet some time next week. And I think I should tell you, he knows all about us."

"Us?" Mahew's brow raised in horror.

"About me bothering you," Sarah corrected. "Vivian knows now, too. They both think it was very wrong of me. . . ."

"I believe I was the first to tell you that."

"Yes, you did." Sarah said. Tears shimmered in her eyes. "And still you have been so kind. . . ."

"Sarah. . . ."

"That's why I had to speak to you one more time. To thank you for your friendship. Although I'm sure my trials seemed silly to you, you've helped me through great difficulty."

"And you helped me, as well," Mahew admitted.

They smiled at each other, Sarah through a veil of tears. Mahew gently brushed one from her cheek with his gloved hand.

"Now," he said. "How to see you home safely with no one observing us. . . ."

"It's still early. I'm sure I can make the walk unobserved."

"What if I followed you at a discreet distance?" Mahew suggested. "Just to ease my mind?"

Sarah nodded in agreement. She started down the path alone, certain in the knowledge that he was looking out for her.

ARTHUR PONSBY NO longer dreaded crossing White's threshold, wondering if anyone would speak to him. He was hailed several times enroute to his luncheon engagement with Lord Sefton.

Sefton was with two other gentlemen, one of whom was George Mahew. Their manner suggested something confrontational. Ponsby slowed his pace and frowned.

"Do you think I've sunk so low as to stalk young girls like jungle prey?" Mahew said in nettled tones.

"Then why were you on Curzon Street?" the unfamiliar gentleman insisted.

"I was traveling from one end of it to the other," Mahew said. "The same as you, I suspect."

"What's going on?" Ponsby asked Sefton in a low voice.

"Preston believes he saw Mahew following Miss Christopher," Sefton replied. "She was outside her residence and turned toward the street. Mahew tipped his hat to her as he passed by."

"Miss Christopher took a drive in the park with me this morning," Ponsby said in a louder voice than he'd intended. Both gentlemen turned, and Mahew bestowed a relieved smile on him.

"I left her at her door," Ponsby continued. "She might have lingered in the drive a while." The idea

Sarah might have waited to see him off filled him with elation.

"There you go, Preston," Mahew said, straightening his already perfectly fitting jacket. "Mystery solved."

Mahew clapped Ponsby on the shoulder and said, "Good luck uniting your team next week," before he passed out the doorway.

"Are you ready for a trial, then?" Sefton asked as he led Ponsby to a private dining parlor.

Ponsby nodded woodenly, his heart plummeting. He'd told only one person about the projected try out. Unless Mahew had some gift of second sight, his contact with Sarah had been more than a tip of the hat.

MARGARET HAPPILY TOLD anyone who would listen that she found the arrangement of the card party almost relaxing.

"Such a simple affair," Margaret declared to Charlotte Andrews as she greeted her on the threshold of their drawing room. "I don't know why we don't hold them more often. And I confess," she said with a wan smile in Portia's direction, "after the stresses of seeing Sarah launched, an evening for my own amusement will be a relief."

"Don't the young people attend?" Portia looked around at the twenty or so guests, assiduously avoiding Castleton's position beside the Duke of Wallace at one of the five tables set up for players.

"I left Sarah in Frederick's hands," Margaret reported. "I think they intended to visit Astley's or some such place."

"Mrs. Andrews," Castleton spoke in a delighted tone as he bowed over the widow's mittened hand. "How good of you to join us." His blue eyes twinkled into Portia's as he offhandedly greeted her, as well. He drew Charlotte's arm through his own and guided her into the company.

"I've set up what I hope will be an interesting match for you," he whispered. "Have you ever crossed swords with Marcus Stavely?"

"No," Charlotte exclaimed in delight.

"I've partnered him with Mrs. Herbst," Castleton said. "They're both shrewd players but I suspect will be at odds with each other in their attempts to score more tricks. And since you've arrived a little late. . . ."

"That was Portia's fault. I've never known her to dawdle so."

Castleton glanced around at Portia. She'd hung back, her lower lip jutting in a disapproval. She'd worn her Quaker clothes—the silver silk dress, her hair drawn back in a severe knot. Her eyes were particularly reproachful. Castleton had to grin. She knew him so well.

"I'm giving you Margaret for a partner," Castleton continued, drawing Charlotte up short. "Don't let her fluttery manner deceive you. She's an astute player of unparalleled concentration. She remembers every card that has been played and knows how to capitalize on it."

"Really?" Charlotte beamed at Margaret as they took their places at table.

Mrs. Stavely and Mr. Herbst, as spouses of serious card players, had already engaged themselves in a frivolous game of piquet. Portia took a seat in the far corner, her intention not to play any game of Castleton's choosing plainly writ in her face and manner. It was as good a time as any to approach her.

"Are cards not to your liking this evening, Miss Kirby?" he asked.

Her hazel eyes raked him contemptuously for a moment, then stared beyond and through him.

He sat beside her. "After the weeks of rest you've had, I confess, I thought you would be fully recovered from the excitement of our last encounter," he continued.

Portia gasped. "You are the most devious and unprincipled. . . ." she whispered hotly.

"And your point, ma'am?"

"You cannot deny you used my aunt's particular weakness to draw us here!"

"No, I can't," he replied. "Just as you cannot deny you are deliberately avoiding my society. I had to do something if I ever wished to see you again, didn't I?"

Portia's eyes dropped to her lap.

"I know what passed between us . . . was . . . agitating," Castleton remarked. "But I did not think you so ungenerous as to allow me no chance to defend my behavior."

"Then you are sorry for what happened?" Portia asked in a stilted voice.

"Actually . . . no," he said. Portia lifted her face to stare at him. "I'm not sorry in the least. Are you?"

Portia's jaw dropped open. Without a word she rose and rushed out the drawing room door. Castleton took one look around to ascertain all were fully engaged in their cards. They were, except for Lucy, who insistently waved him toward the door with her gloved hand.

Castleton quit the room. Footsteps sounded on the staircase, but no door opened below stairs. He glanced over the balustrade in time to see Portia disappear through the cracked study door.

The room was lit only by the smoldering coals in the grate. It took a moment to discern her form among the shadows. His ears were better tuned to the muffled sobs of her weeping.

He latched onto her shoulder, drawing her back to him with firm insistence when she tried to pull away. Just as suddenly, she surrendered. She fell on his chest, allowing him to wrap her in a comforting embrace as she let loose a tempest of tears.

"Shhh," he soothed. "I will press you no more. I promise."

She raised her face, her nose grazing lightly along the curve of his cravat. Echoes of embers danced on the surface of her eyes. He brushed the trail of tears from one full cheek. She leaned into the pressure, fitting herself into his palm.

A passion to secure her grew so strong he could not contain it. "Portia."

She pulled his face down to hers and kissed him full on the mouth. One kiss led to another, and then a countless bounty. Had he not just sworn to control himself, he could have made her irrevocably his right there, her response was so unmistakenly reciprocal.

As it was, he could not stop his hands from wandering her curves—stroking her hips, grasping her waist. When her open mouth not only received his tongue but her own twined past it to tease at his palate, his senses overloaded.

His fingers circled around a breast that hardened despite the silk and lace and supportive stays that protected it from his touch. His thumb dallied on the nubbin beneath the cloth. Portia gasped and tossed her head back, arching her body toward him. He trailed soft kisses down her neck, angling toward the hint of cleft between the rounded globes.

"Castleton?"

They sprang apart at Margaret's uncertain call from abovestairs. Portia covered her swollen mouth with her hand and turned away from him.

He gripped her shoulders. "This is neither the time nor place to ... discuss this," he whispered, pressing a soft kiss to her temple. "Why don't I call on you tomorrow?"

"Castleton?" Margaret was closer now. There was no time to wait for Portia's response. If they were discovered together, she would be profoundly embarrassed. She needed time to compose herself. He released her and strode toward the study door.

"I'll tell her you're resting. Join us when you feel up to it."

Then he withdrew, and Portia's breath returned. She sank down into the nearest chair and shut her eyes, praying as she had never prayed before. "Dear God," she whispered. "Give me the strength to resist him. I swear to you, I cannot do it alone."

It was easier to gain a private word with Vivian Barstow than Ponsby expected. Sarah and Frederick argued about the care and feeding of bears and rushed off to see who was actually correct by inquiring of the poor fellow's keeper.

"Did you have a pleasant time on your excursion yesterday?" he asked.

Vivian blinked. "I don't know what you mean," she said.

Ponsby sighed. "I didn't think you would." He glanced at Sarah, now united with her brother in total absorption as the keeper regaled them with his knowledge of wild beasts. "She met with George Mahew again."

"She wouldn't!" Vivian declared, but sobered as he quickly laid his evidence before her.

"This is all his doing," Vivian declared. "It has to be. He must have designs on her. We must tell Lord Castleton."

Ponsby shook his head. "I am loath to cause dissension if it's not warranted. Mahew is Miss Kirby's cousin."

"All the more reason, sir. If Lord Castleton weds Miss Kirby, Mahew will likely gain unobstructed access to Sarah. He's a man who lives off the largess of the women he charms, and Sarah is a considerable heiress."

Ponsby continued to shake his head. Reputation or not, he had a hard time believing Mahew would use Sarah so badly. He'd sensed nothing calculated in Mahew's behavior in any encounter he'd witnessed. On the contrary, they'd shared a mutual easiness Ponsby feared he'd never be able to achieve.

He proposed an alternate plan. "If we tell Miss Kirby, she can speak to her cousin without the ugliness that might erupt if Lord Castleton were to confront him. And should she think your concern warranted, she may be in a better position to safeguard Sarah than either of us."

"Yes. That will work better. Shall you do it or shall I?"

"I will," Ponsby said.

"What are you discussing with heads together?" Sarah asked from above them. They sprang apart, making Sarah laugh.

"You aren't flirting with Vivian, are you, Mr. Ponsby?" she teased.

"No!" he exclaimed, though a guilty flush suffused his face all the same.

"Of course not!" Vivian declared at the same time.

Frederick glanced from one to the other of them with a disturbed frown on his face.

Ponsby shifted away from Miss Barstow and fixed a smile on his face. "So," he asked. "Which of you was correct?"

"Oh, Frederick," Sarah said dismissively as she took the seat beside Vivian. "That's why I had to disturb his peace by pointing out how famously the pair of you get on."

15

THIS TIME CASTLETON did not curb his impatience. Armed with a dozen roses, he was off to Leicester Square at the earliest opportunity. He had considered making arrangements for a special license as he waited for his valet to tie his neckcloth. But as much as he would like to have Portia safely wed before the week—or day—was done, he thought a large wedding at St. George's would suit the situation better. He wanted the world to know he was proud to have secured her as his wife.

He would take particular delight in sending the Wilkeses an invitation. And watching Alvenia try to worm her way into Lady Castleton's good graces.

The bald butler opened the door for him as before. Portia was waiting for him in the sitting room. Her eyes were heavily shadowed. Castleton knew how she felt. His night had been sleepless as well. He held his arms out to her, but she did not fly to him as he expected.

She turned away.

Castleton tossed his roses on the chair by the fireplace and touched her lightly on her shoulder.

She slipped from beneath his hand. Not in any violent way, but certainly determined.

"What is this? I thought all was well between us."

"Lord Castleton...." she began in a voice barely above a whisper.

"David," he corrected. "Call me David...."

"Lord Castleton," she began again, as if he hadn't spoken. "I must apologize to you for my untoward behavior. I can well understand how you might think, however erroneously...."

"Portia," he seized her by the shoulders, "what are you going on about?"

"I thought ... I thought I could, because you wished it." Her eyes rose to his, anguished but resolved. "But despite a genuine regard for you, I cannot ... it just would not be right to...."

His throat tightened to the point of near strangulation. "Are you saying," he managed, "that you will not be mine?"

"I'm so very sorry," she said as she nodded. "Please do not be...."

He had to get away. Before he howled or hit something. He barely registered the last word as he strode out the door.

"... angry."

Portia collapsed onto the nearest chair, crushing the heads of the roses Castleton had so hastily discarded. She threw them on the floor. How could she bear it? He was lost to her forever. No more smiles. No more shared laughter. Her heart ached as if she'd ripped it from her chest and cast it into the fires of Hell.

"But it was the right thing to do," she told herself.

She had never despised her conscience so much.

CASTLETON WALKED AT the pace of a forced march, letting the growing heaviness of his lungs explain the vise-like squeezing in his chest. My god, she had *played* him.

"I thought I could, because you wished it. . . ."

She must have known his heart all along. Where had she decided to dissemble and hope some tender feeling would blossom in her own? At Welton, of course. All that ground he thought he'd gained was only Portia playacting—making herself into what he wished. In a way, it served him right. He'd done it himself a dozen times over—but never to someone he truly cared about.

He slowed, breathing in great gulping sobs of air. He thought of those kisses, so seemingly full of passion on both their parts. The idea she had only submitted herself like some puppet dancing to his tune fair to sickened him.

But he could not credit her with any malice of motive. Had she wanted to destroy him utterly she could have confessed her lack of desire after they were wed. With some inkling of what married life would entail, she'd wisely understood how repugnant intimacies would be without real emotion to sustain them. In the end, her honest nature had prevailed. She could not be what he wanted in her own heart.

How heartbreaking that, even in rejection, she was still exactly what he wanted in his.

CASTLETON'S TURBULENT RETURN to his house was witnessed by more than just his own family and servants. By afternoon it was generally known his suit was past tense, though most gossips doubted it had gone as far as a declaration. No woman in Miss Kirby's position could be so foolish as to refuse a man of such high ton. The prevailing suspicion was that she had done something that had given Castleton a disgust of her.

"She is related to George Mahew, after all," Mrs. Trent told Mrs. Cray. "Perhaps some secret of her past has come to light...."

"Perhaps some secret *involving* her cousin," Mrs Cray mused.

"You are most likely right," Mrs. Trent replied. "It's said he is the only visitor she's admitted to her home."

What the gossips did not realize was that George Mahew had forced his way into Mrs. Andrews's residence. Not that he got any farther with Portia than friends turned away at the door. She was stubbornly silent on the reason for the break.

"They are saying you refused him," George declared.

Portia's laugh was brittle. "Their imaginations must be taxed to the extreme. Lord Castleton made me no offer."

"Then what happened?"

"We have decided our friendship can no longer continue. Just in time, judging by the wagging tongues."

"Portia...."

"No more, George. I beg you."

Castleton would brook no conversation on the matter, either. His affable manner was transformed to something steely and cold overnight. Even good friends like the Wallaces were warned to keep their distance. By the second day it was decided the truth would never really be known. Just as quickly as it had been added, Portia's name was struck from guest lists all over London.

That same day the rains came, as if the heavens had decided to match Portia tear for tear as they poured forth grey misery. Portia ventured out in the deluge only once—to procure a dozen caps. When she appeared at table wearing one, her aunt shook her head but made no comment.

Rain fell for four days, the weather finally breaking on a brisk grey morning that better resembled November than June.

A summons from the butler directing Portia's attention out to the street brought her out her door at last. The ghost of a smile touched her lips at the prospect of Arthur Ponsby clutching the reins of a perfectly matched pair of bays hitched to a gleaming curricle. He released his grip long enough to doff his hat to her when she emerged from the house for a better look.

"I am bound for the park," he said. "I could not fathom the journey without you somewhere nearby. Won't you accompany me?"

"Are you sure it's safe?" she asked, crossing her arms before her as the wild west wind tore at her gown.

"It is safe."

"Give me a moment to change, then."

"MAKE SURE YOU'VE got a good hold of the lead line, sir," Stubbins instructed, as he once again checked Frederick's hold on the reins of the chestnut pair. Frederick tightened his grip accordingly, and the horses pawed the graveled drive impatiently. The head groom's plain face sobered, but Frederick made another adjustment of his hands and the pair quieted.

"Are you sure you wouldn't like me to drive you out in the landau?" Stubbins asked. "Then your lordship could go, too."

"Everything will be just fine," Castleton said as he handed Sarah up into the curricle beside her brother. "Remember, both Frederick and the horses have been trained by the same hand."

It was the first light remark Sarah had heard him utter in near a week. She smiled and squeezed his hand. "You should come, sir," she said.

"I won't cast a shadow on Ponsby's triumph," Castleton replied, taming his windswept hair. "Have him drive you home for a private viewing of this magnificent new pair. I'm sure Stubbins would like that, too."

Stubbins stammered an affirmative reply to this suggestion.

Frederick flicked the reins, and the curricle lurched into motion. Sarah clutched at her tightly tied bonnet. Driving with Frederick was not like driving with Ponsby. He constantly moved his hands about; she wondered how the horses knew which way to turn. But as they entered the park, he maneuvered them into the increasing traffic with little difficulty.

"Is it my imagination, or are far more people here than normal?" Sarah asked, as they passed four carriages and a group of Corinthians on horseback.

"More than I am used to," Frederick confessed as he concentrated on his driving. When safely positioned on the road, he hazarded a look around. His blue eyes widened, and a grin of pleasure lit his face. "Sarah, they've come out to *see*...."

"To see the team?!" Sarah looked around. Numerous sporting gentlemen rode or drove about. Lord Sefton was present along with other members of the Four-In-Hand Club. Traffic increased with each circuit of the park. Ladies were being driven around, or were riding with their grooms. Not quite as many people as the typical afternoon, but enough to mark this an occasion.

"Oh, there's Vivian!" Sarah exclaimed. Frederick steered toward Miss Barstow, and drew to a halt.

Vivian cocked her head charmingly as she waved her maid forward. "I thought we would never arrive the way Constance walks," she complained. "I doubt you'll wish to alight and join me." She eyed the chestnuts enviously.

"Not to join you. But I'll trade places with you." Sarah gripped the side of the curricle and hopped down. "Frederick isn't half bad at this...."

"Really?" Vivian smiled up at Frederick. He shyly smiled back and offered his hand to her, leaving Sarah with the dawdling Constance. Sarah watched them drive away, thinking how wonderful it would be if they married.

And then she thought about her uncle. As much as a match with Miss Kirby would have been wonderful, the loss of her had changed him in a frightening way. No being should hold that much power over another's happiness. Maybe a lack of lovers did have its better points. She was genuinely glad no one in her life could tangle her heart that way.

"Gad, Mahew," a nearby rider called out, "I haven't seen a monstrosity like that since I was in leading strings." Sarah turned around to see George Mahew perched on the highest phaeton she'd ever seen in her life.

"Mock me if you must," Mahew said. "But I have an unobstructed view of the park from this vantage, and, ten to one, I could outrace any carriage here."

"I'll take that challenge someday soon," the rider said. Mahew flashed his dimpled smile. It broaden when he noticed Sarah.

The rider moved off, and Sarah glanced around. No one paid any particular attention to her, and the carriage was odd enough that curiosity seemed only natural. She stepped toward Mahew, and he reined his team in.

"It's quite splendid," she remarked.

"Isn't it?" he replied.

Sarah stepped a little closer. "Mr. Mahew, do you know what happened?" she asked quickly.

Mahew shook his head. "Has your uncle told you anything?" he asked, in turn.

"No, but I will never forget his face when he returned home that morning." She shuddered. "Your cousin's refusal shattered him."

"He never asked her."

"What do you mean? Of course, he asked. He told my mother his intention before he left the house."

"Portia said he didn't," Mahew repeated. "And she looked as if I'd sprouted wings at the suggestion that he had."

"No, no, no," Sarah said vehemently.

Mahew's horses skittered at her tone.

"My horse grows impatient," Mahew said, as he tightened his grip to still them. "I cannot stand here to discuss the matter with you, ma'am."

Sarah set her jaw and gripped at the large yellow wheel looming before her. Mahew gaped as she nimbly settled herself in the seat beside him.

"What on earth!" he exclaimed.

"If you cannot stand, we can ride about and discuss it."

"My god, are you so intent on your own ruin?" he whispered.

Just then, Melinda Trent and her mother rolled past in a barouche, mouths agape. And others stared. Mahew's old-fashioned equipage might have drawn notice otherwise, but the whispering was clearly about the pair of them.

"I'm sorry," Sarah said. "I didn't think. . . ."

"Do you ever?" Mahew flicked his whip and the phaeton glided into motion.

Sarah clutched the seat as he urged his team to greater velocity. She briefly registered Frederick's and Vivian's shocked faces in the traffic moving the opposite direction.

"I don't suppose I could prevail upon you to scream," Mahew asked as he whipped the horses to an uncomfortably high speed.

"Why would I want to do that?"

"It's what gently bred young ladies usually do when they realize a rake is running off with them," Mahew replied.

Sarah didn't scream, only stared at him, white-faced, as he steered them out of the park gate.

THEY WERE HALFWAY to the park before Ponsby attempted to discuss Sarah.

Portia rubbed her brow. "Arthur, I have an

inkling of your feelings for Sarah, but I cannot deal with tales of her at present. . . ."

"She has placed herself in potential jeopardy."

"Then you should inform her uncle. She is his concern."

"Forgive me, Miss Kirby, but I don't think you would wish me to relate these particulars to Lord Castleton. . . ."

"Why ever not?" Portia said as they reached the park gate.

A tall carriage sped past. George raised his hat, while Sarah, sitting beside him, clutched her bonnet and stared at George with her mouth hanging open. They disappeared from view.

"Oh," Portia murmured.

Momentum took Ponsby's curricle through the gate. Portia faintly registered Vivian Barstow's voice calling, "Hurry, hurry. We must go faster!" as the backs of carriages dangerously approached. Ponsby threaded his team through the traffic on the path, then negotiated a particularly tight turn to head them back toward the gate.

They overtook Frederick Christopher urging Castleton's chestnuts to a speed he was clearly unable to control, while Vivian Barstow clutched at his arm.

"He's getting away!" Vivian shrieked in a clear voice for anyone to hear. "Go faster or we will lose him!"

"I can't," Frederick said. He motioned Ponsby past. "Go," he yelled. "You have the better chance!"

"Find your uncle," Ponsby called back, checking his speed to match Frederick's. "Miss Barstow can explain the whole...."

"You are wasting time!" Vivian said, trying to shoo Ponsby forward. "We won't know where they go if you lose sight of him."

"If he hopes to make anything honorable of this, there's only one direction he can go," Ponsby replied grimly.

"No!" Portia exclaimed. "You are mistaken."

"Hold tight, ma'am," was Ponsby's only reply as he made the turn out the gate, taking the road north. Portia glanced back to watch Frederick and Vivian continue forward. Toward Curzon Street and Castleton.

Oh, my God, she thought. *He will kill George.*

"Talk to me, Arthur," she said, trying to fix it in her mind but failing miserably. "Tell me the whole."

"MR. MAHEW," SARAH gasped. "Please let me down."

Mahew checked the straightness of the course ahead of him before hazarding a glance over his shoulder. "I don't see them yet. We shall have a good lead, depending on how fast Ponsby turns that carriage around."

"If you don't let me down, I ... I will jump into the road!"

One hand came off the reins to grip at hers.

"Don't," he said. "At this speed you will surely kill yourself and me, in consequence.

Panic rose in Sarah's throat. "Oh, please, sir," she begged. "You are frightening me...."

"This will teach you to act without thinking, won't it?" he said. He glanced over his shoulder again, and a broad grin lit his handsome face. "By all that's marvelous, there he is already."

Sarah glanced back too, and saw Ponsby's curricle. It seemed to draw closer but was still too far away to tell with certainty.

"Let's give him a real test before witnesses," Mahew said. "I'll need my winnings to set myself up on the Continent."

He steered them down a narrow street at a pace that had Sarah hunching her shoulders in the vain hope of slimming the carriage. Her relief on emerging onto a wider street quickly died as they nearly struck an apple cart, which overtipped behind them. They darted to and fro on the busy thorough-fare. A plodding horse, hitched to a heavy wagon, reared up in the road as they glided past it.

"Ha," Mahew exclaimed in jubilant voice as he glanced back at the chaos he'd wrought. "That should gain us another mile...."

"You act as if this were some game," Sarah said.

"Of course it's a game. Individually, Ponsby's horses are better than mine, but are untried as a team. My team is seasoned. He's the better driver, but I have the advantage of the faster carriage. We may make it out of London before he catches me."

"If you expect him to catch you, then why won't you stop?"

"Because if I did that now, everyone would know what this was, instead of what it appears to be," he replied.

"You're not really abducting me, are you?" Sarah asked.

"Of course I've abducted you," he replied, although he smiled in a way that made Sarah's heart light again. "You have asked me several times to let you down...."

"But you don't intend to carry me off to some remote lair to have your way with me."

"Are you sure about that?" he asked with an arching brow.

"Yes," Sarah said. "What are you about, Mr. Mahew?"

"YOU ARE WRONG," Portia insisted in as calm a voice as she could muster as they squeezed down the street they'd seen the phaeton turn into a few minutes ago. "George has no interest in Sarah. Not that way."

"I cannot discuss this with you at present, ma'am," Ponsby said, skirting a tipped cart of apples and making a turn onto the street beyond it.

Her breath caught in her throat as a draft horse, four hands taller than either of Ponsby's bays, danced in the road with a wagon dragging behind that blocked most of the road.

Ponsby transferred the reins to one hand. He latched Portia's shoulders and forcibly pushed her across his lap. "Hold on," he said in a too-calm voice as he drove them underneath those rearing hooves.

He instantly released his hold on her and his face turned a fiery red. "I'm sorry about that," he said.

"You should be," Portia retorted, straightening herself. "You're being reckless, Arthur."

"I should have told someone weeks ago. I was foolish to trust Sarah's judgment. And yours."

"If George had designs on Sarah, he would not secure her this way," Portia replied. "He's smarter than that."

"You present me with a credible explanation, and I will consider it," Ponsby returned. "In the meantime, I think it best to catch them as quickly as possible."

So Portia shut her eyes (it was easier to sit beside him with some composure if she did not watch him weave through the streets of London relying on a pair of bays that had never run together before) and thought about it. George would never pursue so young a girl. Even in his youth, his tastes had run toward experienced women. Besides, according to Ponsby, Sarah had pursued Mahew.

Perhaps he was acting on some suggestion of hers? No. Portia had seen Sarah's bewildered expression. She'd been shocked when George drove her out of the park.

He had to know someone would try to stop him.

Frederick. Castleton. Thoughts of what Castleton
would do if he ever caught George iced Portia's
insides.

If George expected pistols at dawn for rescuing
Sarah from the tree, surely he knew this would
provoke a challenge with certainty. Why risk Castleton's enmity? Not for the sake of possessing Sarah.
At the least, this escapade would banish him from
good society forever. He would not wish such a fate
on his worst enemy, let alone himself.

Or Sarah.

Portia sucked in her breath. Her eyes flew open.
They were on the Great North Road now, nearly out
of London's environs. There was less traffic here.
She could see George ahead, still too far to hail.
Sarah was twisted clear around in her seat, but her
posture seemed more relaxed than it should have
been under the circumstances. George also glanced
over his shoulder once, and flicked his whip with a
flourish to urge his horses to a greater speed. Ponsby
adjusted his own speed accordingly.

"Slow a while, Arthur," Portia said.

"Slow? I cannot. . . ."

"Indulge me but two minutes. Two minutes can
make little difference. Please. . . ."

Ponsby frowned at her. He drew back on the
reins. The left bay skittered in his harness, but Bright
Promise dropped to a trot obediently. After a touchy
moment, the other bay matched his gait to the geld-
ing's steady pace.

Portia counted softly to herself, eyes intent on

the carriage ahead as it sped farther and farther away. Ponsby clutched the reins tightly but not enough to disturb his horses.

George looked back over his shoulder again. And then, suddenly, the distance between them began to close.

"He reined them in," Ponsby exclaimed in confusion.

"He depends on you to catch them before we get too far."

"Why would he want that?"

"So you can take Sarah back. She must be seen in Town in a matter of hours or she'll be thoroughly ruined."

"If her ruin was not his aim, then why take this course of action?" Ponsby asked in an angry voice.

"Because this way, the fault is entirely his. He lured off a pretty heiress, but her friends and relations rescued her from his evil clutches. Who could blame an innocent girl for that?"

Ponsby turned to look her full in the face. "Are you saying he's doing this *for* Sarah?"

"How do you suppose he got her into his carriage?" Portia mused. "Dragged her all the way up there? Hard to do and control a team of horses in the bargain, wouldn't you say?"

Ponsby slowed his team further, puffing out a disgusted breath. Portia patted his arm, then clutched it hard.

"Oh, you have to stop!" she exclaimed, looking around.

"But he's turning eastward," Ponsby said, as he watched Mahew make a turn at the crossroads ahead.

"Toward Hackney," Portia replied. "A mutual uncle lives there. You can lose him now. I know where he's headed." She spied a boy in the adjacent fields and again urge Ponsby to stop.

"If we must return Sarah to Town, don't you think we should get on with it?" Ponsby asked.

"I know where he's headed," Portia repeated, as she alighted from the carriage. "But Lord Castleton doesn't. Best to calm his fears if we can, don't you think?"

"Best for Mahew, you mean," Ponsby grumbled, but waited patiently as Portia summoned the boy and spoke to him earnestly.

A MILE OUTSIDE of London, a boy jumped into the road, frantically waving his arms. Castleton was tempted to run him down. In the muddled explanations of Sarah's abduction, and Margaret's inevitable fit of hysteria, they'd wasted too much time already. But Frederick was driving and had the steadier temperament, at present. His nephew pulled the chestnuts to a halt, and the boy scampered up to them, studying Castleton with a critical eye.

"You be the baron?"

"I am Castleton."

"I gots a message for you." The boy screwed his face tight in an effort to make his words straight. "Pour-tea-a says you gotta take the road east."

"Did she?" Damn her. He couldn't believe she was in league with her cousin. But she must know George was a dead man in Castleton's mind. To save Mahew, she might seek to delay him.

The boy nodded earnestly.

"What happened to her?" Castleton asked.

"She and the ruddy man took the east turn. Bang up horses, though nothin' to compare to that high flyer the other 'un was driving."

"Did the high flyer take the east turn, too?"

"Surely did. Pour-tea-a, she said somethin' bout tryin' to guide you to Leahull Bridge, but said she'd leave you a sign or two instead. . . ."

"I'd rather have directions," Castleton replied, and the boy accommodated him with a rambling set of detailed instructions. Castleton flipped the boy a coin.

The child gazed at it, owl-eyed. "Lady done said you'd give me but half a crown!"

"The lady doesn't know me quite as well as she thinks, then," Castleton said, nodding to his nephew. Frederick took the turn toward Hackney, as Castleton fondled the pistol in his hand.

THE WIDE STREAM ran into the Lea about a half-mile ahead, Mahew told Sarah. "We don't know the purpose of the shack," he said as he reined his team in along the bank. "Most likely this was a toll bridge at one time, but I swear this road's seen no regular traffic for ages."

He jumped down from the carriage seat and then took the reins from Sarah. He tied his team to a half-rotted post before helping her down from the high seat.

Sarah looked around her with interest. The stream, swollen with rain water, pooled briefly at the bridge before rushing down its twisting course. Mahew led her to the bridge.

"This was our secret castle," he said, looking about with fondness. "We thought my cousin Ralph the luckiest devil for having such a splendid playground and a father who supported that aspect of his nature. Of the Mahew siblings, Uncle Doddy is something of a black sheep in that regard."

"Mr. Mahew, what will happen to us?"

"Nothing will happen to you, Sarah," he asserted. "Ponsby will drive you back to the park and ensure everyone sees you. They may whisper about you, at first. Wonder if I had enough time to ravish you. . . . But that will fade in time, I assure you."

"And you?"

"Ah. I'm afraid that's a different matter," he said. "I will be banned from most ton functions. They may overlook my pursuit of widows and wives. But the attempted seduction of the young niece of Lord Castleton is too gross an error to ignore."

"But you didn't seduce me. When I explain. . . ."

"You will be labeled 'fast' and ostracized," Mahew finished smoothly. "Do you truly intend to make my sacrifice for naught?"

Sarah gasped as the enormity of the whole

engulfed her. While she'd realized befriending him could have dire consequences, it never occurred to her he could lose anything in the process.

Slow tears trickled down her cheeks. "I'm sorry," she whispered.

Mahew sighed and offered her his handkerchief, but the kindness released a torrent of sobs. He circled her shoulder with his arm and let her weep on him.

"There, there. All will be well. Not between us, perhaps. . . ."

"Can you ever forgive me?"

"If it will help you in any way . . . yes."

She threw her arms around his neck, and he held her close, savoring her warm affection. Unconditional friendship. Only Portia had ever cared for him this way. Tears pricked at his own eyes. It must end now. For her sake, if no other reason.

The sound of rapidly approaching hooves signaled the end of their intimacy. Mahew pulled back to watch Ponsby execute a wide turn around his own team and pull the pair of bays to a halt. "Here is our knight errant now," he murmured.

Sarah pushed away from him and dabbed her eyes with his handkerchief, as Ponsby stalked toward them with Portia frowning in his wake.

"Unhand her, sir," Ponsby declared.

"Spoken like a true knight," Mahew said with a light laugh. "She is already unhanded, however."

"Then step away," Ponsby ordered, his swarthy features flushed.

Mahew stepped farther onto the bridge.

"Are you unharmed, Miss Christopher?" Portia asked, although it seemed more for Ponsby's sake than for Sarah's.

"Yes," Sarah replied. She latched Ponsby's arm. "He meant me no harm. It was entirely my fault...."

"I must see my team cools a while if I am to escort you back," Ponsby replied stiffly and turned his back on her.

"Oh, for heaven's sake," she exclaimed. "Not this again!"

She dogged his steps back to the carriage, imploring him to see reason as he steadfastly ignored her, lavishing praise on his horses instead as he walked them back and forth.

"George...." Portia said in an exasperated voice, but he held up his hand to forestall her.

"You needn't say anything," he replied. "My wicked deeds have at last been meted the ultimate punishment."

"If we return to Town fast enough maybe we can claim a race...." Portia mused.

"Forget it, my dear. Mrs. Trent watched her climb into my carriage, unassisted. And while Sarah did not scream when I asked her to, Miss Barstow's voice carried clear out to the road."

Her head drooped and Mahew embraced her.

"Now, now ... perhaps it was a good thing you refused Castleton. I might still be permitted to call on you...."

"I didn't refuse him," Portia asserted. "Though

you are right. I doubt you'd get within ten yards of him without provoking some act of violence."

"And that's why I intend to repair to France until this scandal cools," Mahew said. He glanced down the lane. "Shall we send the children back to town, then visit Uncle Doddy? I'm sure he'd float me a loan against the six hundred pounds I just won."

"You are being remarkably cool," Portia retorted.

"I'm sorry. There was nothing else I could do."

She hugged him tightly. "I don't know how I will bear it when you are gone," she said. "I feel like I've lost everything."

"Me, as well," he said. "But there is only one remedy, Portia. Begin again. It's difficult. But if I can do it, you can, too. After all, you are the stronger of us."

For the second time in a quarter-hour a woman clung to him, weeping. Mahew was deriding this emotional effect he had on the fairer sex when a grim sight drove every thought from his head, save survival. He gasped as Castleton drove into their midst, the coldness of his blue eyes boring straight into Mahew's soul.

Portia looked up at Mahew's gasp. Her own breath shortened as Castleton jumped from the curricle, not even waiting for Frederick to bring it to a complete stop. He was coatless, the harsh wind whipping at his open waistcoat and tugging at his fair hair. He didn't look at her. He didn't look at anything except Mahew, naked fury in his features and a pistol in his hand.

Sarah bounded before him, exclaiming it was all an error and she could explain everything. He displaced her with a firm hand and continued onward toward the bridge.

Portia instinctively placed herself in front of her cousin and whispered: "George, I think you'd best run."

"Two months ago I might have had a chance at outdistancing him," George replied. "But now. . . ."

"I'll speak to him," she said.

"That is not the face of a man who will listen to reason, Portia," George said, gripping her shoulders tightly. "He's out for blood, and I doubt there's much that would put him off the scent. Which is why I am so fortunate. . . ."

"Fortunate?"

"That I taught you to swim." And without ceremony his gripping hands toppled her over the side of the bridge, into the rushing water.

16

THE WATER WAS a shock. She hadn't gotten a good breath. She was caught in the current when at last she righted herself, flailing her arms, which suddenly seemed made of lead.

"George...." She grimaced. She'd been twelve when she learned to swim, dressed in her shift that James, Ralph, and George had assured her had approximated a bathing costume. Now she was weighted down with a dress, petticoats, and a saturated pelisse. Her fingers fumbled under the water, undoing the buttons of her coat. She could not maneuver with its confines about her.

Divested of its weight, she began to shiver. It had obviously offered some insulation against the cold water. She'd already missed the place where they had left the stream as children. The bank hereabouts was rocky and high, hence the need for the bridge. Portia let the current carry her, exerting herself only to angle her course toward the shore.

She was roughly pulled back into the tug of water.

"It's all right," Castleton said. "I have you."

He hooked her waist, paddling them straight to the high bank. Considering his frightening ire, she decided not to inform him there were easier places to get out of the water if they proceeded farther downstream.

He clambered up the rock face, his white shirt clinging to his body, his hair plastered down his forehead. He aided Portia onto the precarious stones and pushed and prodded her upwards. The climb proved to be the most exhausting part of the ordeal. She collapsed in a heap on the grass.

Castleton crouched beside her, drawing her up into his arms and rocking her tight against him. "Are you all right?"

She managed a weak nod.

"Thank God." Castleton brushed his lips against her temple.

Portia lifted her face, and his mouth came down on hers, claiming it with such sweet insistence she was helpless against it. But eventually she wriggled her hand between them to extricate herself.

"You shouldn't have done that," she said.

His handsome features hardened in pique. "I am not made of stone, ma'am. I've just had the fright of my life. Can't I feel some measure of relief that you are safe? Do you think my pain would be any less had you drowned, simply because you sent me packing? Don't ask me to stop loving you simply because you rejected my suit. My heart is not that capricious."

Portia stared at him. She was suddenly conscious

of the wind blowing straight through the layers of her wet clothing. Her teeth began to chatter.

Castleton shook his head and sprang to his feet. He offered a hand to her. "Come on," he said, clenching his own chattering teeth. "Let's get back to that damn bridge before we both expire from pneumonia."

Portia licked her lips. "I'm sorry. Did ... did you just say you are in love with me?"

"Of course I am in love with you," he snapped at her. "Why else would I have asked you to marry me?"

Portia shook her head. "You didn't ask me to marry you."

"Yes, I did," Castleton insisted.

"No, you didn't." Portia scrambled to her feet, unassisted, her breath ragged.

"I won't argue with you about this," he said, crossing his arms over his breast. "I am freezing and you must be, too. At least, we must start walking."

"You didn't ask me to marry you."

"For the love of God!" He took her by the shoulders, letting some of the anger and disappointment he had struggled with for the past week show clearly in his features. "I asked if you would be mine and you said no! How much plainer could I be?"

"You could have said, 'Portia, I love you, will you marry me?'" she snapped back. "But since neither love nor marriage entered your declaration, I thought...."

"What?"

Her face flamed. She ducked it away from him. "I thought you offered me carte blanche."

"Oh, my God." Hope flooded through him like a well-spring. "And if I had said, 'Portia, I love you. Will you marry me?'"

She turned her head self-consciously. Her soft response was snatched by the wind and the noisy arrival of Frederick and Ponsby.

"Uncle David! Miss Kirby!"

"Thank heavens, you're all right," Ponsby exclaimed at the same time.

Castleton waved them off in annoyance. He forcibly turned Portia to read her expression. What he saw there was encouraging.

"I'm sorry," he said. "I missed your answer."

Portia smiled shyly. "After pinching myself, I would have said yes, of course."

Castleton grinned. "That is what I hoped you said." He took her back in his arms and kissed her soundly and completely, not drawing back until Ponsby cleared his throat.

"Forgive me, sir, but . . . we left Sarah alone back there."

"Sarah is in no danger," Portia said in an earnest voice.

"You think not, ma'am?" Castleton laughed. "I intend to see she pays for leading us all on this merry dance."

"I can supply you with the names of some strict schools in the North," Ponsby informed him in a stiff voice.

"Sarah's already been to school," Frederick said.

"Give me your coat, Frederick," Castleton said. The boy obligingly stripped off his jacket, and Castleton draped it over Portia's shoulders.

"Would you like mine, too, sir?" Ponsby asked, gripping his lapels without waiting for response.

Castleton forestalled him. "You'll need it. Do you think your team is up to the return trip?"

"A stretch of the legs. I'll run them on the country roads, and cool them with a few circuits around the park."

"Take your time," Castleton said. "Amble them everywhere. I want her seen."

Sarah stood by Ponsby's carriage, petting Bright Promise when they reached the bridge. Mahew's phaeton was gone.

"Are you all right, ma'am?" she asked, rushing up to them. "Sir?"

Castleton cast a stern eye at her.

Sarah backed a step but lifted her chin. "Mr. Mahew did nothing wrong. It was all my fault." She turned to Portia, eyes soft. "He extends his apologies he cannot see you safely home."

"Did he?" Castleton gritted his teeth. "That damnable...."

Portia placed a hand on his sleeve. Her fingers looked slightly blue.

Castleton covered her hand with his own. "I must get you warm." He turned to his nephew. "Go directly home and have Stubbins return with the coach."

"We can all squeeze on the curricle," Frederick said.

"And two of us will catch our death," Castleton replied.

"But we cannot just leave you here, sir," Sarah exclaimed.

"Worried what people will think, Sarah? How novel of you. But if you think I will be forced to offer for her again, I can tell you that I already have and she's accepted, so there is no need for concern."

"Oh, oh!" Sarah launched herself on the pair of them.

Castleton took her hand and escorted her to Ponsby's carriage. "We are not finished with this business," he told her. "I am seriously considering torching the garden at every residence we own."

"You wouldn't!" Sarah regarded him with anxious eyes as Ponsby took the seat beside her.

"Probably not," Castleton said. He offered his hand to Ponsby. "But I will accept that list of boarding schools from you, Ponsby."

Sarah exclaimed in outrage as the carriage departed.

"Technically you cannot take such drastic measures at the Rise, sir," Frederick said. "It is my house, after all. . . ."

"Frederick . . . the coach?"

"Oh, yes." He climbed into the curricle and took the reins from his uncle. "I'll hurry back."

"If you must," Castleton murmured as the

carriage rounded out of sight. He turned to Portia. "Well," he said. "Shall we see what accommodation this structure affords us?"

"A table with benches, and a cot, as I recall," Portia remarked. "There is a fireplace, too."

"I was thinking of a more pleasant way to keep warm," he replied, drawing her toward the shack.

She pulled back in confusion.

"The coach will not arrive for an hour or more," he explained. "I don't know about you, but I don't intend to stand about in these wet clothes."

"Oh." Portia flushed, but ducked inside the shack.

Castleton stripped Frederick's coat off her shoulders and draped it on the cot. He nestled his cheek against the crown of her dripping hair as his hands moved under her arms to tug at the tabs of her gown.

"Before we go any further," he said between tiny kisses down her brow and cheek. "I think I should warn you that your life is about to undergo a drastic transformation. No more sitting in corners. I intend to have you always at my side."

"Do you need some help there?" she asked breathlessly as his hands slipped off the ties for a brief moment. Every time his fingertips brushed her she felt dizzy.

"No, I have it." He turned her in his arms and eased her dress off her shoulders. He kissed her softly, and she drew her arms out of her sleeves to wrap them around his neck.

"And I will dote on you," he said in a thick voice as he lowered her onto the coat, then reclined above her. Your every wish, however large or small, will be granted immediately."

"Really?" she panted. "Can you do *that* again?"

"This?" he asked, his hand caressing under the damp petticoat pushed up to her thighs.

"Yes. . . ."

"Anything else?" he asked with a grin.

"I'm not sure yet. I'm afraid imagination is a po . . . oh . . . poor substitute for experience, at present."

"I am glad to hear it." He silenced any other talk with a series of penetrating kisses while his hand continued to roam her in a most delightful way.

The combination of sensations left Portia exhausted and exhilarated at the same time. She trailed her mouth away from his to follow the line of his jaw up to his ear lobe. "I have to tell you something," she whispered.

"You want to stop?"

"No."

"You're afraid?"

"Surprisingly not."

"Not nervous?" He drew back to meet her eye. "I am. . . ."

"You are?!"

"I want to please you. This time more than any other. . . ." He grinned at her. "You're still free to change your mind, you see."

"That will never happen," she said, tracing the

planes of his face with her fingertips. "I love you. That is what I wished to say. I thought I should before. . . ." She colored. Everywhere. Delightful.

He brought his mouth back to hers. She met him kiss for kiss, moving her body in ways that inflamed him, regardless of hesitancy or awkwardness.

"I suspect you will learn to best me in this game," he said as he drew his shirt over his head and tossed it aside.

"Will that bother you overmuch?" she asked as she softly tested the texture of his naked skin with strokes that made him tremble toe to crown.

"Not in the least," he assured her. "I shall rejoice in your every victory."

And he did.

About the author

ONE OF SEVEN siblings, Barbara Satow has loved stories all her life. After reading massive stacks of library books in her teens—including the work of her favorite author, Georgette Heyer—she decided to write her own novel in her twenties. That traditional "will never see the light of day again" first book was followed by multiple false starts.

She spent the rest of the decade selling books instead.

For a time she channeled her creative energies into screenplays for contests (she was a Top 250 Finalist in the first Project Greenlight) but she returned to novels in 1999 when she joined Romance Writers of America. In 2005, she was finalist in the Regency category of their Golden Heart contest for unpublished writers.

Barbara is single and is a life-long resident of Northeast Ohio.

This is her first book.